Praise for Night Swim

"Jessica Keener steps boldly into the terrain of Eugene O'Neill, conjuring up the pathologies and quirks of a besieged Boston family in stark, quivering detail that never entirely distracts us from the looming sense of crisis. This gripping first novel announces the arrival of a strong, distinct and fully evolved new voice."

— Jennifer Egan, Pulitzer Prize winner, author of *A Visit from the Goon Squad*

"Like the adults in Rick Moody's *Ice Storm*, the central couple in this novel of 1970s suburbia are remote alcoholics. 'Love was something distant that retired to a room on the second floor,' Sarah, the 16-year-old narrator, says, referring to her stay-at-home yet absentee mother. This is a woman who makes a divot in the soil for her drink glass while tending her roses ... This earnest debut centers on Sarah as she tunnels through new depths of loneliness ... moving."

— *The New York Times*

"Keener's observations perfectly capture a certain kind of 1970s adolescence: the adults who tried too hard, the sudden appearance of a joint when in the presence of older cousins, the way a grownup party could spin from fun to disturbing in a blink. Most exhilaratingly, she taps into the thrilling moments when a girl of 16 can see her future, whether in music or books or a boy's smile."

— *The Boston Globe*

"Rooted in personal sorrow, this memorable debut will strike a universal chord with readers: 'Life was full of befores and afters.'"
— *Booklist*

"Keener understands deeply that scene writing creates powerful moments for her characters. We learn of Sarah's irritation, fear, reticence, and desire not through discussion, but through her actions and interactions with others. And Keener's writing is lovely; she manages to build sentences that are both precise and ornate. While Keener's *Night Swim* tells of a girl who has lost her bearings, her hold on her novel is both assured and poised."
— Jewish Book Council

"Jessica Keener's debut novel *Night Swim* is a masterfully told tale. Dysfunctional family dynamics are revealed in language evocative and honest, and her characters so well drawn they could be our own kin. The emotional depth of this novel has me constantly recommending it to friends in book clubs."
— Large-Hearted Boy

"An amazing new literary voice, Jessica Keener explores the fine-laced network of tangled familial relations in language both bold and intricate. *Night Swim* is the deeply moving and devastatingly beautiful work of a fearless writer."
— Sara Gruen, *New York Times* bestselling author of *Water for Elephants*

"Jessica Keener has an ear for the nuances of family life and manages, in this book, a small miracle — describing, convincingly, a family suffering the rigidity and opaqueness of a small-scale tyrant, yet honoring his authority and treating his painful struggles with kindness. Keener's heroine, a 16-year-old girl impatient to achieve womanliness, is a marvel of curiosity, impulsiveness, and generosity. What a lovely book!"

— C. Michael Curtis, Fiction Editor, *The Atlantic*

"Reading this was pure pleasure. Just gorgeous. Jessica Keener's *Night Swim* is a poignant and sensual examination of a life and a nation on the cusp of change. Sixteen-year-old Sarah brings us a moody and burgeoning wisdom as she pulls us toward secrets we recognize — the desire to hurry past pain and loss toward adulthood, the pull to belong and yet not be absorbed completely into the will of others. In a delicate balance of rebellion and compassion, Sarah teaches us to listen and hold tight to our dreams."

— Susan Henderson, author of *Up From the Blue*, a Shelf Awareness top 10 pick for 2010

Night Swim

Night
Swim

A novel by

Jessica Keener

THE
STORY PLANT

The Story Plant
Studio Digital CT, LLC
P.O. Box 4613
Stamford, CT 06907

Print ISBN-13: 978-1-61188-105-9
E-book ISBN-13: 978-1-61188-107-3

Visit our website at www.thestoryplant.com
Visit the author's website at www.jessicakeener.com

The following excerpts from *Night Swim* originally appeared in: *MiPOesias*: "Night Swim"; *Eclectica*: "Saving the Fish Tank"; *Wilderness House Literary Review*: "Solo"; *Night Train*: "The After Party"; and *The Huffington Post*: "Mother and Daughter."

"Nylons" received a finalist award in fiction from the Massachusetts Cultural Council Artist's Grant Program. "Solo" won a Chekhov Prize for Excellence in Fiction, chosen by the editors of *Wilderness House Literary Review*. "Night Swim" was nominated by the editors of *MiPOesias* for a Million Writers Award.

The author gratefully acknowledges:
Lyrics from "A Case of You" by Joni Mitchell used by permission. Alfred Music Publishing Co. Inc.
Lyrics from "The Circle Game" by Joni Mitchell used by permission. Alfred Music Publishing Co. Inc.; Westminster Music LTD
Lyrics from "Both Sides Now" by Joni Mitchell used by permission. Alfred Music Publishing Co. Inc. Westminster Music LTD
Lyrics from "Time and Love" by Laura Nyro used by permission. Hal Leonard Corporation
Lyrics from "Corinna Corinna" by Bob Dylan used by permission. Music Sales Corporation Inc.
Lyrics from "Aquarius" by James Rado and Gerome Ragni used by permission. Alfred Music Publishing Co. Inc

Previously Published by Fiction Studio Books,
January 2012
First Story Plant Printing: September 2013

Printed in the United States of America
0 9 8 7 6 5 4 3 2 1

Constantly in the darkness
Where's that at?

Joni Mitchell
"A Case of You"

So winter froze the river
And winter birds don't sing,
So winter makes you shiver
So time is gonna bring you spring

Laura Nyro
"Time and Love"

For Barr

1

Prelude

Mickey Fineburg's email brings everything back again.

Hi, Sarah. Remembering those good 'ol days in the neighborhood. Saw your CDs online. Sampled the links. Wow! Impressive. How did you end up in California?

I kissed Mickey under a broken pool table in my basement. We were eight, his lips warm as play dough, pressing with earnest intention. I pressed back, happy and unafraid, oblivious to Mickey's younger brother watching us. That night at the dinner table Mother looked stern and surprised. She said: *Mickey's mother called me. You're too young to start, Sarah.*

Start what? I wondered.

I do a quick search online. His company bio says he resides in Greenwich, Connecticut, after living in London for twenty-three years. Married with three children. I write Mickey back — "Thank you so much. I moved west after high school. Just read your company bio. Did you like living overseas?"

Mickey answers right away. *Loved London. New England is a shock. Remember those fires we burned? Can you believe our parents let us do that?*

I write: "Your dad wasn't too happy about it."

In the fall, Mickey's dad and my father raked leaves from our lawns, scraping and pushing leaves into piles on our small, dead-end street, then setting those leafy mounds aflame, Mickey and I poked at truant sparks. We lit sticks and spun smoky spirals in the air.

Another message: *Lost Dad last year. Mom's doing pretty well in assisted living but her memory's gone. What about your father?*

I write back: "So sorry to hear that. My father lives with his second wife in Florida. He can't walk — bad hips — but his memory is intact."

Mickey lived next door. I knew the Fineburgs the way I knew the border of fir trees dividing our properties: always there, a part of my neighborhood. That kiss was a childhood game we played once like other games, like war or kickball or hide and seek — nothing more; his dad was someone who waved to me from behind a lawn mower.

Then Mickey writes: *I hope this doesn't sound too personal but you're up late...*

I've been through this hundreds of times, this stirring about the house at three, four a.m., this deep hour when people closest in my life — Alan, my husband — and three sons, dissolve like particles in a sea. Time at this hour doesn't follow lines but circles and dips into underwater caves. My kids all live on the East Coast, post-grads in Maine, Vermont and Massachusetts. Alan would be asleep in our bed, but he's in New York on a business trip.

I write one last time. "So nice to hear from you after so many years. Thanks for getting in touch." Then I turn off the computer, switch off my desk light, and in the darkness move down the hall to bed, returning to the past for answers, skipping as it is easy to do in my older mind from one year to the next, to a place that is no longer there. It's as if I'm swimming toward forever, only backwards.

Chapter One

The Dinner Table

I grew up in a six-bedroom house in Soquaset, Massachusetts. Nobody spelled the name of our town correctly. Letters came to our house that said Soquashit or Sacquatics, or Socket. And Massachusetts always invited too many esses and not enough tees. The town, seven miles inland, was close enough to water by car but a good hour north of Boston. In the fifties and sixties the town flourished and became known for its excellent school system and lush neighborhoods. By the time I turned seven, Mother let me — the second oldest and only daughter of four — walk to Soquaset Square without an adult.

Our blue, clapboard house had slanted ceilings in the attic bedrooms where my oldest and youngest brothers slept; window seats in the den; and closets full of Mother's gowns, high-heeled shoes and cedar shoehorns. Neighbors admired our house for its stained glass windows in the turn of the stairs and in the dining room windows facing west. At dinnertime, when the sun exited the front yard, it left a trail of orange shadows across my plate.

"Anybody home? Hello? Anybody home?" On weeknights at a quarter to six, Father trudged up our driveway, flung open the kitchen door, and bellowed his greeting as if he expected our house to be empty and the furniture cleared out. He was a tenured professor at a small, private college, who rarely modulated his voice between podium and pantry. To think there might be a difference didn't occur to Professor Leonard Kunitz.

"Hello? Irene! I'm home!" The kitchen door closed with a determined thud.

"Irene?"

"Coming, Leonard."

In harmonic contrast Mother floated down from the bedroom to meet him for a pre-dinner drink. She moved without gravity, a cumulative effect of her pain pills, the ones she took three times a day. Together in the den, Father flipped two shots of vodka down his throat while Mother drank Scotch with a twist of lime and one ice cube. She took medium swallows. They smoked cigarettes in flowered armchairs, embraced by the arc of the bay windows that gave us a grand view of the backyard.

Usually dinner lasted all of twenty minutes — a frantic rush to gulp down firsts, then seconds.

"There's more chicken in the kitchen," Mother said. "Luanne? Could you bring what's left?" Luanne was our black maid from Haiti.

Father sat at the head of the table and ate like a starved child, his dark, quick eyes scooping up the slightest imperfections in everyone around him. He had small shoulders, a slight paunch, and wore loosely tucked in shirts, blazers, knit ties, and crumpled corduroy pants, which set him apart from Mother's fastidious appearance and those of her country club peers.

"Leonard, there's plenty of rice."

Opposite him, Mother sat straight as a violin bow, her back to the kitchen. The kids sat two and two on either side. Mother's dyed blond hair was short and layered like rose petals, her favorite flower. Adorned in a suit and matching scarf, she looked streamlined as a glass vase, and fashionable, even when she came in from the garden in slacks, the dirt and thorns clinging to her gloves.

"Why don't you start the coffee now," Mother said, as Luanne carried in more chicken and rice in a covered dish and set it on the table.

"What are we having for dessert, Irene?" Father asked.

"Cookies."

Mother had petite features — tiny wrists, slim calves that she liked to show off at parties — and the largest collection of shoes in the neighborhood. On her side of the family, Grandpa Joe built a successful shoe manufacturing company, which my uncle took over and managed. Mother was the silent partner and the reason people said we were rich.

On our small street, an elderly lady, Mrs. Brenwald, lived on the other side of us. She never went outside. Every Saturday a boy from the town market delivered grocery bags to her front porch. When I had nothing to do, I crouched by the living room window and waited for her to appear behind a curtain at night. Did she have a secret? An ugly past? My younger brother, Robert, said she was a witch but I believed that she floated in a world between earth and heaven — a harmless ghost, a lost angel.

The only evidence that Mrs. Brenwald once had an existence outside her house sat in her driveway. An antique Ford covered in a sheet was anchored to tires profoundly out of breath, squashed by endless seasons passing. More than once, Father called the police to take the car away. "A pile of crap," he called it, but the car remained impervious even to him.

This proved to me that Mrs. Brenwald made a pivotal decision many years ago, and that she had willed her life into its present shape. I found this idea both mystifying and attractive. To form one's destiny seemed monumental, like exploding holes through a mountain to get to the other side. But, in fact, that's what I wanted to do.

I'd like to believe that Mother wanted that too, choosing an alternate path that even she didn't expect.

~~~~~

"Sarah, bring me *The Complete Works*, will you?" Father said. He waved his fork like a sword, stabbing it in the air while he chewed his last bite of chicken breast.

I dashed through the rooms, across carpeting green as the fairways at the country club where we belonged. In the den with its built-in bar and book-shelves, I found the book of Shakespeare housed behind a picture of Father dressed in toddler's clothes. His thick hair fell in ringlets to his shoulders, his white apron — a popular outfit of the period — rimmed his ankles.

My great grandmother, Sarah Davida, was there too, on the shelf, staring out from her tiny village in Russia. Her name, which I inherited, meant "beloved princess" in Hebrew. She wanted to become an opera star but that was an absurd dream for a poor, Jewish farm girl. Instead, she milked cows and married a teacher from the old country, a quiet, studious man who peered over the Torah. I stared at her picture and wondered what it must have felt like to give up a dream, to stand before the mountainside, the beautiful sky beyond, and realize that she had to turn away and go back down into a small, grimy town. I didn't want that to be my fate.

She sang at *shul*. She sang to lighten her chores, she sang to her five children before bed at night; and through those children, she transported her musical seeds and they grew inside me.

Somewhere over the rainbow, way up high—

Judy Garland's voice bubbled in my mind as I scanned the family line-up. Further down the shelf, my grandmother looked square-faced. Tired. She died when I was too young to know her, a cold turned to pneumonia. Father told us she had blue periods, dark phases signaled by closed shades. In their Brooklyn apartment, his mother drank tea on a couch "the color of flamingos!" On better days, something would shift in her, he said — the sun warming the kitchen table in the morning — and soon the house filled with her friends from the sisterhood, temple organizers, and bake sale fundraisers. The smell of cinnamon and coffee meant good times at home. Maybe this is what Father saw in Mother when they met: a darkness familiar to him in his childhood.

"Sarah? Are you lost? We're waiting for you!" Father called to me.

I carried the book back to the table and sat down. By then, Luanne had cleared away the plates for dessert. She was a shy, comely woman with walnut brown skin who spoke in hushed, guarded tones around my parents. She became another person when my parents went out.

"Please, sing me that bridge song again," I asked when I found her dusting a lamp in the den. I sat on the couch and squeezed my knees to my chest to show her I meant it. *Please?* She held a dust rag in her hand. The smell of lemon polish made my nose itch. It opened the pores in my brain.

She looked out the bay windows and opened her mouth in a wide "*O — Oh, Lord, show me that bridge. I'm standing at the water, and I can't see that bridge.*" It surprised me how she talked in a whisper yet sang solid and penetrating as an oboe.

On Sunday, her day off, she wore white hoop earrings, purple lipstick and a torso-hugging blue dress with matching hat. She walked to the end of our street. A black man picked her up in a white Dodge

Dart and brought her back late the next evening, after I was asleep.

"We'll have our dessert and coffee now," Mother said to Luanne. Mother straightened her shoulders whenever she spoke to what she called *the help*. Luanne nodded and headed back to the kitchen.

"Hamlet was riddled with ambiguities," Father explained, opening the book and licking his lips. "I'll do the openers." He took a deep breath and boomed out the first line, "*Who's there?*"

"Leonard, don't shout," Mother said, tapping her ears.

"You do it then," he said, supremely offended. He pushed the book at me and I passed it over to Mother.

"I'd like to read Ophelia's part." She turned the thin pages, squinting at the words. "*Could beauty, my lord, have better commerce than with honesty?*" She over-enunciated 'commerce' and 'honesty' as if her mouth were pained or tied down by something I couldn't see.

"Ophelia doesn't hiss, Irene. Read it again."

"I'm not hissing. *Could beauty, my lord...*"

Luanne nudged open the swinging door and placed a platter of oatmeal cookies in the middle of the table.

"Coffee?" Mother said, turning toward her.

"Yes, ma'am."

"I thought we were starting after dessert," Elliot said. My youngest brother reached for a handful of cookies but Mother stopped him.

"Start with one, luv," Mother said.

Elliot looked like Uncle Max. Soft around the stomach, and wide-faced, he was the baby but possibly the wisest of us all who kept his deepest thoughts to himself, preferring sedentary activities. Slow to speak, he gave the impression of excessive dreaminess.

"Okay," he said.

"I'll read Or-feelya," Robert said. He spoke in high grating tones.

"O-feel-ee-ah!" Father corrected him. "Say it."

"I'll feel ya," Peter joked, grabbing a cookie with long, dexterous fingers. He was pale and light-haired like me. The oldest at seventeen, he sank into his chair, lanky — all arms and legs, a shadow of a mustache defining his upper lip.

Father pounded a fist on the table. "Enough!" The storm perpetually brewing beneath his skin surfaced and made his face turn red.

Everyone was silent except for the swinging door. Luanne walked back in with two cups of coffee.

"Bring the coffee here, girl." Father fished a cigarette from his shirt pocket and separated his saucer from his coffee cup to use it for an ashtray.

"Don't talk to her like that," I wanted to shout, but my words stayed mute inside my head.

"Luanne, the ashtrays are in the cupboard," Mother said. "Above the refrigerator." She spoke slowly, a careful movement of her lips.

Robert jumped up, pressing his hands to his ears. "I can't listen to this family!" He ran upstairs howling. Craven and overexcited, words spat out of Robert's mouth from the time he had taught himself to read when he was three. We heard his footsteps and the bedroom door slam. Mother pressed her lips until they whitened.

"Give me the book, Irene."

She obeyed.

"Sarah, tell Robert to come back down here. He was not excused." He took a cookie and pushed it whole into his mouth. His cheeks changed shape, sticking out like miniature fists. The oatmeal crumbs settled on the corners of his mouth.

"Do it now."

I slid out. We all knew Father's rule. Families who ate together got excused together. Anyone who veered from this cardinal regulation risked punishment. I feared for Robert who upstairs was hanging over the side of his bed reading a book. His dark hair shot up like his thoughts, abruptly and sharp.

"You're invading my privacy," he said.

"Dad wants you to come down."

"I'm reading."

"Just come down," I said in an attempt to offer an older sister's advice, "or he'll blow up again." I was three years older than Robert and knew if I stood still, he would calm down enough to reconsider. He prickled and folded his shoulders, then shoved the book under his bed and followed me down.

By now it was pitch-black outside and the large globe light above the table reflected off the windows like a bloated fish.

Robert stood in front of Father.

"You will not," Father said, smacking Robert on the cheek, "leave the table without permission. Now you may be excused."

Robert burst into tears and tore back upstairs. Father headed to his den office and slammed the door. Elliot started humming. I couldn't move, paralyzed by my unintended betrayal of Robert.

"Elliot, time for a bath. Sarah, Peter, you have homework," Mother said.

"You've got to be kidding!" Peter said, shoving his chair out from the table.

Ashamed and horrified by what I'd done, I went upstairs to my desk and stared out my bedroom window at the weeping birch tree that hunkered over the driveway in the dark. Later that night, I knocked on Robert's door to apologize but he wouldn't let me in. He had pushed his bureau in front of the door.

"I'm really sorry," I said through the keyhole.

I went to bed and stayed awake a long time waiting for sleep, my raw stomach unable to settle down. The hall light shone into my room. I tried humming. The vibrations of notes calmed my nerves. Ahhh, ooooo, eeeee. *Oh Lord, show me the bridge.* I mimicked the way Luanne opened her mouth and felt the tone change on my tongue, then shiver along the path of my cheekbones.

I watched the treetops out my window, thin tall pine trees like still figures watching back, and the long backyard that curved up to the stars. The bright moon gleamed on the wooden floors and made my floor melt and become liquid as a pond. I invented songs. In this universe away from my

father's explosions and Mother's thin voice, I imagined standing solo on stage singing to an auditorium
filled with understanding faces. *Come and see what I
see.*

    I sang to the moon, the hall light, and my mem-
ory of the honey summer light when the low sun
slunk into my room in warm weather. I hummed. I
changed my notes from high to low. I rolled them on
my tongue. Singing was like eating. It filled a hungry
feeling.

Chapter Two

Black Maids

In the kitchen, Luanne snapped green beans for dinner. She wore pink, pearl-like earrings and she was humming. She seemed different, more distant after a day off. For two nights of the week, she lived in Roxbury, a poor, black section in Boston that white people avoided.

"What you want, Sarah?" she asked in a Haitian accent. Her skin looked creamy. She had high cheekbones and moist, glowing eyes.

I sat by the window overlooking our driveway. Through the cluster of fir trees, Mickey Fineburg's bedroom window lit up, shiny and lemon-colored. I didn't see him much. He was my age, but he went to private school. I knew his family's routines. The Fineburg's white Colonial made different sounds at different times of the day. Doors opened and shut. Their station wagon hummed in their driveway in the morning before backing out.

"You've got some thought in your head. I can see it."

"Isn't it hard living somewhere else and coming back here?" I asked.

She nodded but didn't say anything. When she finished with the beans she placed whole potatoes in the oven and asked me if I wanted to watch television with her. In her small room beside the kitchen, I sat on the linoleum floor beside a basket piled with pink rollers. She had draped a blue scarf across her window. It darkened her room, making it soft and cozy. On her bureau, she kept a paper cup filled with earrings. She sat on her cot behind me. Together, we watched a movie about the Wild West on her black and white television perched on a fold-up chair. During the commercial I said, "You could ask my mother for another day off."

She shook her head. "Always trying to be the adult. That's not your business."

"Luanne!" Mother called from the kitchen.

Luanne left the room. I wasn't an adult, but at fifteen I noticed things.

"We'll need a salad," I heard Mother say.

Luanne's room felt safe as a warm secret. I didn't want to leave and stayed to watch the rest of the movie. I heard cooking utensils clattering. Father came home, slamming the door. "Anyone home!" He went into the hall to hang up his coat. Luanne moved back and forth through the swinging dining room door, setting the table. Finally, Mother called to us. "Elliot, Peter, Robert, Sarah! Wash your hands. Dinner is ready!"

Not long after, when winter's icy roots plunged deepest and seemed destined to stay forever, I came home after school, plopped my books on the kitchen counter, and went looking for Luanne in her room. Oddly, her bedroom door was wide open. The room appeared lighter, her bureau top swept clean of perfume bottles. I stepped inside. Her scarf over the window was gone. Where were her cups of earrings?

I ran upstairs to find Mother in her bedroom. She was sitting on her red upholstered loveseat reading a fashion magazine.

"Where's Luanne?"

"She left, honey. I've called the agency. They're sending someone next week to replace her." She removed her reading glasses. "She quit, dear."

"Why?"

She explained that Luanne had left a note about finding a different situation. "Just as well. I always thought she was too young. Not like you, Sarah. You're such a mature girl for your age, beyond your years."

Stunned, I turned away from her. My parents' bedroom had views of the front, side and backyards and a dressing room with a wall of closets. It was a spacious room but I felt suddenly squeezed in. I ran upstairs to the attic to see if Peter had come home. I was mature enough to know that our family was a problem and I wanted to tell him. Instead, I found Elliot playing with miniature plastic animals in his room. He occupied himself well for a young child.

The following Saturday afternoon Luanne rang the doorbell to pick up the rest of her clothes. Father answered the door.

"Taking off to shack up with someone?" he said as I ran downstairs to see her.

She was already walking back to the front door with her suitcase in hand when I called to her.

"Leonard, please," Mother said standing next to him. "Are you sure you have everything, Luanne?"

She barely nodded and headed for the door.

"I'll miss you," I wanted to say. Instead, I said, "Bye, Luanne," and looked at the rug, ashamed.

She went through the front door and hurried down the flagstone walk. A black man waited for her in a white Dodge Dart. At the last minute, something pushed me and I ran to the open door and shouted, "I'm sorry!" But it came out in a whisper that only I could hear. By then, Luanne was in the front seat closing the car door. The car flew off down our road in a cloud of exhaust and sand.

"Come inside, Sarah. It's cold out. You don't have shoes on," Mother said.

I went back to my bedroom and shut the door. A sharp pain threaded my chest to my stomach. I tried singing a lullaby, leaning on my windowsill — *Kumbaya My Lord* — the notes low in my throat. Where was Luanne now? Would she think of me ever? My imagination failed me. My heart felt cumbersome on my lungs. Yet the tears wouldn't rise up or drain out of me. I went downstairs again to Luanne's closed door in search of her quiet, kind essence. I turned the doorknob and went in. Bare bed. Bare floor. Bare everything.

Mother heard me. "These things happen," she said, stopping in the hall outside Luanne's old room. "It's too bad. But there's nothing we can do." She turned and went into the kitchen.

Mother filled her days with bridge and luncheons during the week. On Thursdays, she went to the hairdressers then food shopping on Fridays. Occasionally, she signed up for a flower arrangement class or joined friends from the country club for communal sessions on cross-stitching. This didn't last. Her rheumatic fingers refused such delicate needle work. But I have a pillow she made: a green and white checkerboard pattern backed with dark green felt. It's a small item but I cherish it.

All these things replaced the musical life she once led: the violin recitals and college concerts, the discipline of rehearsals and practice replaced by a need for order in the house, the need to perform taken up with these social gatherings, a way to keep herself on public display. Something else inside her was not keeping up. I just didn't know it then.

~~~~~

After Luanne, different black maids came and went. No one lasted more than a few months. One white maid from Ireland stayed for five days. None replaced Luanne. Then Dora, another black maid, took the position. She was different. She was obese, squat, and surly. She came from Florida and didn't care about earrings or singing. She said, "You can't fool me. I have five grown children." She looked at me as if I had hidden things and she was going to find them. But, not by inviting me into her room. Her door was closed. She was efficient down to the minute. "When I tell you to wash up you go right ahead," she said. "Your dinner is waiting. I don't serve hot food to eat it cold. You hear?" She talked as if she knew everything about life, as if nothing could shock her, as if she had seen it all.

Chapter Three

Somewhere, a Promised Land

I hurried down the cement steps to the car on my way to Aunt Annette and Uncle Max's house to commemorate the Jews' escape from slavery in Egypt. "Moses is off to the Promised Land!" Father shouted from the kitchen. He wrestled his knit tie into a knot and headed out. The door slammed.

Snow was gone but the trees had not yet poked their greening fingertips to test the air. Mother took her place in front, looking crisp in her pale blue suit and taupe shoes. The car absorbed her perfume and waxen scent of lipstick. She turned around to survey us.

"My beauties," she said, approvingly.

My brothers, including Peter, wore matching navy blue blazers and gray slacks. Mother insisted they look this way for Passover seder but Peter re-belled, unbuttoning his blazer so that it slid down one shoulder. My velvet maroon dress confined me in a narrow, boxy shape, better suited for an eleven-year-old, not someone heading for high school next year. I don't think Mother noticed my emerging breasts and hips pressing against my dress seams. Or if she did, perhaps she wanted to slow this part of my growth, like pruning rose bushes, which she said brought out fuller blooms. I crossed my legs and flicked the toes of my patent leather shoes, up and down, up and down, impatiently.

"Let's pray Uncle Max doesn't drag things on," Peter said.

We were sometime Jews. On high holidays, mother shooed us off to synagogue while she stayed home and baked potato pudding in her apron and fine leather pumps. Next to her, a half glass of water for washing down pills stood sentinel on the kitchen counter. "Go with your father," she said.

Father popped the car in reverse and I jerked backwards against the seat. In the short drive to the Klines' neighborhood in the hills, we passed older houses set back from the street. The Klines' home, a Greek Revival with enormous white pillars, appeared at the end of a long, horseshoe driveway.

Grandpa Joe greeted us at the door. "Must we wait for holidays to get together?" he asked. Approaching ninety, he suffered from angina. When he felt a pain in his heart he excused himself from the room and popped a tiny white pill.

"If I saw you every day, it still wouldn't be enough," Mother said, kissing him on the forehead.

"How's my other princess?" he said, touching my chin gently.

He had a skinny face and didn't rush when he spoke. I smelled the cologne he always wore: a combination of cinnamon and lime. His companion, a woman in her seventies named Lilly, greeted me with a firm handshake. Energetic and quick talking, she lived in the same apartment complex as my grandfather. She tinted her hair a golden brown and was the widow of one of his former business associates. I spotted my dead grandmother's opal ring on her finger. Grandma died when I was six but I still remembered the rings she wore.

"Why don't we see each other more often?" Aunt Annette said when we entered. "It's a shame we can't find the time."

"You're the world travelers," Mother said, a jealous lilt in her voice. Her rising inflections seem most pronounced around the Klines.

We lived close to each other, yet our lives and the Klines' didn't intersect. The Klines' two sons, Kenneth and Edward, were much older, college graduates long gone from the house. The Klines' house was often empty because my aunt and uncle traveled so much.

"Hello, beautiful," Kenneth said in his loud, sonorous voice. He was a handsome giant who picked me up and swirled me around the downstairs foyer, until the yellow divan and gilt-framed pictures became a colorful blur. Kenneth was my demi-hero. Hefty with wavy, brown hair and hazel eyes, he went to college on a ship that sailed around the world. He lived in places beyond the horizon. He lived faraway in San Francisco where Mother said he was "peddling leather goods to those hippie boutiques." I thought Kenneth handsome and slightly dangerous.

"Hello, yourself," I said when he set me down.

"Here's my man," he said putting his arm around Peter. The two wandered into the living room and sat by the couch near the fireplace.

Cousin Edward, the oldest and more reserved one, was a lawyer in Boston. He nodded to me but much preferred to talk with the adults.

~~~~~

The Klines' mahogany dining table, twice the length of ours, had a double set of claw-foot legs and matching chairs with carved wooden backs. Mother fondled a linen napkin. "Look at your table. Just lovely. Where did you say you got these? Your trip to England?" She lifted a crystal goblet and held it up to the light. "Exquisite, Annette."

"Yes. A dealer located the set for us."

At the far end of the seder table, Uncle Max put on a studious, half-sleepy face as he and Father droned on through long Hebrew passages. Every few pages, Uncle Max eyed me, staring at my neck. I looked down to see if I had spilled something on my dress.

When it came time to name the plagues, I dipped my pinky finger into the juice and stabbed my clean, white china plate. The drops grew into a small, bloody puddle.

Dam (blood)!
Tz'Farday'A (frogs)!
Kinim (lice)!
Arov (wild beasts)!

Dever (cattle plague)!
Sh'Chin (boils)!
Barad (hail)!
Arbeh (locusts)!
Cho-Shech (darkness)!
Makat B'Chorot (slaying of first born)!

"Slaying of the first born?" I asked. "I do not understand this."

I smeared my white linen napkin with grape juice.

"You don't have to understand it. It's tradition," Mother said. She kept her left hand under the table and pushed her empty wine glass toward Father. He filled it to the top.

"It's not tradition, it's murder," Peter said. "Let's slay the first born, kill some children. Start a My Lai Massacre. *One two three four, what are we fighting for?*" He started singing the Country Joe and the Fish song, the one they sang at Woodstock.

"Peter. Stop. That's enough," Mother said. "Of course I don't mean that. I'm talking about rituals — foods, gathering together every year with the family." She lifted her chin. "I believe those things are important."

"Change is better."

"You say that because you're young, dear."

"Since when did you get old, Irene?" Father asked.

"Old? What are you talking about?" Granpa said. "She's perfect."

"Perfection is a lost horizon," Father said. "Isn't that right, Irene?"

"Never mind. Let's not turn this into a seminar," Mother said. "Let's enjoy each other." She smiled at me but I saw a flicker in her eyes, like a small animal fleeing.

From what? *From what, Mother? What?*

These questions churned in my stomach as I slurped down matzo ball soup. I was a thin person with a fat person's appetite. I ate gefilte fish, two chicken breasts, multiple helpings of noodle pudding, candied carrots. The Klines' Irish housekeeper, a stooped woman in her sixties, whisked away our dirty plates. "You have enough, dear?" We ended the seder in a burst of traditional songs.

"When Israel was in Egypt Land,
Let my people go!
Oppressed so hard they could not stand,
Let my people go!"

Afterwards, Elliot and Robert went to the TV room. Kenneth and Peter headed upstairs to Kenneth's old bedroom to play guitar.

"Sarah, will you come with me a moment?" Uncle Max said, rising from his chair.

I followed my uncle to the basement where he had portioned off a part of the room for his sculptures: a clutter of small nude clay models, big-breasted women with thick thighs, which he lined on a table covered in an old painter's sheet. I counted half a dozen nudes, some without arms and legs, a few lying down. One nude, the size of an upright watermelon, was perched on the floor and served as a doorjamb to the boiler room.

"Take a look at my new piece," he said.

He switched on a floor lamp and putting his hand lightly on my shoulder, steered me toward the table. Then he stood in front of me, staring.

"I was thinking of using you as a model," he said, touching my neck. He explained how he wanted to do a nude of a younger woman. "Ask your mother. See what she says."

"I couldn't do that." I shook my head.

"Think about it," he said, nonchalantly reaching for a cigar from his breast pocket, setting it aflame with a butane lighter. "But I wouldn't want you to be uncomfortable. It's for art."

"I'm going up now."

"Yes. Let's go up."

I ran back up to the first floor, to the powder room, and locked the door. Uncle Max followed behind but passed the bathroom and continued on to the living room where the adults had settled. He called out to Aunt Annette to see if she would play the piano.

I calmed down in the bathroom, dawdling with the sink faucet, until the smell of my uncle's cigar subsided. It was an odd request and he knew it. Art or no art. I wouldn't do it. Upstairs, I heard Kenneth and Peter singing Bob Dylan songs.

Corrina, Corrina, Gal, where you been so long?

I ran upstairs to join them.

Chapter Four

Stupid Talk

On the car ride home, Mother said something to Father about Uncle Max having trouble with the business. It was dark now, the street lights flicking past faster as Father headed down the hill toward our street.

"I think he's hiding something from us."

"Yes, yes, yes, I heard him," Father said, irritably. "He's concerned he might have to work for his money."

"He asked me to pose nude for him," I said.

"Really?" Mother turned. "I'm surprised."

"I said no."

"Good," Father said. "I'll give him a piece of my mind."

"Let's just let it be," Mother said. "You said no and that's that."

"Guy's a creep," Peter said. "Dad, watch that car."

Father braked hard but not soon enough, lightly bumping into a brown sedan that had stopped at the stop sign at the bottom of the street.

Father turned. "Everyone okay?"

"He's waving to you," Peter said. "He wants to talk to you."

"Jesus Christ! I barely touched him."

"Leonard, lower your voice."

"Let me take care of this." Father rolled down the window but didn't get out.

The man sauntered over and introduced himself.

"Officer Riley." He flipped open his wallet and showed his police badge.

"Very impressive. Looking for an excuse to show your badge, Mr. Riley? Look, there's no damage."

Peter covered his eyes.

"We're coming from the seder," Elliot said, holding up a plastic frog. "Do you know about the plagues?"

"Shh. Not now." Mother waved a finger from her good hand, her right.

The policeman leaned in. "Going pretty fast with kids in the car."

"Well within the limit."

" — Leonard, please."

"Tell you what; you can bring that up at a hearing." Officer Reilly flipped open a ticket pad and began writing. He was ordinary looking. Brown hair and eyes, thick wad of nose, small lips. "I'll be right back."

The policeman went back to his car and sat behind the wheel to finish writing the ticket.

Father tapped on the steering wheel. "Mr. Know-it-all on his day off. You'd think he was writing the

Great American Novel. Man's got nothing else to do."

Mother's face tightened in that old, familiar way. But when the policeman returned, she tried to smile. Robert started squeezing and opening his fists in unison. "I would like to go home," he said.

"You have a better rest of the night, sir." The man handed Father a ticket.

"I'm not through with you," Father said. "You wait. I'm going to retrieve my camera and document this."

"Go right ahead," the policeman said, smiling. "I've got plenty of time."

Elliot started humming one of the Passover songs, an annoying repetitive sound.

"Forget it, Dad," Peter said.

"I won't forget it. I want silence in this car!" Father slapped the dashboard, his face turning purple. Mother stiffened into plaster of Paris. Robert, too. Then Father put the car in gear and drove around the corner into our driveway.

We couldn't get out fast enough. Each of us clambered up the back stairs to the kitchen. Father headed to the den. I got to the second floor when I heard glasses, the clattering of Father making another drink. My brothers heard too and gathered around me on the second floor landing. We flattened ourselves on the carpet and looked down through the railing.

Mother called to Dora to bring a cold glass of water. Dora walked across the hall to the den and returned to the kitchen, her face closed up like a cardboard box.

"I'll be fine," Father kept saying. He sounded stupid.

We watched as he stepped backwards, then sideways.

"You're not fine," Mother said, steering him into his office. The door shut.

"He looks like he's going to faint," Robert said, beside me.

Elliot was limp and silent.

"What is she saying?" I wanted to know.

"Come with me," Peter said, getting up.

We all followed him down to the basement. He had rigged up a sound system from Father's office, feeding a wire through a hole in the basement ceiling and attaching it to extra stereo speakers. We heard Mother say: "Get ahold of yourself. I can't take it anymore."

"You should have married a richer man."

"It has nothing to do with money. It's your behavior."

I yanked the wire from the speaker. "Don't listen to them," I said.

Elliot started crying.

"It's stupid adult talk. They don't mean anything," Peter said, wrapping his arm around Elliot.

Robert's shoulders bent inward. "You're all stupid."

I agreed with Robert — even stupider as we crept back up and ran into Dora at the top of the stairs, waiting for us. She looked at Peter and me.

"What did you do to upset your brothers?" She put one arm around Elliot and the other around Robert, who didn't like to be touched, and brought them into the kitchen. "Nothing that some hot chocolate can't fix," she said to them.

Peter and I mounted two more sets of stairs to his room. We shut ourselves in his closet, sitting on the floor under a forest of shirts dangling on hangers. "What's wrong with them?" I didn't understand my parents' talk. It tangled like knotted strings.

"It's not your problem. Listen to this." He sat crossed-legged and positioned his guitar over his knees, making sure the neck didn't bang against the wall. His confidence, tinged with disgust, galvanized me. If he could dismiss them, so could I.

"I'll teach you some new chords."

I nudged closer to his knees and let him arrange my fingers on the frets. Cramped in this narrow space, the sweat under his arms smelled like wet cotton and rubber. But nothing was sweeter and safer. *If I had a hammer —*

The metal strings thrummed a beautiful, round sound of The Weavers' folk song. Peter strummed harder and our harmonies gelled "*I'd hammer out love —*" until our voices and Peter's guitar formed a nest high in the trees, untouchable as I sang and my lungs vibrated with deep breaths and melodies and invisible wings. Whatever existed below me, in the lower floors, became inconsequential. No one interrupted. No one came up to tell me to stop.

~~~~~

Days after the police incident, Mother developed a mild discomfort in her shoulder. The ache traveled up the left side of her neck and down her arm until it took over the house. The family doctor prescribed more pills to relieve the pain. She took green capsules three times a day: one with her coffee in the morning, one before dinner, and one before bed. At first the pills worked. Her tight-lipped smile softened. But the pain returned worse than before. When I came home from school, several times I found her lying on the living room couch sipping a drink, one arm draped to the floor.

"Can I do something?"

"No, hun. How was school today? Much homework?"

Homework was not an issue for me. I got A's. She knew that.

"Same as always."

I waited for her to say something else but she seemed to be half-asleep. She tried to sit up. I reached over and helped her shift into a sitting position.

"I'm in a terrible mess, aren't I?" She shook her head and looked at me. I looked at the rug. Her pleading eyes discomfited me like getting snagged in a web.

Steroid shots offered her temporary relief, but again the pain rebounded. She couldn't bend over to tie Elliot's shoes. That became my chore, as did getting Elliot dressed before school in the morning unless Dora intervened, which she often did, and marshaled us all out the kitchen door with slices of buttered toast in our hands. "Let's go. Come on. All of you. I don't want anybody late for school. Go on!"

Mother visited doctors, took pills, tried different exercises. Nothing helped.

"You're going to have to have surgery," Father said.

She wore a neck brace. It no longer seemed unusual to find her upstairs in her bedroom sitting on a straight-back chair with a sling and rope contraption wrapped around her chin. The rope looped over the top of the door and was weighted down on the other side by a sandbag. In theory the sling was supposed to relieve the pressure in the spine, which had something to do with her neck pain. When she sat in this contraption, she braced herself against the back of her chair and talked through her teeth.

Today, I stood in front of her inspecting the ropes and pulley.

"What will you do if this doesn't work? Surgery?"

"I'm running out of options. Tell Dora to bring me up a drink," she said. "Don't forget a straw."

~~~~~

I went down to find Dora. The room that had once been Luanne's and a little bit mine was no longer. Instead of Luanne's scarf across the window, Dora kept her shade wide open to let sunlight in. Her spotless bureau top smelled of lemon wax. The gray linoleum floor shone like polished silver.

I knocked. The door opened suddenly and fat Dora loomed over me. Her stout presence cast a wide shadow.

"What is it, Sarah? Dinner's not ready for another fifteen minutes."

"Mother wants her drink upstairs."

Dora nodded but looked disapproving at me.

"What?" I said.

"Money don't solve everything," she said and went into the den to make the drink.

Did I say it did? My silent voice created waves in my head. I went to the kitchen window and looked out at the Fineburgs' house. Mickey's window shade was pulled half-way down. I heard Dora thumping up the stairs. She liked to make her all-knowing presence heard. I didn't know what to do.

Below, I saw Father walking up the driveway from the commuter train. He wore a long, black overcoat and carried a briefcase, the kind that stood upright on a tabletop and opened accordion style. He was proud of the fact that his briefcase was fifteen years old, as if holding on to old things proved something about his worth.

"Everyone's home," I said, as soon as he walked in.

"How's your mother?"

"In her sling."

He went to the hall closet and hung up his coat.

"Mrs. Kunitz is upstairs," Dora said, emerging from the hallway. "She's going to have to have that surgery. I know it."

"Irene!" Father shouted from the bottom of the stairs.

"Mrs. Kunitz can't talk. She's in her sling. You have to go upstairs."

"*Christ!*" Father said, trudging up the staircase.

"What are you staring at, Sarah?" Dora said. "Go wash your hands. Get your brothers. We're about to eat."

We took our seats at the table and watched Father and Mother slowly walk down the stairs together. Mother moved like an old, crippled person, straining to keep her back straight while Father held her elbow and guided her down.

"I think the sling's making it worse, Mom," Peter said.

Father led Mother to her chair and eased her down on the seat.

"Your mother has a heightened sense of pain." He looked apologetic, as if something about the pain in her neck was his fault.

Then Dora walked in as if on cue and began serving. She put five chicken wings on Father's plate, four on Peter's and three on mine.

"I'll have another," I said.

"When you're through with what you got, I'll give you more. And, don't forget to say, *please*."

I made a face. I didn't know if she hated me because we had money or if she just hated me. I looked over to Mother for help.

"Let it be, Sarah," she said. "There's always more."

Chapter Five

Adults

I wondered what Mother was thinking about in her hospital bed. Tomorrow morning, the surgeon would fix her herniated spine. Was she scared? Was she looking forward to a new life after surgery? I finished my homework and piano practice. I took a shower, but I couldn't sleep. In my flannel night-gown, I went downstairs and wedged myself between the bookcase and window in Father's office. He was correcting papers.

"The doctor says she'll be home in four days. Twelve hours from now it will all be behind us," Father said.

"I can't wait. I hope it fixes her."

"Me too, pumpkin." He took off his reading glasses.

I looked out the window where the cherry tree grew. At night, the branches looked arthritic in the darkness.

"What are you working on?"

"A story about love." He handed me a paperback copy of *King Lear.* "The king has three daughters. He wants them to each prove their love to him. Think about that. How do you prove love? Climb mountains? Put yourself at mortal risk?" He stood and began to pace, walking toward me, then back to the desk.

"At work you have to prove you're worthy. No matter what you choose to do in life, princess, you'll have to prove something. How do you do that?" He didn't wait for an answer. "Well, it depends. Sometimes you have to do certain tasks to please the king or the boss as the case may be. In my case, the person who wants to be pleased is the head of the department.

"The boss is the person who gives you the money. Do you go along with the boss? I'll tell you the answer," he said, slapping down the book. "Some people do what the two elder daughters did. They do what they think the boss wants. A few do what they believe is morally right. Those few, a minority I might add, are ostracized, just like Lear's youngest daughter. Are you getting the picture?"

"What does your boss want you to do?" I asked.

"He wants me to teach *my* classes *his* way and I'm not going to do that!" He shook his finger at the book.

"Mr. Kunitz," Dora said, walking in with a dishtowel in her hand, "Sarah needs to be in bed. She has school tomorrow."

"Yes, yes. I know."

~~~~~

The night after her surgery, Father took us to see Mother at the hospital. We filed down a wide hallway. A nurse wearing a blue dress and white shoes smiled and showed us to Mother's room, which smelled of sour rubbing alcohol and sweet perfume.

"Here they are," Mother said, sounding tired. She lifted her arm and flopped it on the bed.

We walked in, clumped together. She lay against a huge pillow, her thin hair matted. She looked pale and sleepy.

"She may drift in and out," the nurse said. "But she's doing great."

Mother turned to the nurse. She closed her eyes. Her mouth buckled as if she were trying to hold back tears. "Yes, I hope so."

Elliot walked right up to her bed and gave her a toy lion. "This will protect you."

She opened her eyes. "Elliot." She tried placing the lion on the nightstand beside her, and missed. The toy clattered to the floor.

"Oh, Elliot." She looked at the night table, then lifted her hand to her eyes. "Please." Tears dripped from the side of her eyes. "I lost it there. I lost the sound. Can you get it, Elliot?" She turned toward the night table.

"Here it is," Elliot said, picking up the lion.

She closed her eyes again.

"Irene. Are you in pain?"

She turned her head. "What did I lose?"

"Nothing, Irene. You're dreaming. You're going to be fine." Father stood by her head and put his hand on the mattress. "The doctor thinks this is going to do the trick."

Peter stood by the door. "Should I get the nurse?" He left the room.

Robert found the switch to the television and turned it on.

"Not now," Father said.

Peter came back with the nurse.

"Why is she crying?" Elliot asked.

"The anesthesia will do that. It takes a few days," the nurse said. She walked over to Mother and looked at her face. "She'll come out of it. She won't even remember half of what she says. You can come back again. She's probably had enough for today."

"Let's not tire your mother," Father said, striding back to the door.

~~~~~

She came home at the end of the week looking like herself: hair combed and washed. Everything back in place. Father was relieved to have her on the mend. We all were. She wore a brace but it was temporary. Friends sent bouquets, and cards, which decorated her bedroom. Each day her neck improved.

Finally freed from all the energy locked in her bones for so many months, a great surge of purpose took over her. She seized on the idea of a summer party. Even her roses responded to the idea, opening in a crescendo of hues and smells in the backyard. The huge flowerbed that dominated the backyard was squared off like a stage and divided into four quarters with aisles for strolling and viewing.

I stood at the edge of her garden watching her fold in new soil with a trowel. On her knees, she felt for clumps of dirt, nudging the silt for weeds with lavender gloves. I treaded the borders lightly not wanting to ruin anything.

"It's the balance of all these things," she said. "Soil, light, temperature in just the right measure."

I tried pulling a green plant out of the garden, shaking the dirt from the balled root.

"Oh, that's not a weed. It's a young rose. Oh, well. Toss it in the pile there." She pointed to a heap. The smell of her drink, a glass of Scotch tucked into a pocket of earth, floated by her roses. "See. Here's a weed." She held up a stringy, green plant. "Pull it out slowly. If it breaks, you won't get the roots and the weed will come right back and take over. You don't want that."

Inside the house, Mother made lists. She sat at the kitchen table, her neck pain gone, though she still took pills every morning just in case.

"The thing is not to let it flare up," she said.

She counted up names of couples she wanted to include from the neighborhood, the country club, and teachers from Father's school. Dora grew more important by the minute polishing silverware. Silver trays sparkled on the kitchen countertops.

Father lugged two card tables up from the basement and placed one in the living room beside the piano, the other in the den near the bay windows. Dora draped them both with white tablecloths, the legs hidden under linens whose hems touched the floor. I put the silverware in baskets lined with linen napkins. Elliot sat at the kitchen counter drawing pictures of dogs and cats.

Robert, as usual, sequestered himself in his room, reading. He disliked social events. They made him nervous. The talking noise gave him headaches. Peter treated the event as if it were a play and he was the stage manager. He rambled back and forth between the main rooms, calmly hooking up extra speakers, then stopping in Father's office to test the sound.

I moved on the edges of activity, preparing myself for the onslaught of adults, not sure what to expect but curious. I loved all the party food and nibbled on salted almonds from a candy dish on the piano. In the kitchen, I snagged a piece of cheese, and a dollop of onion dip.

"Want to draw?" Elliot asked me. He handed me a crayon and I drew a cat playing a guitar before Father called me into his office.

"Sarah! Take a look at these."

One by one, he handed me albums he planned to use for the party. I stacked them on the floor. His office was a cave of papers and books, shelves filled with books, and a mahogany roll top desk from a yard sale that was dented and scratched, and old. "Buy a new one," Mother said when he complained about sticking drawers. His Royal typewriter on a metal stand by the window gave off a metallic, inky smell. When he prepared a syllabus or exam, he typed with two fingers, the keys clicking with happy purpose. A stereo system was stacked high on a shelf near the window.

"Music is the essence of a party. Without it, you have nothing." He looked at the ceiling to consider his words, then started up again. "Music is to parties as darkness is to night. The party is the music. 'Are you the leaf — '" he asked, quoting his favorite poet Yeats.

"Okay, Dad. I get it."

I wasn't in the mood for pontifications.

"How can you get it? I didn't finish so how can you understand? Are you the dancer or the dance?"

I shrugged. "I don't know."

"Good. You don't know. My best students, princess, admit their ignorance."

I sat down beside him on the rug and flipped through his selections: Cole Porter, Gershwin, Artie Shaw, Glenn Miller, Ella Fitzgerald.

"You will learn to love these people," he said. "And once you love them you will never want to leave them and they, my dear, will never leave you."

I looked at him.

"What did you decide to do about your boss?"

"I told him what he wanted to hear."

"That's not what Cordelia did."

"True." He unsheathed a record and held it up to the light, looking for scratches, avoiding my gaze. "However, I will continue to work my methods. I haven't given up, my princess. I'm just going underground for the time being."

"So Cordelia did the wrong thing?"

"Not at all. But some have argued that she was foolish, perhaps she shouldn't have been so brash." He stood up and puffed out his chest. "Truth is, I listened to your mother and took her advice."

"What's that?" Mother stopped in at the doorway. "Don't forget to get dressed," she said to me, smiling. She leaned against the threshold in her white, quilted robe. "How about your blue dress?" Peter came in and adjusted the wires on the speakers again, coiling the wires into two neat piles on the floor.

The doorbell rang. Dora walked into the living room cradling a bright yellow flower arrangement.

"Gorgeous," Mother cried. "They match my dress." She bent over the flowers and inhaled. I did too.

The back doorbell rang and a triplet of women caterers entered with plates and casserole dishes for the buffet dinner. They lined the kitchen counters with trays of stuffed mushrooms, crackers, cheese, sour cream dips, chicken wings, pastries filled with cheese. Lobster seafood pasta was the main entrée.

As the day progressed, so did the summer sun bearing down on the house. It grew warm inside. Father hollered. "Peter! Fans! Bring up the fans!"

Fruit and cheese platters decorated tabletops in the den as did small vases of Mother's roses. One of the card tables in the living room had been set up as an extra bar with all the bottles of gin and vodka, scotch, whiskey and ice buckets. Beer was kept in coolers in the basement. Bottles of wine stood in formation on the liquor tables alongside empty, crystal glasses. The smell of squeezed limes, olives, and hors d'oeuvres crisping in the oven was intoxicating. Every inch of the downstairs rooms had been surveyed and dusted. Peter brought up standing fans and fans that fit into windows. It put us all in easy but alert tempers. I placed a paperweight on top of a stack of cocktail napkins to keep them from scattering.

I shaved my legs and dressed in a pink skirt and shirt, and white sandals. Peter put on his newest uniform: bell-bottomed dungarees, a red bandana around his neck. Though Mother disapproved, she swiveled away to attend to other details.

As the sun lowered itself, releasing colorful ribbons into the sky, Father swung open the front door and kept it open.

"Here we go! I see our first guests!"

I stood at the bottom of the carpeted stairs and greeted the adults as they arrived.

"Hello, Sarah. Don't you look beautiful. So grown up. How old are you now?"

"Fifteen."

Two by two, they entered through the door as if our house were Noah's ark itself. Dora methodically whisked away decorative purses and scarves, which she sequestered in her room for the night. Assured that their valuables were in reliable hands, guests turned toward the living room. The men strode anxiously to the bar in the den. They joked and patted each other's backs. Father gripped the necks of unopened wine bottles.

"This way," he announced to new arrivals.

Aunt Annette and Uncle Max brought a box of candies. My aunt kissed me. Uncle Max nudged Mother's elbow and took her into the back hall for a talk. When they reappeared together in the living room Mother looked worried, shaken over something. She quickly engaged herself in greetings and instructions to Dora and the caterers. I found Elliot hiding under the card table next to the piano in the living room. The fans blew a gentle breeze through his pajama top.

"Hi ya," I said, slipping underneath the tablecloth to sit with him and his collection of plastic animals. I offered him a handful of salted almonds. He had an elephant, a tiger, and a hippopotamus. Together we viewed a parade of spiked heels and wing-tipped shoes. Many women wore sheer black or gray-tinted stockings.

"How long will they be here?" Elliot asked. He put one nut after another into his mouth, munching loudly.

"Hours and hours."

We watched the night gathering speed. The rooms filled with tangles of smoke, conversation and laughter. I felt pleasantly submerged under the table, giddy from the smells of mushrooms, the tangy scents of vodka and lime, gin and bourbon. The music Father selected swarmed through the rooms. Outbursts of giggles or someone blasting forward to make a joke punctuated different corners of the rooms. A group of men, including Uncle Max, settled on the couch in the living room.

Elliot leaned harder into my shoulder, his body laden with sleep.

"Come on. I'll take you up."

Upstairs, the air was cleaner. We drank tall glasses of water and snuggled on top of the sheets as I read Margaret Wise Brown's *Goodnight Moon.* Elliot knew it by heart.

In the great green room
There was a telephone
And a red balloon

The rhyming patterns of the story took him away. He stretched out and turned over, hugging a satin pillow, his bunny rabbit from his crib days tucked under one arm.

"See you in the morning," I said, kissing the side of his head.

I passed Robert's room. He had returned to his place on his bed, disinterested in the adults tugging on his cheeks and ears. He didn't care how much he had grown. He had fantasy books, his world of space ships and alter-planets to tend to. But I wanted to see how the party was progressing. The noise level had risen to a happy, high tide. I wanted to see more. When I came back down, Dora looked me over and decided that I was old enough to do something useful. "Why don't you pass these around," she said, handing me a tray of hot mushrooms with melted cheese.

I entered the living room and made my way through.

"So *you're* the girl?" a man with blond gray hair reached out and stopped me. "Shell Garrison," he said, putting his drink down on the piano. He tapped my chin and whistled. "A beauty like your mother. How old are you?"

"Fifteen."

He nodded, lighting a cigarette.

"Let me give you some advice," he said, pulling me to one side of the room. I held the tray with both hands waiting. "Got a boyfriend?" he asked.

I shook my head.

"You hold out for the one you want," he said, blowing smoke in my face.

"Okay."

He was a handsome man and I was both intrigued and unnerved by his directness. I excused myself and continued passing around food. Father introduced me to one of his associates, a woman with cleavage in a cream-colored dress. Miss Delgarno's long fingers dove down to pick up a mushroom, which she promptly plunked into her mouth whole. Her breasts bobbed up high over her v-neckline. I couldn't stop staring at her chest. She wore a startling blue sapphire necklace. Her thin dress clung to her bra so that her nipples and bra straps popped through.

"You've got quite a dad," she said to me, smiling broadly. She wore pale pink lipstick and had a small mole on her upper lip. Father took two mushrooms and stuffed them into his mouth, obviously pleased.

"What do you think about all these zany adults?" Miss Delgarno asked me. She jostled a gin and tonic in her hand, then sucked on her cigarette until it turned bright red.

"I don't know."

Actually, I thought the question was one she was asking herself. But I said nothing and continued on, past Uncle Max and the group of men on the couch. Mother stood at the far end of the den near the bookshelves talking with Shell, who kept leaning over, whispering into her ear. Mother spotted me and came toward me.

"Having a good time, honey?"

She touched my cheek on her way to the kitchen. Miss Delgarno and her cream-colored dress went into Father's office and came out again swaying to a Glenn Miller recording of "Moonlight Serenade." Father cruised over to the bar and refilled her drink. Shell found me in the den next to the windows that looked out to the backyard. The roses were in full bloom, all colors that shone in the spotlights that Mother had turned on. The spots cast bright, intricate shadows across the lawn.

Tall as a tree with sizzling blue eyes, Shell leaned over me, swaying lightly, and asked me to dance but I was too embarrassed.

"Well, then. Where's your beautiful mother?"

He lumbered off toward the kitchen. I watched him reappear with her. He took her in his arms and they started dancing the rumba. This set off another level of glee in the living room. Peter appeared next to me.

"We've got some desperate people here," he said, shaking his head.

We stood near the piano watching. Father left Miss Delgarno and cut in on Shell so Shell grabbed Miss Delgarno. But I saw Shell look over at Mother as he danced with Miss Delgarno, his eyes skipping across the walls. Others joined in while my parents danced together, tipping forward and back, taking quarter turns, their hips shifting together like college sweethearts. It embarrassed me yet I stood mesmerized, drinking three glasses of ginger ale in a row until my stomach felt bubbly and full. Father took smooth control of my mother and she liked that, tilting her chin upwards in approval. Maybe she was remembering their college dance where they first met, in Boston. My father, seemingly assured and wild, gave my mother license to be less than perfect.

"See that? I know how to lead," Father called to me.

He directed Mother past Shell who tried, again, to switch partners, but Father refused to let Mother go. It was a game between the men, a way to compliment my mother, the hostess. Then the song changed. Mother stopped next to me and laughingly informed me that Shell owned a chain of restaurants called Shell Fish.

"Richest man in this room. You should have danced with him dear."

"I don't care about that."

"You will." She flinched impatiently. "Come and help with dinner."

Buffet dinner was served then cleared. Dora and the caterers laid out a new cloth, gold-rimmed dessert plates and silver forks. Coffee brewed in large silver urns. Dora moved intently from one cluster of adults to another, ushering them back to the table. Everyone gathered around to admire the strawberry layer cake. "Irene is the pearl in my oyster," Father said, then called out: "Irene! Where are you?"

Mother emerged from the kitchen all smiles, her cheekbones piqued with the heat and the wine she had been drinking all night long. She stood next to Father and he put his arm around her. "Ah, the insouciance of time. The eternality of family and friends."

After the cake, Aunt Annette and Uncle Max said their good-byes. They were the first to leave. Peter slipped a beer from the cooler, sneaking it up to his room. At midnight Father announced to everyone, "The backyard! We must go out to view the full moon." Some of the women told him he was crazy but laughed and followed him out, including Miss Delgarno.

The remaining adults looked overheated, red-faced, and woozy. More couples asked for purses and the room began to thin out. Dora insisted I go upstairs to bed. I looked into Robert's room. He lay sleeping with his mouth agape, his light still on. A pile of open books fanned around him like a rapt audience. The air in my room was markedly cooler and deafening in its tranquility. I looked out at the round moon from my bed and saw Father and Miss Delgarno talking alone in the yard, smoking cigarettes, and gesturing up at the sky. She kept shaking her shoulder-length hair and smoothing it back behind her ears, then hugging herself. I disliked her adulation of Father. But he inhaled it. I could see his puffy cigarette breaths jumping in the spotlights.

Mother walked out and greeted them, then wobbled oddly between them. Father put his arm around Mother and kissed her, then took her inside. Someone turned the spotlights off and the backyard grew still and soft and not quite dark in the moonlight. I heard the guests' cars starting up and simmering away down the street. Then Miss Delgarno reappeared again as a darker shadow in the dark, moving toward Mother's garden, past the tall oak and the two smaller cherry trees and into the back woods. She wore a long, cape-like coat this time. Shell followed behind practically invisible except for the tiny glow of a cigarette that zigzagged like a firefly. He crossed the lawn and headed for the woods. I saw him drape his long arm around her shoulder before they disappeared into the trees.

Chapter Six

The After Party

In the dark hours after my parents' dinner party, a police officer found Mother at the edge of Gooseneck Lake slumped over the steering wheel. The car hurtled over the embankment, a low dirt mound, and drove into the shallow water. The jolt broke her nose and bruised her forehead. Emergency workers removed her from the front seat and took her to the local hospital for observation.

"Very, very lucky," Father said, shaking his head.

He stood at my bedside looking crumpled. The early morning sun nudged the windowsill behind him. His hair was askew, his clothes buttoned wrongly.

"I didn't hear the car leave," I said. "Where was she going?"

"The lake. The lake. You know your mother. Full of whimsy. Beautiful night. Party. She went on a drive to get some fresh air, those aches she gets and the point is, she's going to be fine. Took those pills. The doctors don't tell you the effects." He fluttered his knotty hands to illustrate what he meant then turned back to the door. He didn't want to tell me more than that.

Gooseneck Lake is where I spent winter days ice-skating with school friends. On one end, it stretched into a long, narrow shape. We skated on the belly section, where it opened up into a round, plump pond protected by shrubs and scraggly trees, where Mother lost her bearings rounding a curve. I shook my head. I felt angry, unable to comprehend.

"I don't get it."

"She'll be fine, fine, fine. Crazy accident. Damn arthritis. Those pills. You and the boys spend the day with your aunt until we straighten this thing out. Get dressed and come downstairs."

He closed my door.

This word 'accident' made him behave in a peculiar shifting way. His voice trembled. I was accustomed to his shouts. But now as I listened to him hurry down the hall, knocking on Robert's door and repeating the word, "accident," in a whisper, I wished he would revert to a louder gauge.

I lay on my back in bed, looking at the ceiling as Robert's reply floated into the hallway, an elongated, twelve-year-old's whining question: "Whyeeee?"

Father said something inaudible.

"I don't want tooooo. Nooooo."

My brother sounded scared, which made him defiant.

"Get up."

Father tromped up to the attic and I heard Peter's voice and Elliot's, then Father stepping heavily back down to the second floor landing.

"Sarah, now, please."

I sat up and got dressed. My three brothers came down one by one and sat on the kitchen stools. Dora, silently poured bowls of cereal and stood at the sink cleaning vegetables, looking stern-faced and military. While we ate, Aunt Annette arrived. She wore a brown and white polka-dotted dress that touched the midline of her knees. Her calves looked surprisingly slender, given her girth, wide shoulders and full bosom. Her dark leather pumps tip-tapped on the kitchen floor. She smelled freshly showered and powdered.

"Hello, dears," she said, bending down to kiss Elliot. She reached toward Robert, but he recoiled and stepped away. So she took Elliot's hand and assured him that Mother would be fine. Elliot snuggled against her thigh.

"What happened to her?" Elliot asked.

"Your mother hurt her nose. She'll be home in a week, so we don't need to be glum," my aunt said.

"How did she hurt it?"

"In the accident."

"But how did it happen?"

Elliot persisted — that part of him that needed to cure all ills, mend animals, fix people, as if his whole being were in a state of anticipation, the hairs on his skin like mini-antennae honing in on what might and could go wrong.

"So many questions, dear. I don't have all the answers right now but when I do I'll tell you. How's that?"

"When will you know?"

"Later, Elliot. Let's think about the zoo."

Father came in shaved and combed, his hair flat. "I'm leaving now. Okay?" He turned to Aunt Annette. "You're all set?"

"I'd like to go with you," Peter said. He spoke with new authority, a new kind of inner confidence.

Father stepped back and bumped into the stove.

"Not today, Peter. I mean it. Please." His voice sounded desperate.

Peter started to speak then changed his mind. Instead, he slid his lanky body off the stool and walked out of the room.

~~~~~

Accident became the operative word, a simple word pockmarked by carelessness and avoidable travesty. The word infuriated me. Fuming, I got into the back seat of Aunt Annette's car. She pushed the master button on the control panel. All the door locks clicked simultaneously like bullets shooting at targets. This didn't help my mood.

"Everybody set?" She looked into the rearview mirror, then put the car into reverse.

"Do we have a choice?" Peter asked.

"No," I said.

The car smelled of my aunt's perfume and had an indifferent air, as if nothing on Earth could soil it or her or us but I knew better. I was the mature one, wasn't I? Isn't that what mother said? *Sarah, you're very mature for your age, beyond your years.* We drove out of the neighborhood, in my aunt's scratch-free black Cadillac with melon-colored leather seats, ashtrays hidden in the doors, down the hill past hedges dried out from summer heat.

On the highway, Peter stared out the window in front, his long, blond ponytail all I could see of his expressions. Beside me, Elliot played with two of his plastic animals — a horse and a sheep. He whispered to himself and tapped the sheep's head against the horse's muzzle, then walked them up and down his thigh, or tilted them on the ledge of his knees. Robert read his book about time travel, his head in an invisible vise, his hand turning pages with a snap that told me he was fending off our shared dismay. No one tried to make conversation.

At the zoo, we filed through the turnstile and headed first to the bird exhibit. Despite the sunny day, the crowds were thin, perhaps because of the heat. We found ourselves alone inside the marshland area, a dark, low-lit room that smelled of old rain and bird droppings. In the water tank, a mallard pecked at a Styrofoam cup floating in the reeds. Robert stopped to look at a school of goldfish. One fish stopped at the glass. Its flat eye peered through murky liquid.

"Why was her car in the lake?" Elliot asked suddenly. He spoke clearly, his voice rising in the dankness.

Peter walked away from the snake tanks and stood next to Robert.

"It went off the embankment. The tire tripped off the side. That's my guess."

"It was an accident, dear," Aunt Annette said. "Another car may have blinded her."

That word again. The more I thought about her driving so late at night, bleary-eyed and oblivious, the more incensed I became. The so-called accident. Why not just say my mother was crazy, caught up in something that I couldn't see or grasp. Mother had behaved irresponsibly. We all knew it.

Elliot took my Aunt's hand.

"Let's go see the monkeys. Okay, everybody?" she said.

~~~~~

We left the birdhouse and followed a cracked walkway to the monkey exhibit, another dark, hollow building. The Gorilla House looked like an abandoned Hollywood movie set with fake boulders, straw piles, a few lean trees. Sky domes let in a hazy light. High on a rock perch, a full-grown male gorilla eyed us disinterestedly. A younger gorilla lingered near the glass front. He picked up a rubber tire and rolled it alongside the glass, then picked it up again and threw it. Elliot crouched down and pressed his palm against the glass.

"He wants to play."

"He must be bored," I said.

The young gorilla walked up to where Elliot knelt on the concrete floor. The two stared at each other. Elliot waved and smiled. The gorilla hopscotched, screeched and ran up the boulders, then down. He thumped on the Plexiglas to startle us.

"Stand back," Aunt Annette said.

"He's playing!" Elliot jumped up and down, de lighted by this.

"Gorillas are highly intelligent," Robert said.

The gorilla ran away and came back again, then danced in a small circle.

Peter said: "Yeah, well. That's why they shouldn't be locked in here."

I wanted to get out of the stuffy building. I started to think about the hours the gorilla spent inside the cage and it depressed me.

"I can't breathe in here."

"But they're protected," Elliot said.

"Endangered," Robert said.

"Not all," Elliot said.

"Shall we keep going?" my aunt said. We were on edge and she didn't want Robert or Peter to start arguing.

We left the building and headed for the giraffes at the opposite end of the park. My aunt walked slowly, stopping to read signposts that explained animal behaviors and foods. Even though the day was muggy, my aunt wore stockings. I wondered if she ever took them off.

Peter began humming a folk tune, the notes falling gently like a stone down a small hillside. *Michael row your boat ashore, hallelujah.* I joined him.

Ahead of us, Elliot, never quick-legged, hurried toward two giraffes grazing in a large open field. A barbwire fence cordoned off the area. The giraffes, tall as palm trees, turned toward him as he approached them. They began to move in his direction, their elegant necks swaying in unison toward a small, faded sign: ELECTRIC FENCE LOW VOLTAGE.

"Don't touch the fence, Elliot!" I screamed too late.

He grabbed the wire and fell backwards onto the ground, shrieking. Peter raced over. I came up right behind. Elliot rolled over onto his stomach and began sobbing.

"You'll be fine, son!" a guard called from the road. A man sped over in a golf cart. He turned to Aunt Annette, who looked horrified. "Don't worry now. The shock don't harm him. It scares them. That's what it is."

"Do you want to explain this?" Aunt Annette asked.

Peter and I both put our arms around Elliot, who sat up looking at his hands. Robert stood with his arms lifelessly at his side, then he began hopping in place. The gray-haired guard assured us that Elliot would not suffer any physical harm.

"It's low voltage and keeps both animals and visitors safe."

Aunt Annette dismissed the man, turning impatiently. "My word. How could you?" I had never seen her upset. Her chin shook. Even with Mother's accident, she had been calm, almost expectant. "Come on, dears. I'll take you to lunch."

We watched the guard drive slowly away.

"Let's go home," Peter said.

Elliot started whimpering. "I want to go to the hospital. I want to see my mother."

"Yes. Why don't we go see her?" I asked.

"I promise you, she'll be home in a few days."

My aunt put her arm around Elliot. He curled his shoulders inward, pressing his chin to his chest. I wanted to cry, too. I turned back to look at the giraffes. They had loped to the opposite end of the field; beautiful, untouchable beasts.

We got in the car. I sat in back again, between Elliot and Robert.

"Did it hurt?" Robert asked Elliot as we backed out of the parking lot. "What was it like? Was it like fire? Did it burn?"

"Shut up, Robert, you sound like a mini-Hitler," Peter said in front.

I held Elliot's hand and rubbed it between my own.

"It was terrible about the sign," I said.

"Did you see it?" Aunt Annette asked me in the rearview mirror. "It was barely legible."

"That place should be shut down," Peter said.

"Shameful. I'd read that it had improved," Aunt Annette said. "It's utter negligence. Low voltage, my word."

"I'm okay," Elliot said. "It's not the animals' fault."

Aunt Annette drove out of the parking lot. There were no indications of betterment here — faded signs, asphalt buckling and curling at the edges. In the rearview mirror I saw her lips pressed into a straight line.

"We'll have lunch. That will make us all feel better. Who wants clam chowder? Elliot, Robert? And we'll have softie ice creams for dessert."

~~~~~

In the evening, I talked to Mother on the phone.

"Are you taking care of the house for me?" she asked.

"Dora is."

"Would you do me a favor, sweetie? The roses need to be fed. In the garage on the third shelf of the metal rack, you'll see a tall can with a picture of roses on it. Take a tablespoon of the white powder and mix it with a gallon of water, then pour the mixture into the roots. Give them a good soak."

I listened. Her voice sounded groggy.

"All right, dear? That would be a big help to me."

"We wanted to come to the hospital and visit you today."

"I know. Your father told me. Put Elliot on, honey. He had a terrible scare today."

I went down to the garage to prepare the mixture. The powder had a putrid smell of old dung. I dumped a dose of powder in the watering can, carried it out to the garden in the backyard and soaked the dirt beneath the rosebushes. Afterwards, I went into my parents' bedroom and opened Mother's toiletries closet. Crystal perfume bottles clustered on the shelf like miniature people whispering secrets. One bottle looked like a flower vase. Another bottle came from Paris. I dabbed sweet stinging perfume down my arms, resting my cheek on the shelves, inhaling the mixed bouquets. Upstairs, Peter was playing a Joni Mitchell record, replaying "The Circle Game" song over and over. *We can't return we can only look behind* — Mitchell's sweet soprano circling my parents' bedroom ceiling like a bird calling far away at sea.

In Mother's clothes closet, I paddled through the hangers, touching one dress after another, her blue taffeta dress next to her red mohair suit. I found matching red silk-dyed shoes in a plastic bag on the floor. The yellow dress she had worn at the party was missing. I imagined it rolled up in a bag, soaked and soiled by the muddy water. I knelt inside the closet and shut the door, fitting my hands into Mother's pointed shoes. Blue taffeta swished across my face. Protected now, I curled up and listened to the music upstairs. Closing my eyes in the darkness, I saw Mother standing at the full-length closet mirror, turning to view herself, highly critical, unsatisfied; moving away, then approaching her image again like a firefighter trying to battle stubborn flames.

What was burning?

Downstairs I heard my aunt's voice interspersed with Father's voice, then the front door shutting. I hurried out of the closet and slipped into my room.

Father checked in with each of us.

"She's fine. Bruised and swollen. Recovering."

He stood at my bedroom door and talked to my rug, not looking at me. "I'm tired now. Let's just be thankful she's all right."

I wanted him to tell me more, explain her to me, but I could see that he was withholding something, not wanting to speak. Later that evening, I heard him scrambling through the downstairs rooms like a hermit crab, searching to inhabit another empty shell abandoned on the sea floor. He walked heavier than usual, back and forth through the house as if carrying his life's belongings on his back, anticipating her return, not knowing exactly where to go without her.

~~~~~

The next morning I woke early and went downstairs. I found Father asleep on the couch, an empty vodka bottle by his feet.

"Dad," I whispered. "Get up."

He opened his eyes, blinking, stirring his brain. He sat up slowly.

"Fell asleep," he said, sluggishly.

He stood up and hobbled over to the stairs. Once he started up to his bedroom, I sat on the couch in the warm indentation of his body and wrapped my robe around my legs. I waited for my brothers to rise. Dora was already up. I heard glasses clinking in the kitchen as she unloaded the dishwasher. Then Elliot came down to watch cartoons on TV. Robert came next and finally Peter. I heard Dora open the cupboard, the carving knife slicing oranges for juice. I took the empty vodka bottle into the kitchen to dump in the trash. Dora turned to inspect me, her arm muscles bulging from pressing oranges for juice.

"Where'd you find that?"

"Living room."

Dora shook her head.

"Glory. My word; what I've seen."

I took a bowl down from the cupboard and poured cereal and milk into it, then slid onto the stool. Dora poured me a glass of juice.

"You have some of this," she said, coming over to me.

She stood close. I breathed skin cream and the scent of oranges on her hands. She poured three more glasses and set one in front of each empty stool.

"I hate the pulp," I said, sipping.

"That's what's good for you. Drink it anyway."

She looked at me sternly but I smiled, comforted by her steady, grim demeanor, her incisive talk; her sweet-smelling dark skin.

"How come you put up with us?"

She started to answer but changed her mind.

"Drink your juice, Sarah."

She went over to the sink and finished unloading the dishwasher.

Despite another round of pleas, Father refused to take us to the hospital. The doctors had put Mother in a special ward for observation.

"I'm respecting your mother's wishes."

She did not want us to see her until her swollen face subsided, which the doctors said would take a week. I heard my aunt tell my father that she needed a different kind of help.

A few people who had been to the dinner party stopped by with offerings: a casserole, a box of candy. Shell showed up in a red cardigan sweater and green pants, carrying a basket of fruit. He scrubbed my head with his knuckles.

"Not to worry," he assured me. "It's that change in season. Makes you drive crazy."

"What change?" I asked.

"Summer heat."

He didn't mention her overdose of liquor and pills. No one did.

My aunt stoked my hair. Her long fingers nudged me to smile.

"What?" I said, accusingly.

"She'll be home soon."

"If she hadn't gone out driving in the middle of the night, this wouldn't have happened."

~~~~~

That night in bed, I floated over the rooftops of the neighborhood. In the darkness I tried to count stars but they had receded like a tide of sand toward another shore. When I saw the quarter moon I fell back on my bed. The crescent light shattered my windows. Mother appeared in the broken pane and smiled. She wore a red woolen skirt and cashmere sweater, a long string of pearls draped around her neck. Her diamond ring was missing.

Mother?

Sweetie.

When are you coming home?

Soon, darling.

I stood in front of her and stared but she didn't say anything else.

Mother returned home after a week, just like everyone said. The first night she came into my room.

"Still awake?" she asked standing in my doorway.

"Sort of."

She moved closer and sat on the edge of my bed, the mattress so thick it hardly registered her weight.

"Homework done?" she curled her fingers around my ear.

"Of course."

"Good."

She got up from the bed and went over to my desk and fidgeted with a pencil, then parted the curtain and looked out. The streetlight scraped against her cheek and made her oval face look empty, like a pretty candy dish. Circles under her eyes cast a greenish halo.

"Fall's coming," she said. "When I was a child I wanted — "

She leaned against the desk and turned up the cuffs of her blouse, exposing thin wrists.

"Wanted what?" I said, propping myself onto my elbow.

"Sweetie," she said, coming back over to the bed and sitting on the end. "My mother used to call me sweetie, isn't that something?" She stroked my bedspread. "She always believed I would be something special, a star. She never liked your father from the beginning. I think she was afraid of him."

"Mother," I said, turning over, tightening the blanket around my neck. "Stop it. You're talking funny."

She looked at me, blinking. Her lipstick had been licked off and only the outline remained.

"Sleep tight, my love." She patted my shoulder and went down the hall to her bedroom.

~~~~~

In the next few weeks, she was apologetic about the accident but distant, becoming wispy again once the bandage on her nose was removed, busying herself with her roses, and taking new pills to help her sleep.

She ordered a custom Cadillac similar to Aunt Annette's, and when she drove it home and parked it in the driveway, it was so big and wide it wouldn't fit in the garage. She looked small at the wheel, frail, I thought.

"Big as a tank," Father said to her.

"Yes. That's what I want. Protection."

After the arrival of the new car, no one mentioned the accident anymore as if we'd made a silent family pact to avoid it; and, I didn't know what else to say to her. She'd already left me. What do you say to someone you've lost?

The answer to that got washed under another pressing matter: an historic dock strike in Boston that severed the legs of the family business. Within days Grandpa had a massive heart attack. He collapsed at his kitchen table on the top floor of his condo building overlooking Boston Harbor. There was no reviving him at ninety-one.

But I remembered when he held all of me in his arms. He didn't rush when he spoke. His voice had a feeling of forever in it. *Light, Sarah. Look.* He pointed to the hallway light outside my bedroom door, his sounds popping like soap bubbles in my ear. On the ceiling, the saucer-shaped fixture shone. He carried me over to the window in my bedroom and pointed to the moon. *Light,* he said again, so that I understood the moon was in my house too.

It seemed to me that such a quick death at this time of his life was a blessing.

2

Interlude

In bed, and almost asleep, my cell on the night table chirps a message. Alan writes: *Flight canceled. Snowing hard. Going to hotel. Will call after I check in. Love you.*

Love you more, I write back, relieved that my husband is safe but worried that he'll rush back for my performance tomorrow night. I don't want him to do that, so I call him.

"How much snow?"

"Four inches. It's supposed to stop soon." His voice is deeper from too much coffee and long meetings, which is what happens when he goes on these business trips.

"Promise me you'll wait until the weather is clear, You don't need to be here for this."

"I know. Don't worry. I promise. Now, get some sleep. Gotta go. The bus is here. I'll call when I get an update."

A peek out my bedroom window, a smudge of pink is bleeding into the eastern sky. Daylight settles my brain. Relieved. Alan is safe.

I settle in again. It's a new morning. Day three of the Festival of Lights. I like this particular Jewish holiday, this proof of miracles. Our menorah is in the kitchen, candle drippings hardened on the plate like cake frosting. I'm not nervous about my gig tomorrow night. It'll be a friendly crowd: animal lovers raising money to sustain an elephant reserve in Africa. My next door neighbor, Becca, arranged the event in nearby West Hollywood and apparently five hundred people have bought tickets. That's a good audience for an indie folk singer like me.

My bedroom is a comfortable sixty-seven degrees, in December, which is still odd to me. Even after thirty-plus years of living here, I'm not used to L.A.'s mild winters as if I am still waiting for those snows and terrible winter freezes to erupt. My two sons — the oldest named after Grandpa Joe, my youngest after Alan's father, Steven, are with their girlfriends on the east coast this year. Strange, too, how almost everyone except Peter and I, are back in New England — Elliot at his farm in Vermont, and Robert, who never left Yale after he graduated, is a tenured professor there. I'm here, and Peter teaches music at U. of Cal. I just don't like the uncertainty of winter weather, and yet that cold side of the world pulls hardest on me at this time of year.

Chapter Seven

Nylons

A month after Mother's accident, I started high school at Soquaset High. Margaret Lucci sat on my right in homeroom, the room I went to every morning for attendance. Her last name followed mine.

"I lost the baby in the bathroom," Margaret said, three weeks into the first term.

"You what?"

"I lost it in the girls' room. I had a miscarriage."

We shared the same desk, a long table divided in the middle by two shelves. I kept my notebook and paper in the bottom shelf. Margaret put her papers in the top shelf.

"Are you sure?" I leaned down to the floor pretending to look for something in my shelf. I wanted to believe her but I couldn't see any bulges anywhere. She wore a straight, tight black skirt and a white blouse so sheer her black bra floated against the cotton. Her breasts bobbed with every movement of her arms. I rummaged around in my shelf and pulled out a sheaf of lined paper. I had never known anyone, personally, who had been pregnant except for Mother with my younger brothers and my memory of her was that of a woman wearing clothes draped like curtains.

Margaret nodded. "I'm sure. Six weeks and four days. Come with me to the girls' room when the bell rings."

I nodded and looked straight ahead at Mr. Giles who was also my English teacher.

"Kunitz?" he called softly. He didn't look as if he had heard what I just heard.

"Here." I raised my hand.

Mr. Giles sat at his desk in front of the wall-sized blackboard and penciled off my name in his attendance book. His hands trembled. The eraser head on his pencil wobbled noticeably. His eyes, always kind, skittered past my face and onto Margaret Lucci's.

"Lucci?"

Margaret nodded.

I turned to her again. She had straight black hair, cut to her jawbone. Tiny hairs darkened the back of her neck. Her bangs fell into her eyelashes.

"I had terrible cramps." She whispered this after Giles called the next name.

"Monihan? Patterson?" Mr. Giles had an ailing person's voice, an uncertain tone.

"Don't you think you should go home and rest?" I worried about her. At the same time I felt honored and exhilarated by her confession. She had picked me, and no one else, as far as I knew.

"No. I can't let my mother suspect anything."

"My mother wouldn't have a clue," I said, trying to keep my lips from moving so Mr. Giles wouldn't notice.

"You're lucky," she said.

"Robertson, Schwartz?" Mr. Giles called down to the end of his list. Even his head shook a little. His whole body vibrated like a tuning fork, as if a ghost of himself moved beneath his skin at a different tempo. His right hand trembled more than his left.

The bell rang and I followed Margaret down a flight of foot-sculpted cement stairs, into the girls' room next to the gymnasium. The bathroom looked like an old dance studio with penny-sized, black and white floor tiles cracked and crushed with age.

"No one ever comes down here," she said, going to a sink, one of many lined against a mirrored wall. She plopped her black purse into the drain. "You can see why. It's a dump. See if anyone's in the stalls. You never know."

I bent over and didn't see any feet resting on the floor. "No one," I said.

"I had really bad cramps in this very room yesterday morning." She rummaged through her bag and pulled out a black eye pencil. "I couldn't walk." She drew a thin line of black on the inside rim of her eyes, pressing her hips against the porcelain sink and leaning forward until her nose almost touched the mirror. "Do you have your period?" she asked. She widened her eyes and inspected every eyelash.

I nodded.

"I've had mine since I was nine," she said.

I didn't tell her that my first one came just this past summer. I went up to the sink next to hers and turned the hot water on but nothing came out.

"None of them work," she said.

She smoothed lipstick, white as confectioner's sugar, over her lips. I licked my lips and realigned my cable-knit sweater so that it hung squarely across the waistband of my green, pleated skirt. For all my colors — green socks and skirt — I looked conspicuously plain in the mirror. Margaret wore nude-colored pantyhose that made her calf muscles gleam. She had long, slim legs. Her black shoes, though scuffed and dull, fit snugly. Her shoes had small heels that made her leg muscles curve. She had pared herself down to an essential something that I wanted.

I looked away from the mirror and counted eight sinks. Every one of them had a crack, either in the drain or near the water taps.

"This place is useless," she said, talking to me in the mirror. "Do you smoke? I've noticed Jewish girls don't smoke. Too busy studying, I guess." She gestured toward her bag. "You can help yourself."

"My parents smoke."

The bell rang again and I knew I had to go to class.

"I better go," I said. "Are you sure you're all right?"

"Yes. I'll see you later, at lunch."

She smiled and I left her dabbing a mascara stick across her bottom lashes.

The halls had already emptied. I went quietly through the back door of the classroom and slid into my chair in the middle row. The biology teacher, Mr. Bingham, looked at me but didn't say anything. He lumbered in front of the blackboard, a tall man with a baritone voice and a black, triangular beard trimmed to a point below his chin. His brown hair looked greasy.

"What did I miss?" I sat next to my lab partner, Sophie Cohen.

"Nothing, yet."

Sophie sat perfectly straight, stretching her long, pale neck. She had hair so thin and light, strands of it floated over her shoulders like milkweed. She wore yellow kneesocks that matched her plaid skirt and sweater.

Mr. Bingham talked about stable and unstable molecular states. He said water molecules adhered with great strength in the liquid state. But I couldn't get Margaret's pregnancy out of my mind. I calculated that she had had sex before school started, on a warm summer night, under the trees, not unlike the night of my parents' party.

Mr. Bingham flicked on the overhead projector. Water molecules looked like sports equipment: round balls with sticks jutting out of them. He told us that molecules, when heated, knocked together and got excited, causing the temperature to rise even more, which explained how water turned from liquid to gas. Sophie pulled a comb out of her notebook and ran it once through her hair, then put it back into her notebook again. Thin strands floated back up in the dry October air.

The bell rang, ending the class. Together, Sophie and I walked to Mr. Giles' English class where molecules slowed to a freezing state. None of the students moved in their chairs.

"Anyone here think the ghost of Hamlet's father is real?"

Sophie passed me a note.

I think Mr. G's wife died, she wrote in pencil. *He talked about her on the second day. He said Hamlet missed his mother and that he missed his wife.*

Sad, I wrote back.

Mr. Giles called on me to read a passage spoken by the ghost, which I did easily and with a semblance of great understanding. Well, in truth, I was all too familiar with Shakespeare's rantings because of Father.

"My hour is almost come
When I to sulph'rous and tormenting flames
Must render up myself."

"Good, Sarah. Tell me, do you think the ghost is real?"

"Yes. I believe Hamlet. I don't think it's his imagination. But, I can see why some people might think he's making it up."

"So you believe in ghosts?"

"Possibly." I thought of Mrs. Brenwald pacing at night. Seeing Mr. Giles vibrating in front of the class, I wondered, again, if he had a ghost inside him, or if his shakes were an imaginary nervous disorder. Like Mrs. Brenwald, he didn't seem to be a person who got mail or phone calls. Surely he didn't have any children.

When the bell for lunch rang, I stopped at his desk.

"May I ask you a personal question?"

"Not if it's too personal," he said, warmly. "What is it?"

"Do you have any children?"

He smiled and stood up slowly. "Three boys, grown up now and living in other states."

"Oh," I said.

"Teachers have children, too," he said mischievously.

"I know. My father is a college professor. He teaches English literature."

"That explains it. You seem to have a good grasp of Shakespeare at your age."

In the hallway, the swirling excitement of lunch hour freed the air. The long hallway filled up with masses of students banging into each other. Voices from the crowd became deafening. Sophie and I headed for the cafeteria in the basement, passing the girls' room where I had been a few hours earlier. I looked for Margaret but didn't see her in the crowds. A clique of Jewish girls passed by and waved to us. They dressed like Sophie and me, in matching skirts and sweaters, white blouses with circle pins. Older girls knew me because of Peter and his rock band. He played at school dances. I rarely saw him at school, though. His classes were in another wing. His lunch breaks at different times than mine.

The school building had numerous additions built onto it, unmarked doorways and stairways. I had heard rumors about a sub-basement with tunnels where janitors smoked and had sex. I would ask Margaret. She knew about things.

As we neared the cafeteria, dank odors of over-cooked food and steamed plastic blew in hot drafts into the hall. I spotted Margaret in the darkest corner of the cafeteria talking to a boy with blond hair. I waved to her and she waved back with one finger, motioning me to come over.

"I'll be right back," I said to Sophie.

I walked over to Margaret.

"Do you want this table?" she asked. "We're going out for a smoke."

The boy turned to look at me. He had beautiful, violet blue eyes, very clear and telescopic.

"This is Anthony Parelli," Margaret said. "My cousin."

Anthony nodded. His dark, blond hair fell into his eyes.

"Sarah sits next to me in homeroom," she explained to him.

"You've got nice legs," he said.

I stepped back.

"Don't let him bother you," Margaret said.

"He doesn't."

"What's your last name, Sarah?" he asked.

"Kunitz."

"You Jewish?"

"Shut up, Tony," Margaret said.

"Yes. I'm Jewish. Why?"

"I like Jewish women," he said, smiling.

I shook my head and looked at Margaret.

"Don't let him bother you," she said, again, zipping up her bag.

"I won't," I said, looking at him.

Anthony smiled and I rejoined Sophie in the food line. Rows of tables, long, pink-topped linoleum tables were claimed by distinctly different groups. It was easy to identify cliques by their dress code. Jews wore sweaters and circle pins. Irish Catholics and Italians dressed in black. None of the groups intermixed. Margaret was an exception. She didn't seem to care. I paid for my lunch and walked back to Margaret's corner table though she was gone. She and Anthony had left a cellophane wrapper from a cigarette pack on the table. Sophie sat opposite me. We both tried a mouthful of the spaghetti.

"Not too good, is it?" Sophie said, chewing.

At the far end of the room, a fight broke out between two Italian girls. Several boys jumped out of their seats and ran to form a circle around the fighters. Just as quickly, Mr. Bingham appeared, pulling two boys away by their shirt collars. A woman teacher ushered the two girls out. The girls wore dark skirts and nude stockings like Margaret.

"Crazy," Sophie said. "Who are they?"

"I don't know. Let's go outside," I said.

The playground was a fenced-in parking lot with fading basketball court lines at one end. We went to a quiet spot near the teachers' cars. Sophie held onto a car door handle of a red Saab and lifted her leg in front of her. She took dance lessons twice a week.

"This is a *plié*." She tapped her foot up and down in a controlled, regulated way, then curtsied. She repeated the same motions with the other leg. "I have to do twenty-five on each side."

The wind blew gently and her hair floated again. I had thicker hair. It only tangled in the strongest gusts. At the far end, a group of Italian boys were playing basketball. I saw Anthony among them. A basketball arced into the pale, blue sky. Someone called out, "Pass it here, Tony!"

Anthony stole the ball from another boy and expertly made his way to the basket. His straight hair flickered over his eyes as he bounced the ball. Two more boys tried to block him but he leapt up and the ball went in. Shouts followed. He applauded himself and surveyed the entire playground as he ran back to his team. He spotted me and nodded. I looked away.

"*Plié*," Sophie said, dipping up and down.

The bell rang twice and everyone headed back in. Sophie walked next to me up the cement steps. It had been so bright outside, the dark hallway blinded me. I moved instinctively beside her.

At the end of the day, Sophie and I walked to the auditorium for chorus. We stood on graduated platforms on stage. The music teacher, Mr. Edwards, had delicate hands for a man and very white complexion. Even the bald spot on the top of his head glowed candle-white under the lights.

"Everyone, listen up." He rapped his director's wand against a metal music stand. The wand was a long, white plastic stick.

"I want to sing the whole piece without stopping. You'll make mistakes but keep going." He scooped the air with his sinewy arms.

"One, two three and — "

I sang second soprano, the range below first soprano. Sophie stood on the row above me. She sang first soprano and her voice, like her hair, had a wispy, airy sound.

Mr. Edwards encouraged us by throwing fake confetti in the air when he wanted us to sing louder, or patting the air softly when he wanted us to quiet down.

"Keep it going, keep it going!" he said, scooping more air. "Don't lose it," he called.

Unlike Mr. Giles whose voice often failed to have any sound at all, or Mr. Bingham, who spoke hyperbolically, blowing pot-clattering sounds into every syllable and word, Mr. Edwards' voice had a clean tone, like a single guitar string humming.

Today, he passed out new sheets of music for the Thanksgiving Day program in November. "To Dream The Impossible Dream" from *Man of La Mancha* was one of the selections, and a song called "Everything's Coming Up Roses," from *Gypsy*. At half past three, the bell for the end of the school day sounded.

Outside, the wind flew between my knees and smelled moist as overripe apples. Sophie's mother waited at the curb in a dark green Cadillac to take Sophie to her ballet lesson.

"See you tomorrow," Sophie said and ran to the car.

I started home, my books a heavy pile in my arms. I carried my biology and math textbooks, three spiral notebooks, my French book; a small, paperback of *Hamlet* on top. Along a chain fence outside official school grounds, I passed a surly looking group of Italian boys and girls smoking cigarettes. All the boys wore tight black pants and pointed black shoes. Two girls wore maroon athletic jackets that zipped in front and had large side pockets. I recognized one of them from the cafeteria fight. She flicked a burning cigarette toward me as I passed her. It hit my shoe.

"Kike."

Stunned, I walked faster and faster. I didn't dare turn around, in shock partly, and in fear, and in anger. I crossed the street, hurrying away from them, keeping my pace until I reached the beginning of Soquaset square. I had never experienced anti-Semitism firsthand. I couldn't believe this was happening. My neighbors were Jewish. Sophie was Jewish.

The familiar storefronts calmed me and I slowed down. I knew these stores like old friends: the hardware store; the record store with its files of top 40 hit singles, owned by a man with balding hair. The dry cleaners smelled of mothballs and dumped hot winds onto the sidewalk.

I looked behind me. Still no one from the chain link fence. Ahead, the corner drugstore with its aroma of bubble gum, the one that supplied Mother with her back pills, which a high school boy delivered once a month. The pills arrived in a white paper bag folded and creased like fine linen. Next to the

pharmacy, a Five & Dime took up the rest of the
block. I looked behind me again but saw no one following. I slipped into the big, discount store. Safe.

How well I knew the aisles of this discount store
sprawling in a messy grid. The green speckled linoleum floor dull and mottled. Aisles of clothes. Shoes.
Women's make-up. Parrots squawking in back next
to dusty changing rooms. At the front of the store,
next to the cash register, a small boy rode an electric
horse. The horse made a whining, thumping sound
as it pumped up and down. I went to the aisle that
stocked cosmetics.

Piles of lipstick filled cardboard boxes on a shelf.
I rummaged through the heaps until I found the col-
or that Margaret wore and slipped it into my jacket
pocket. The electric horse stopped and the store
grew quieter, except for a few squawks in the back.
I heard the child plead with his mother for another
ride. The thumping sound resumed.

In the next aisle, I spent a long time studying
the packages with nylon stockings in them. I picked
through the cellophane files until I found a pair
that fit my measurements, five feet one, ninety-two
pounds. The Nude color had a brownish tone. I took
the nylons to the register and paid for them, then
hid the package between my notebooks. The horse
stopped again. The child moaned and wrapped his
arms around the horse's neck. I went back outside. A mother with her toddler walked by. Across
the street, in front of the library, two young boys
skipped down the sidewalk, tossing stones in the air.

I headed home, passing the town sign: **Town of Soquaset Incorporated 1689**. Cars picked up speed and raced past, making water sounds. The sun eased down toward the rooftops. I felt the lipstick, again, deep in my jacket pocket.

"Starting here!" I began singing — whispering at first, then with more force — the song from chorus practice. I opened my palm the way I'd seen professional singers on TV dramatize songs with their hands. "Starting now!" I twirled as I passed Soquaset's local junior college: a small gathering of Victorian, red brick building with windows so old the glass looked wavy. I knew from Mr. Bingham's class that glass was really in a liquid state not solid like most people thought, which is why it rippled over time. Gravity pulled it down. Behind a hedge, a boy and a girl were kissing on a bench. I walked faster, anxious to get home to my room.

When I entered the kitchen, the house was distinctly quiet. I hung up my coat in the hallway and headed for the stairs. Mother lay asleep on the living room couch in a turquoise mohair suit. A glass lay empty on the green carpet beside her.

"Mother?" I stood over her. The glass had the same sweet, tangy smell as her breath. "Mother?"

She moved and opened her eyes.

"What time is it?" She sat up and smoothed her hair. The stocking on one leg twisted around the knee.

"Aren't you feeling well?" I asked.

She stood up and straightened her stocking.

"My back's acting up again. I'll go upstairs."

She moved slowly away from me and started up to her bedroom. The tangy perfume covered me like a veil. I waited until she reached the upper landing and shut her bedroom door, then went up to my room. In the dusk, I put a desk chair in front of the bedroom door to keep anyone from coming in and held my new stockings high, dangling the silky legs like puppets. I tried them on and walked in grand arcs back and forth around my room. My legs felt cool and delicious and daring. I wondered what Anthony would think.

The sun slid below the edge of the earth leaving a sky layered in purple and brown outside my bedroom window. The weeping birch tree in our driveway had dropped its leaves early. Vine-like threads hung straight down to the blacktop. I imagined Anthony standing in the driveway calling to me. I went down to him in my sheer stockings, feeling light and beautiful, and together we walked into the darkness like bathers wading in a warm sea.

Chapter Eight

The Closet

I took the stockings off, hid them in my underwear drawer, and opened my jewelry box. Buried in
a nest of silver bangles, I found a necklace with a
Jewish star that Aunt Annette had given me on my
eighth birthday. The star was the size of my thumb-
nail. I put it on and went down the hall to see who
else was home.

Robert's door was shut. I knocked.

"Who is it?"

"Me."

I opened the door. He sat on his bed reading
a science fiction book. The yellow light in the fish
tank flickered on the surface. Streams of bubbles ex-
ploded rhythmically.

"Isn't the air coming out too fast?" I pointed to
the tank.

"No."

"What are you reading?"

"*Time Planets.*" He held the book cover up for me
to see. "It's a series. There are twenty-two books.
Twenty-two is a power number."

"Power for what?"

"I'm on number one," he said, ignoring my question. "I'm going to read two a week. In eleven weeks — eleven is another power number, by the way — I'm going to know everything about ancient numerology. Numbers have energy levels. I made a chart, see?" He pushed a piece of paper to the end of his bed. On it, he had written book one and a box ready to be checked off beside it.

"So, if you'll excuse me, I'm busy," he said, looking at his watch. "I have to stick to my schedule."

I went up to the third floor.

Elliot looked puffier than ever. He lay on the floor on his elbows, cleaning his plastic animals with the bottom of his shirt and repositioning them on the windowsill that overlooked the backyard.

"Has Peter been home?"

He shook his head and went back to rubbing one of the elephant's legs.

Peter had started a rock band called The Symbols. The group had a drummer and bass guitar player. Peter played lead guitar and sang. During a practice session in his friend's basement, Peter jumped off a chair singing a Rolling Stones song and fell on his ankle, causing a hairline fracture. In the last few weeks, he had been getting rides from friends, coming home later and later every day.

I went back down to my room and started on homework: twenty-five math problems, an essay for English, French sentences on future tense. Downstairs a clatter of pots and dishes began but not from Dora's hand. Dora was gone for two weeks to care for an ailing aunt. Mother had called a maid agency for a short-term replacement. Clarisse from Jamaica had gray hair, a quiet speaking voice and kind eyes. She moved with great deliberation and I quickly felt sorry for her bad luck. Had the agency warned her about my family? Would Dora return? In her absence I found myself missing her. What if she never came back like every other maid? Over the months, I'd grown used to her tough comments, her sharp eyes watching us. She paid attention to me.

The kitchen door thumped shut.

"Anybody home!" Father called out.

I heard him go to the hall closet and hang up his coat. Mother walked past my door and went downstairs to join him, then called us down to dinner. Downstairs, the dining room shone. Clarisse had draped the table in white linen. Mother still looked sleepy. She held a glass of red wine and took a long sip, then sat down at her place at the table. Father put the wine bottle at his end and sat down.

"Where's Peter?" Father asked no one in particular. He looked toward the kitchen. Elliot and Robert shrugged.

Clarisse came back into the room carrying a casserole dish of noodles and fish.

"Set it down right here," Mother said, gesturing to a spot in the middle of the table. "And would you get the children their milk?"

Clarisse nodded and went back into the kitchen through the swinging door.

"Monsieur Robert," Father said, smiling. "Let's hear about this new series of books you're reading.

Your mother told me." Father dished a spoonful of the casserole onto a plate and waited for him to answer.

"It's about time."

"And what about time?" He smiled and looked at Elliot, then at me and then Mother.

"It exists on twenty-two planes."

Clarisse came in holding two glasses of milk and placed them beside Elliot and Robert.

"Next time you can bring out the glasses and pour at the table," Mother instructed.

Clarisse nodded and went out.

"How many times have you told her that?" Father asked.

I looked into my glazed china plate and saw a reflection of the ugly round chandelier hanging above. Appalled, again, by my father's rudeness toward our maids, words kicked inside my head: *get the stupid milk yourself!*

"Where's Peter?" he asked again, lumping the casserole onto my plate. "He's late."

"What's this about time?" Mother asked Robert, repeating what Father just said. She sipped her wine, sensing a blow up I knew was coming.

"We live on the third plane of time," Robert said. "Our house exists in the third plane of time."

"Third?" Father asked. "Why not the fourth?"

"That's the way it is," Robert said, irritated. "The first is before we're born. The second is in the womb. The fourth is after we die."

The kitchen door opened and Peter walked in. His foot was healing but he still limped.

"You're late," Father called to him.

"My watch says six-oh-three," Peter said, stripping off his jacket in the hallway. He wore a dungaree shirt and red bandana around his neck. His hair fell to his shoulders.

"It's six-twenty-three. You've been late every night this week."

"I've been busy." My brother sat down in his chair and reached across the table for the casserole dish.

"Don't be fresh," Father said.

"You didn't wash your hands, dear," Mother said.

"I got my first paying gig. That's why I'm late."

"You could have managed that earlier. You'll have another excuse tomorrow."

"It's not an excuse. I'm not excusing myself. You don't even care about my music. You should be congratulating me. But you don't give a shit. All you care about is time!" He pushed his chair back and stood up.

"What do you know about time?" Robert asked.

"You sit down," Father commanded.

Peter laughed a bitter laugh as if he had made up his mind about something.

"What's fifteen-twenty minutes?" Peter said, raising his voice. "Nobody lives in such rigid time zones. It's insanity."

"I said don't be fresh with me, young man," Father said, standing up. His face turned red. His eyes looked big as bowling balls. There would be no stopping him now.

Peter stepped back and began to move away. "I'm going to my room. I'll eat later." He looked at Mother.

I stared into the jumble of noodles and fish, to avoid the molecules that I knew would fly. Mr. Bingham's theory couldn't be entirely correct. In my house, things heating up made the volume of space decrease. I felt claustrophobic. I couldn't breathe.

"You'll sit down and eat now!" Father thumped his fist on the table. "In fact, you'll stay in for the weekend."

"Leonard, please."

Mother flinched and reached for her wine glass.

Peter widened his eyes and looked up at the chandelier. "You can't be serious," he said, waving his hand.

"Sit down!" Father yelled. "We're not finished here."

"You're not but I am." Peter walked behind Mother and started for the first stair.

"Get back here!" Father pushed out of his chair and charged toward Peter, catching his elbow. Peter twisted away. Father almost lost his balance and tripped backwards.

"Don't touch me," Peter said. He started to climb the stairs again but Father lunged up and yanked Peter's shirttail.

"You listen to me, young man."

"You listen to me," Peter shrieked. He shoved Father on the chest and Father fell onto the carpet. Robert wailed and charged around the fist of bodies, upstairs to his room. He slammed the door. Mother closed her eyes.

"Leave me the hell alone," Peter said, standing on the stairs. "I'm not a little boy anymore, understand me? I'm almost eighteen."

"Go. Go," Father said waving a weak hand.

Peter's chest heaved. "I don't have to pay for your failures, either," he added. He turned away from Father and walked upstairs.

Father nodded pathetically but didn't speak. Slowly, he returned to his chair. Mother said nothing. Elliot tugged at his hands. I didn't speak but I knew things would be different now. Peter had won. I felt oddly gleeful, inwardly cheering for Peter who I knew was plugged into his earphones by now, soaking in music, already far away upstairs.

At the table, Father looked boneless and lost. I studied my lap until Father picked up his fork and resumed his meal. He took bite after bite of the casserole, chewing endlessly. Mother emptied her wine glass. Dinner was over when Father swallowed the last forkful, wiped his mouth, scrunched up his napkin and placed it beside his knife on the table.

"I'm done."

"Clarisse," Mother called.

Clarisse entered and cleared away the plates.

"Can I be excused?" I asked Mother.

She nodded.

"Elliot, come with me." I looked at my brother. He slid from his chair and walked beside me up the stairs.

I knocked on Robert's door.

"Go away."

"We'll only be a minute."

I opened the door. He lay on his bed hugging his book. The fish tank bubbled, all the golden fish mouths opening and closing, fins gliding along the glass edge, dipping behind the greenery.

"Want to come up?" I looked at the ceiling, meaning Peter's room.

"No." He tugged at his pillow. "I have to finish my book."

Elliot stepped closer to the fish tank. He smudged his finger slowly across the glass.

"Don't touch it!" Robert barked. "It's the rule, remember?"

"Elliot won't hurt the fish."

"You're not supposed to touch the glass. It upsets them. Go away."

He put his hands over his ears and started humming loudly.

"Okay, shh!" I said, touching his foot.

Mother called up to me, her high voice penetrating the door. "Sarah! What about piano?"

I took a deep breath.

"I'm coming."

"Robbie, I've saved your dinner," Mother called. "Don't you want it?"

"No. I'm not hungry!"

"Elliot!" Mother called for the third time. "Time for your bath. Clarisse will be up to help you."

I went back downstairs. The dining room table had been cleared of all dishes, but the tablecloth, yanked up on one side, looked undressed against its will. The chandelier glared like a searchlight. I turned away and stepped down into the living room. There, the piano waited, so patient and tranquil. I slid onto the bench and surveyed the pattern of black and white keys. Rosewood gleamed from furniture polish. I opened my red Thompson book and began finger exercises. The small reading lamp cast a hot, intense yellow light on the pages.

My fingers moved up and down the keys, stroking the black sharps and flats exactly right. After I finished my finger exercises, I turned to simplified versions of Beethoven sonatas. But as I worked my left and right hands so that combinations of notes and chords fit together in a sound puzzle, I heard them again, arguing in Father's office.

I tried to play louder, pressing the pedal down and holding it to the floor. But I heard... *"Do you understand me?"* Father whined. After a short silence, I heard his shrill high-pitched retort. "Christ, Jesus, Irene."

I tried to play faster and louder but their voices outplayed all the notes. My fingers couldn't move quickly enough, so I started to sing: "To dream, the impossible dream!" I let my voice shout out the words, changing to a higher pitch like a kite taking a sharp turn in the wind. My fingers stopped. "To dream!" I sang, hoarsely, holding the word "dream" as long as my breath sustained it. Mother opened the door.

"Sarah, please. Go upstairs. Have you done your homework?"

I slipped off the bench.

"This house is driving me crazy!" I stomped up each carpet-covered step, straight to the bathroom and locked the door. I turned on the bath and undressed while the tub filled with hot water. In the bathtub, I held my breath and put my head underwater to muffle sounds. But I still heard my parents' bedroom door slam. Father walked heavily down the stairs and down again to the basement stairs.

In my bedroom I put on a flannel nightgown, one with small, green flowers. The steamy air hung between my legs. A colder, dry air splashed against my neck and face.

Father marched back up the basement stairs. He stopped in the kitchen. I heard a crash, then the banging began. The banging sounded different, exuberant, like a proud call for attention. I snuck down to see what he was doing.

I peeked into the kitchen at the very moment he let go of the toolbox. The box was a large, oblong metal container filled with mechanical objects that are a mystery to people like Father who lacked an aptitude for tools. A vial of nails broke open and scattered across the white kitchen floor.

"Christ!" He grunted and looked around, spotting me.

I stepped back.

"Oh, so you want to help?" he said huffing. He knelt down and turned the toolbox upside down. A hardware store of hammers, nails, clippers and screwdrivers fell out.

"What are you doing?"

"See that?" he said pointing to the small broom closet. "I'm going to rebuild it. It's a terrible configuration of space. Under-utilized."

"Now?"

I looked around me. Clarisse had packed the kitchen away neat and tidy, except for the mess Father was now making. Every glass and dish had been rinsed and carefully placed in the dishwasher; the lights dimmed except for the spotlight above the sink. The dishwasher had already begun its ritual of clicking followed by a series of small explosions. I smelled the dishwashing soap, as if it were God's breath exhaling into the room. The floor had been swept. Countertops scrubbed, every last crumb, spot and drop sponged away. The aluminum sink and faucet towel-dried and left smudgeless as polished pewter.

"If you want to help, you can go downstairs and bring up the small boards." He got on his knees and plucked the hammer off the floor.

I went down to the garage. I could not recall a single day Father had used a hammer well. Then I heard another thud upstairs. I picked up two boards, one under each arm, and started back up. I heard another bang. He started hitting repeatedly, faster and faster, a flurry of banging and thudding.

Father swung the hammer toward the ceiling then down again on the broom closet's flimsy walls. Half the closet had caved during my short absence. The destroyed closet put me over the edge and I started laughing uncontrollably. The night had been a snake pit of bad behavior. Everything about it came launching out of my mouth in giggles to the point of tears.

He stopped and stood back to catch his breath.

"Piece of cake," he said, looking at me.

Both Robert and Elliot came down to see about the noise.

"Stand back, now."

He lunged forward and hammered on the other wall until he broke through.

"Watch it, watch it."

We three stepped back out of the kitchen. Splintered closet walls, a scattering of old nails on the floor toppled haphazardly around Father. He used the claw of the hammer and pulled out more nails and pieces of plaster.

"Stay away from the nails. Stand back."

"You never build things," Robert said.

Father puffed and leaned on his hands and knees. "This should be very easy." He stood up and wiped his wet forehead. The hammer dangled from his hand. The dishwasher clicked again and went into the rinse cycle, whooshing and throbbing, the fan inside spinning round and round.

"Clear out. Go on. Let me finish in here."

He waved us away good-humouredly, looking highly satisfied, almost calm after so much wood bashing.

I went to my room and put my stockings on again, then put them away. Above, I heard Peter strumming his guitar, stopping and starting, something he did when he was writing a new song. The guitar came through as a faint humming through the walls. I was proud of him. He had dared to speak up, make a change. Mother, by contrast, resumed her usual night activities in the bedroom with the door closed, talking on the phone with a country club friend.

"Oh, shit. *Christ*!"

Below, Father's chopping stopped. The house grew densely quiet. I went into the bathroom to brush my teeth. The heat from my bath earlier had cooled to water droplets, covering surfaces in liquid lace.

Father climbed the stairs and went into his bedroom. Water pipes squeaked as he turned his shower on. Mother came out and urged Robert to bed, calling up to Peter to get Elliot settled.

When it seemed Elliot would be asleep, I went up to the attic. Peter lay on the floor with his earphones, listening to music in the dark. I parted the curtain of beads hanging in his doorway and tapped him on his knee. His bedroom shag rug felt warm and fuzzy between my toes.

"You okay?" I asked.

"He's brain baked," he said, sitting up. A thin melody came out of the earphones like far away traffic. He turned the volume down. "He thinks he's normal. It's amazing."

I sighed.

"You know how hard it is to get a job playing music? Six bands tried out for the dance. We beat the guys that played last year."

"That's great."

"What's his problem? What's he got against me?"

"Maybe he envies you."

"Right. He's a creep. Certified. Graduation and I'm outta here," Peter said, surveying his room.

I went over to the window and looked out. It was too black to see the long backyard, but if I were a bat hiding in the eaves, I would swoop in and out of everything.

"What do you want to hear?" Peter crawled over to his record collection. He had over two hundred albums stacked on the floor.

"You pick."

"What are you two talking about?" Mother asked, standing at the door. She had changed into a white blouse and black slacks and had combed her hair, but she did not look refreshed.

"Nothing," Peter said.

"Don't wake Elliot. Keep the music down. It's a school night."

She went downstairs.

"She acts as if nothing happened," Peter said, disbelieving. He pulled out an album by Jimi Hendrix. "Listen to this song. I want to play it at the dance."

He played "Crosstown," lifting the needle and replaying sections of the song at different points in the melody. He hummed accompanying parts for each instrument — guitar, piano, bass guitar. He played the drumbeat on his knees, stopping the song again when he missed a beat, over and over until he got the rhythm right. I felt privileged to be included.

~~~~~

In the morning, I heard Clarisse putting pots on the stove downstairs. The smell of coffee and the sound of Father's gruff voice percolated brightly.

"Up and Adam everyone!" he shouted from the front hallway. "Time waits for no one. Sarah! Elliot! Rob-hurt! Everyone up! Good-bye!"

The door shut with a whomp. Farther started his car and drove to work instead of walking to the train. He did that sometimes. I got up and inspected the clothes in my closet. I didn't have anything black so I put on a red plaid skirt and matching red sweater. My Jewish star gleamed against the red wool. I reminded myself that if someone said "Kike" again, I would say something and if things got bad I would go to the principal, or Mr. Edwards. I would make those people at the fence understand. I tucked my stockings inside my French textbook.

Downstairs, Mother stood at the stove in a blue silk robe, stirring hot cereal.

"I'm late," I said, crossing the kitchen, one arm in my coat jacket.

"What about your breakfast?"

"Can't."

I tiptoed around the lumber hive, which rose to a peak high as my shoulders, in the middle of the kitchen floor.

"Elliot, sit down and eat," Mother said.

I opened the back door. A cold breeze shook me as I ran down the steps to the driveway. When

I reached the library in town, I went to the girls' room, a tall, narrow room with green and white square tiles. The steam radiator clanked with rising heat. I put on my stockings and lipstick. I felt glamorous when I stepped outside again, the chilly air shimmering like metal springs up my sleek, almost naked legs. I hurried to school without running. I wanted to see Margaret and Sophie — and Anthony. I couldn't wait to get back inside those dim, overheated halls.

Chapter Nine

Solo

Peter and I prowled the halls of New England Conservatory looking for Mother. We were not in the best part of downtown. The Conservatory bordered Roxbury and the South End in Boston; a jewel set between decrepit buildings and heroin addicts. Mother had dropped us off to find a parking spot.

It had been years since Mother had seen Mrs. Janson, whose amazing daughter, Justine, excelled as an opera singer. The idea of seeing an old high school friend and her prodigious daughter spawned happier expressions on Mother's face at the dinner table and later, when she came into my bedroom to kiss me goodnight. She sat where my sheets folded over the blanket, and talked the way she sounded before parties or outings at the country club.

"Justine started singing when she was two," she said standing in the middle of my bedroom. She's simply one of those people who knew what she wanted right from the start." Mother pointed her small chin upwards to reinforce this idea.

"Is she nice?" I asked. "Is Justine friendly?"

"Friendly?" She turned to look at me, lying on my back. "I imagine. Her mother certainly is."

For Justine's recital, Mother wore an aqua blue wool pantsuit, which looked arresting next to her short, blond hair. Her mohair coat smelled of plastic wrap and bittersweet dry-cleaning chemicals. Peter threw his army jacket over his bell-bottom jeans, the ones he never washed, which caused mother to grimace as usual, but it was the only way he would agree to go. I wore lined woolen slacks and a navy blazer with silver buttons the size of radio dials. Mother looked at me with approval, which mattered to me.

Dora was back but it was her day off on Sunday, so Father stayed home with Elliot and Robert. Peter would have driven, but his foot, wrapped in an ace bandage, was re-injured from leaping off our high school stage during his Rolling Stones-inspired guitar performance. The doctor told him he had to wait two more weeks. I sat in back of the Cadillac, all eyes on Mother's driving. Peter sat in the passenger's seat.

Ever since she half submerged her Thunderbird in Gooseneck Lake, she avoided driving at night. But she made an exception today. She did not want to miss this chance, as if witnessing Justine's greatness might infect us all.

"Justine's a true prodigy," Mother said, gripping the wheel. "She knew what she wanted and pursued it. That's what it takes. Beverly told me that Justine sang the National Anthem in first grade, in front of her entire school. Isn't that something?" Mother's voice shifted to higher, emotional registers. When we didn't answer, she said, "Isn't that something?" as if Peter and I were already heading down a road to anonymity.

I drew circles on the car window, certain I could offer something important to the world, too, like Justine, I just didn't know exactly what, yet. Peter and I sang, but not opera. I wanted to wrap myself in soulful folk harmonies, not satin gowns. Laura Nyro. Joni Mitchell — singers like that. Peter played rock guitar. But that didn't count for Mother. Classically trained in violin from the age of six, she considered our newer forms of music substandard.

As she exited the highway and entered the city, she braked and accelerated at the slightest provocation — a car passing to our right, a pedestrian waiting at the crosswalk. Snowbanks from the last storm narrowed the lanes. The February sky swept us into early darkness. Then, a light snow started.

"You're braking too hard," Peter said. He looked miserable in front. Pale brown bangs covered his eyes as if to block a harsh view of life ahead. On the sidewalk, strangers wore hurried looks, rushing to finish errands before stores closed.

"I can only do what I can do." She took a long, jittery drag of her cigarette, leaving her pink lips on the filter. We didn't say anything again. I'd heard this phrase from her too many times, but it still unfurled inside the car like her cigarette smoke, flattening against the ceiling, flattening us.

Finally, Mother said, "Beverly also told me that Justine practices four hours a day, but that's what it takes when you strive for greatness." She leaned toward the windshield. "There are no shortcuts about that."

"Is that how long you practiced?" I asked because I had no idea. She rarely talked about her musical days playing violin.

"Yes, centuries ago," she said, sighing.

~~~~~

In the car, she reached for her cigarette again, her middle finger and thumb wincingly misshapen. She took extra pills before this trip because her finger joints throbbed like suffocating hearts, especially in damp, cold weather. Did all mothers take pills?

Downtown, we circled around the block, past several filled-up parking lots.

"I'll let you two off," she said.

"What will you do?" Peter asked.

"I'll find a spot. Go."

"We'll stay with you," I said, leaning forward. I hung my arms over the front seat.

"Hurry. Go on. I don't want you to miss the beginning. It sets the tone."

She dropped us off at the front entrance and we watched her turn in the direction of nearby Symphony Hall, where Mother played once in college. Her red brake lights flickered as she merged with other cars.

Now her violin lay in a cool corner of her bedroom closet like a dated history book. Once a year, she picked it up and tapped the strings, stroking the bridge with one finger. She'd place the chin rest under my chin and for a moment I'd see her face change, soften, open up to a world beyond the one she found herself in, and that included me. She held the bow for me, then sawed my arm back and forth across the bridge and together we listened to the breathy, sleepy strings.

"All dried out. They sound terrible."

She stopped sawing and her mood changed.

"You could buy new ones."

"What's the point?"

When people asked why she no longer played violin, she said, "arthritis and children," and gave a quick smile, as if having children was some kind of ailment. I know she didn't mean to hurt me when she said that, but she did.

~~~~~

Inside the conservatory I saw ornate plaster ceilings, moldings wide enough to curl up in, chandeliers intricate as beehives. The building captured some essence of beauty and hope, seemed to offer a permanent escape from ugliness and despair. Maybe Mother was right to bring us here, after all.

I started to feel excited about the recital as Peter and I followed a curved hallway to a small room at the building's rear. He limped and sounded one-footed in the hall — the padded sole of his special boot silent while my heels clapped in double rhythm against the shiny floor. A poster on the wall showed a picture of Justine Janson, her hair pulled back. She looked much older than twenty-one.

As soon as we entered the recital room, Mrs. Janson came over to us and introduced herself. I shook her small hand. She was a short woman with frizzy hair and wide, hula-hoop hips.

"You're dears to come in this weather. Where's your mother?"

"Parking," Peter said.

Mrs. Janson made a face, one that sympathized with the plight of finding a parking spot in Boston. She smiled and thanked us for coming. We took our seats in a row near the back. Peter draped his army jacket over Mother's empty chair to reserve it for her.

Soon, the lights dimmed. A man in a tuxedo crossed the stage and took his place at the piano. The door to the recital room closed. I looked back instinctively for Mother, still circling the building, I imagined, looking for an elusive parking space. A spotlight brightened and Mrs. Janson's daughter Justine glided to center stage swathed in purple chiffon. The pianist began a roulade of scales. Justine parted her lips and began to sing in Italian.

The program notes translated each aria into English so I read the words while she sang about loneliness and longing, the beauty of the woods and the path she walked on. She shaped her lips around high notes. She trilled about her aching breast and lost love.

"What good is the exquisite flower lighting her path with no one to share it with?" the notes translated. *"What good is the sweet air if only I can breathe it?"*

While Justine's voice hovered in uncertainty, trilled and twirled and rose again, I counted fourteen rows of wooden seats.

"Where is she?" I whispered to Peter.

He left his seat and slipped out the door. I went with him.

The long, marble hallway was empty except for two women taking tickets at the front entrance of the main Jordan Hall. The Vienna Choir Boys were singing in there.

"Did you see a woman in a mohair coat?" Peter asked a girl with thin hair and freckles.

"She's our mother," I said.

The girl shrugged. "A lot of people pass through here. Where is she supposed to meet you?"

"She's parking the car," I said.

Peter pointed in the direction of the small recital hall to the left. "If you see her, please tell her to go to there."

The woman nodded.

"She's very pretty. She has blond hair," I added.

We walked down the foyer steps and looked outside. Snowfall covered the roads in a crusty membrane, the falling sky lowering itself upon us.

"Is she lost?" My breath fogged up the glass door.

"Possibly."

We waited together, staring at the snowy street lined with parked cars turning into white ovules.

Peter looked at his watch. "It's icy out there," he said, his voice quiet as the snow.

We went back up the stairs and stood near the ticket takers unsure about what to do next.

"Isaac Stern is playing at Symphony Hall. There's a lot going on today," the girl offered as a way to explain the parking situation.

"Let's go back," I said. Maybe Mother had come through a side door.

Back inside the recital room, the audience clapped. Justine left the stage. Lights brightened for intermission. I wanted to tell Mrs. Janson. Perhaps she would know something. As soon as Mrs. Janson turned around I started toward her.

"Not here yet?" she asked, looking a bit worried herself. "They did say parking was impossible today."

"It's snowing," I said. I looked for Peter at the door. He motioned to me.

"Let's go back to the front," he said.

We walked down the marble hallway again, past doors I now recognized. Some had gold leaf numbers and others did not. This time when we reached the front lobby we ran into the intermission crowd for the Vienna Choir Boys. People smoked furiously. The doors to the main concert hall opened revealing cathedral-sized organ pipes above the stage and gold-rimmed railings. It was a beautiful room steeped in carved wood and plush green chairs. It looked happy inside there, the opposite of how I was feeling, a squall brewing in my stomach.

"I'm calling Dad," Peter said testily.

Peter spotted a telephone booth off the lobby. I stood against the folding glass doors while he dialed home.

"No answer," he said, thumping the receiver into its metal holder. "Let's go outside."

We went out without coats down one block toward Boylston Street. City lights twinkled red, white and green, indifferent to my cold-stiffened fingertips. Peter surprised me by lighting a cigarette.

"I'm thinking of calling the police." He took short puffs, impatient intakes.

"Where do you think Dad is?"

"I don't know," he said, stamping out the cigarette.

"Where could she possibly be?" I was freezing, scared, my head covered in a doily of ice. I looked over at Symphony Hall lit up with a border of lights the size of onions. The building looked secure, unperturbed by the disorderly streets cutting around it.

Back inside the lobby, overhead lights flickered. The crowd drained into Jordan Hall for more Vienna Choir Boys, leaving the marble stairway empty again.

"This is insane," Peter said.

An hour had passed since Mother left us at the curb. Behind the thick doors of Jordan Hall sounds of the choir crescendoed and receded like underwater currents. Peter went back to the phone booth and called Father again. No answer.

"Something's wrong," he said, unfolding the glass doors, still clenching the phone. His face was wet, his hair stuck in moist bands across his forehead.

"I'm calling the police."

He folded the doors shut. I listened to the dime click and ring through the slots. Someone answered. Peter nodded and waved his hand. He looked at me as he talked but his clairvoyant blue eyes saw beyond my face. His voice lacked intonation. He nodded again and hung up.

"What did they say?"

"They thought an hour was long. They're looking into it."

He walked out of the booth and back over to the front door, which is when we both saw him: my father's face distorted as a runover grocery bag.

"Dad!"

He veered abruptly, his shoulders pushing an invisible burden up the stairs.

"Your mother's in the hospital. Get your coats."

The ice crystals left a glistening halo on his large forehead. I scrambled down to the recital room, careless this time when I opened the doors. The light caused Mrs. Janson to turn. She must have seen a look on my face because she raised her hand to her chin but that is all I remember of my mother's high school friend that day. We ran back outside.

In the backseat of the car, Elliot and Robert scrunched together on one side. I got in and sat next to them. Peter got in front.

"What happened?" Peter said.

"A furniture truck hit her. Goddamn it! They don't know." Father pounded the dashboard. When the light turned red, he looked both ways and ran through it.

"Jesus Dad!" Peter said. "Don't kill us!"

"Your mother can't wait." Father swiveled the steering wheel, his eyes twisting all over the road.

I froze, but not from the cold. Father sped past Symphony Hall. A stray dog hunting for food in an overturned garbage can wore a sheen of snow on its back. Elliot kept wiggling his pudgy fingers like bugs caught under stones. Robert held tightly to a book and read, his body hard, unmoving.

I prayed as we raced toward the hospital. Father honked at every car in his way. I prayed for everything to be as it was before this moment, until the sound of my father's murderous expletives dulled, and the stinging lights of the city became shadows. I imagined Justine in the deep woods singing alone as if only God were listening. I wanted God to hear me now. *Please, please let her be all right.*

Father swerved into Boston City Hospital and parked in front of the emergency entrance.

"Stay here," he said.

He pushed open the car door and ran inside. The motor idled, warming the car with a moist, leathery smell. Every five seconds the windshield wipers cleared the glass, making Japanese fans.

"I'm going in," Peter said, opening the door.

We all piled out.

Inside, we caught up to Father arguing with a woman behind the nurses' desk. The woman had a hairclip, which she scooped into her hair as she stepped around the counter. She was thin and small.

"I'm calling the police if you don't tell me where my wife is."

"The doctor is coming to talk to you now — please hold on. I will get him."

"Hold on to what?" he said, shadowing her. "Where's my wife? Goddamn this fucking hell hole!" he screamed.

A doctor hurried down the main hallway, his white coat flickering. He wore gray slacks and black tie-up shoes.

"Mr. Kunitz? I'm Dr. Greer. Why don't we go into the waiting room? No one's in there right now."

The doctor pointed to a small room off the hall.

"How is she?" Father said, grabbing the doctor's elbow.

The doctor paused and made some kind of calculation. He turned his head slowly. His face was long and flat as a clipboard.

"I'm sorry — "

"What?"

He looked at Father and the rest of us in the waiting room. I heard words about concussion. Shattered spinal cord. Pills. The man's beeper pulsed and he turned it off. Another nurse walked in.

"She's in recovery," she said.

"Recovery? You said she was — For Christ sakes! Which is it?" Father jammed his face up to the doctor's.

"It's a holding room for you and your family, if you choose," the doctor said, glancing at my brothers and me. But there wasn't any choosing. Father dashed out and we hurried with him to the door where the man had pointed. We moved as one conglomerate, sidling into a room at the other end of the hall. I smelled rubbing alcohol.

The woman's face was swollen inside a helmet of bandages twice as big as her head. She would have been horrified by how ugly she looked. It wasn't her. She didn't move. She lay still as a branch ripped from a tree. I floated to the top of the room, dizzy with the height.

Father collapsed on top of her, wailing and barking in shredded yelps. Elliot, who was more flesh than bones, sank into a corner. I heard him moan. Robert stiffened. Peter stood at the end of the bed shaking. The room convulsed, a spasm of contractions, as if Mother were giving birth again, over and over, pushing us back out.

"Shut up. Shut up. She'll hear you," I heard myself say. "Shut up, everyone."

This is when my Aunt Annette came in. Nearly six feet tall in her navy pumps, she looked military in her blue suit, white pearl earrings and hair swept tightly into a sailor's knot at the back of her head. "Good Lord, Leonard. The children." My aunt tried to gather us up like a bushel of apples that had spilled across the floor. But that was impossible. The bitter bucket of life had spoiled everything or would if I let it. Mother said there were no shortcuts. It was up to me to know. Whatever life I would lead, whatever greatness I hoped to achieve, would take hours of practice, she said. Years. I turned. My aunt took my arm and led me away.

Chapter Ten

Stay

They buried Mother five days after the car crash. The adults called her death a tragic accident — that word again — as if she had not been trying to leave us. But she finally succeeded, and the whole town knew. Aunt Annette couldn't get over the fact that a photo of the accident had appeared in a paper with a circulation of half a million. Front page of *The Boston Globe* metro section, a twenty-five-year-old driver from California was moving his wife and toddler to the city. He had never seen snow before and certainly didn't know how to drive in it. His U-Haul truck broadsided her.

"The Cadillac stopped in the middle of the street," an eyewitness was quoted saying in the article. "But the light was green." The truck barreled across the intersection, unable to brake in time, and skidded into her. Unconscious, internal bruising, head concussion, broken ribs, the driver lay in the same hospital where Mother died. Uncle Max was worried about getting sued. I hated him even more than the day he wanted me to be his nude.

"Let him sue," Father said, despondently. "He'll get nothing from me."

The morning of the funeral, a day streaked with elephant-colored clouds, I stood in a small reception room of Reuben's Funeral Home, a dim-lit holding room, and loitered inside a cold, foggy hole, which is what life is reduced to when your mother dies. Aunt Annette thought Elliot and Robert were too young to attend. Father disagreed and for once I felt grateful toward him. It was our mother, not hers.

"I think it'll be too much for them," she said.

"She's not yours," I snapped.

The organ music in the other room grew louder, a whining but distant siren with one long note ramming the air as if the organ player's finger had been scotch-taped to the key. It sounded ugly and rough. An usher in a black suit came up to me to let me know that the service would soon begin.

"Sarah. It's time. You'll sit in front, next to your father. Follow Peter."

The cool draft from the larger room sucked me toward the doorway. Father left the room, tears soaking his face. He had gone into his own world of suffering alongside Hamlet and Lear, coveting his grief as if God had a limited supply to pass around. But Father was wrong. He couldn't see that God had an endless source of it and it flowed through me and Peter, through my younger brothers.

The organ pitched higher, more insistent and unkind. As I entered the room, I heard the hush of strangers and looked down at my feet. There is nothing worse than the pity of others. It was as if this consensus by adults to feel sorry for me was a way of levitating themselves, nailing me to a display board. It demoralized any effort to appear normal. I pulled the veil of my hat over my face, turned toward the altar, and saw Mother's casket covered in white roses. I looked away. My stomach twisted and I strangled an impulse to vomit.

In the wooden pew, an usher placed a paper program in my hand. Father let out another wail and I heard the crowd shiver in response. People take on the opinion that children can't handle moments like these but it is precisely children — not adults — who are in sync in the presence of death. As the nausea subsided, I sat calm as a tulip bulb buried in the earth. In my dark pit, I simply asked Mother to *stay with me*, I prayed. *Stay close. Closer.*

I listened hard for her faint, intelligent voice. I just didn't hear her then. She might still be catching her breath. Anyone killed by a truck would need time to recover. Knocked out, she swam in a different universe, breast-stroking to the surface. It would be the very opposite of her life on earth where she didn't swim at the country club, but waded up to her thighs to keep her hairdo dry. She might start playing the violin again. Her fingers would straighten; her back would no longer hurt.

~~~~~

Up on stage, Rabbi Meyers took his place at the podium and began the prayers. The organ sounded again, quietly nudging the crowd to join in. I didn't turn the pages in my prayer book. The rabbi asked everyone to stand. Again the sounds of muted sobs came from behind. I grew dreamy and *drifted down my school hallway. I walked alone to the art classroom in the basement. Lights were dimmer here, floors made of a harder material, concrete. Side stairways spiraled up narrow passages. I had gone to the girls' room to put on more lipstick, nearly late again so that the hall was deserted when he appeared at the opposite end; his blond hair combed back and wet looking. He must have just come from gym. Anthony walked up to me. I couldn't turn away.*

"What are you doing here?" he asked. He smelled of fresh cigarette smoke and English Leather cologne. I inhaled his scent, wanting more of it.

I pointed to my art class at the end of the hall.

"Who's your boyfriend?"

"Who's your girlfriend?"

"Maybe you."

He touched my lip and walked away. I turned to watch him. He hunched his shoulders, but sauntered down the hall with a football star's innate confidence.

"He likes you," Margaret told me during morning attendance. "I want you both to come over after school."

~~~~~

Father let out another piercing groan. Aunt Annette reached over and touched his arm. Her hand crossed my lap. Her fingers were long and pudgy, tapered to nails that glistened with a pale, pink glow. Though she was taller than most women, and overweight, she had a gentle refinement. I wondered what it would have been like if she had been my mother.

Then I remembered Uncle Max. He sat up front, behind the podium, twisting the program in his hands. Aunt Annette kept folding a small, white napkin. Everyone rose again. Uncle Max came to the podium and talked about Mother as a girl.

"Sarah, Peter," he said, leaning forward on the podium. "Your mother had a musical gift, which she passed on to you. Cherish it." He went on to talk about her love of gardening, her artistic sensitivity. Then he turned to the casket. "Irene, you'll always be my little sister — " His voice sputtered and snapped. He walked back to the chair and put his head into his hands.

The organ started again, another meager effort. Aluminum, grimy notes offensive to what Mother, my musical mother, should expect. I hated this crowded room. People nodded and mumbled the words. People obeyed.

Then, everyone stood and six men, including Uncle Max, but not Father, walked up to the stage and spaced themselves evenly around Mother's casket. The rabbi nodded. The men picked up the box and descended down three steps to the middle aisle. As they passed through the room to the back exit, a ripple of sobs and murmurs followed. An usher leaned over to me and said I could return to the small room reserved for the family of the deceased. He wore a ruby on his middle finger and his brown hair was capped by a black yarmulke. My aunt came over and led me outside.

I sat in the hearse with my brothers, Father, Aunt Annette and Uncle Max. A quartet of policemen on motorbikes escorted us through intersections in town and a road that led to the highway.

Father bunched a handkerchief and shook his face at a spot on his knee. Peter looked out the window. I imagined Mother up front, smelling of perfume and talking gaily as if the next excursion would be the one that would take us out of our troubles, clear away the unhappiness that cluttered our life. I was deep in my capsule with nothing to say and I could tell Robert, who sat beside Elliot, was too. He pulled at a crease in his pants, as if he had been put in this car by mistake and was waiting for someone to figure this out and take him away. He turned to the window and watched the police while Elliot beside me took my hand and cried. Aunt Annette handed him a Kleenex. I listened to his sobs: quiet, gentle gasps. A policeman drove alongside us, directing the hearse driver to turn off the next exit, and then the policeman took off again. Another policeman raced ahead to forge an opening for the procession of cars that trailed us. We all turned our eyes to this motorcycle display, this speed-chasing dance. The zigzagging design distracted me. My brothers watched too. But not Father. Nothing dragged him away from the centrifuge of pain.

The cemetery looked like a snowbound prairie with a few hedges and occasional tree. Headstones lay flush to the ground, an attempt, I think, to equalize the dead and therefore the living. No one could mount a statue larger than the next. In this place, it was the size of the family plot that mattered. Hedges cordoned off our plot. A canopy had been raised on metal poles.

The hearse stopped. Father got out first, then the others except for Peter, who waited for me, but I couldn't move my legs. A crowd gathered outside under the canopy. Elliot and Robert stood beside Father. The rabbi put his arm around my younger brothers, bent over and whispered something to each of them — another adult outside the family, taking charge. Elliot nodded. Robert shook his head. Other cars drove up and parked along the roadways that sketched lines through the flat, white field. Then, Peter turned to me.

"Coming, Sarah?"

I looked over at a mound of shoveled dirt and shook my head.

He moved to close the car door.

"Don't shut it," I said.

The rabbi looked over at me and nodded.

Even in this chilled season, I couldn't think about her without thinking of her roses. The garden lay underground and dormant now, but in summer, Mother's weather, the roses appeared everywhere — in crystal vases in the front entryway, in single stem vases lined up on the kitchen windowsill like models posing in a fashion magazine. Every other day, she emptied the vases and replenished them.

"Makes them last twice as long," she explained.

Each stem was stripped down to display the lean form of its silhouette against sunlight. And the garden, of course, in full bloom was rife with roses. Bushes and bushes of roses.

She once told me: *When I walk outside in the morning, I feel the plants trembling, bending toward me in greeting.*

All summer long, she passed hours in her wide-brimmed hat kneeling among the thorns, snipping and pruning. Father sat close to the house on a lawn chair as Benny Goodman's clarinet swan-dived out of his office window. On those warm afternoons she secured her glass of Scotch in a hole she scooped in the soft ground.

But to me it seemed that roses were meant to fail at every moment. Just as one bush might bloom, another wilted under attacks of bugs tinier than my eye could see except for the damage done. I can only conjecture that this was precisely why my mother adored them.

I believed she could have won prizes for her flowers if she had tried. Every person who came to the house said so. Such a profusion of roses, including vases of dried buds that stayed all year on display in the downstairs vanity and her bureau top. It got so I couldn't smell them anymore.

Occasionally, she made arrangements for the local hospital. For these, she used cakes of green oasis. Her designs, like her style, were spare — not more than eight roses in a vase cut different lengths, with some leafy greens to fill out the spaces.

"Too many in the vase takes your eye from the individual flower. No rose is the same, you know. They each have character and temperament."

Perhaps she was mourning her garden at this time of year. Her flower heads had turned brown, her petals wrinkled as old peoples' faces. The smell of mulch, those cans and pails of mixtures labeled and shelved in the garage, those bitter odors are all that remained, until another spring.

~~~~~

The officials in black overcoats passed out a sheet of prayers. The rabbi said something about the life of loved ones lived on in spirit and memory. The cantor sang in Hebrew. Then the men from the cemetery went over to the coffin and began lowering it.

I pulled the door shut and looked out through the window. The rabbi walked over to Father and handed him the shovel. Father punched it into the mound of dirt, then stood at the edge of the hole and let the dirt fall. He fell apart again, wailing. Peter put his arm on Father, who hunched over sobbing grey puffs of cold air into his hands. Max took the shovel and filled it with dirt, dark and crumbling like frozen chocolate cake. He flung the dirt into the hole and then he too collapsed in tears, turning toward Grandpa's stone, whose grave lay in the same large plot. Annette walked over and touched his arm. Then the rabbi handed Peter the shovel.

My brother went over to the dirt hill and shoveled deep into the middle, filling the shovel to the brim. He walked to the edge and turned the shovel upside down. When half the dirt clung to the metal, he began shaking it violently to free the dirt. The rabbi came over and gently took the shovel out of Peter's hand. With Elliot, the rabbi held the handle and helped Elliot push a small clump over the ledge.

One by one, attendees formed a line behind the mound of dirt and took turns with the shovel. I couldn't imagine Mother in there. I saw her floating above us, fluttering in a light wind, a shape long and silken as a scarf that stretched over the whole cemetery. In the distance, a few gray clouds worried themselves into one large cloud. I would have liked to join them as they moved toward the horizon to find out where she had gone.

Chapter Eleven

Shiva

The reception and week of *shiva,* seven days of official mourning, took place at Aunt Annette's. Father did not want to return home. He said he was ready to put our house on a raft and *shove it out to sea.*

The rabbi stood in my aunt's dining room and led more prayers. Time stepped on my heels. No matter where I stood, in a corner in the living room, in the hall by the coats, in the dining room by the coffee urn, it nudged me to move. By mid-evening, cigarette smoke had filled the room up to my shoulders, absorbing food smells — bagels and lox, cakes and plates of cookies. A large tuna fish platter massacred by forks and spoons.

Father sat in the living room on a couch as people crowded around him. Some people leaned over to hug him. Others knelt down on the floor for longer talks. Mostly, he cried or let out a groan or a sudden shout that paralyzed the room like a siren in a traffic jam. Everyone stopped talking. Then the noise in the room resumed. Many people, especially the men, came over to me and patted my head as if

I were a puppy dog that hadn't learned to bark. The women stopped and brushed my hair back around my ears, maternal strangers, as if such simple motions could neaten the pain, tuck it away.

People came in like tides. When the front door opened, I bobbed on sudden currents of cool, quiet air that flew in.

Neighbors showed up on the second night. The Fineburgs next door. Mickey. Like silent trees, like organisms who share the same sunlight, the same moon at night. Mrs. Janson came by without her daughter.

"I'm so sorry, Sarah," she said, making a grim face. She tightened a black shawl around her shoulders.

I was thinking Mother might want to know about Justine.

"How's your daughter?"

"Just fine, Sarah." She squeezed my elbow.

I nodded and walked away.

Aunt Annette kept a large pot of coffee brewing. A caterer refilled trays and trays of pastries. The people who had come to my parents' parties filed in now in gloomy procession. The women dressed in black suits and dresses. Some wore diamond brooches on their collars, or small, glittering earrings — stylish but not gaudy. Miss Delgarno showed up wearing a turquoise sweater, Mother's favorite color. She was younger than Mother's friends and she came alone.

I disliked the way she took Father's hand, squeezing it as if she could offer him a measure of solace that no one else could. She tried to do the same to me but I stepped away. This time, I wasn't serving hors d'oeuvres. I didn't have to be polite.

"How are you doing, Sarah?" she asked.

"Great. What do you think?"

My rude answer kept her at bay so successfully I employed this new tactic on Uncle Max. He leaned over to kiss me.

"Don't touch me."

He jerked up as if I had whacked him with a paddle, and though in normal times he might have ventured to tell me to be polite or nice, he accepted this statement and crossed the room to light up a cigar. I couldn't understand what my aunt saw in him. His lips had turned brown from so many years of cigar stubs melting in his mouth. The putrid smell of cigar smoke penetrated every crease in their house.

"You have your mother's eyes," Mr. Garrison — Shell — said, taking my face in his huge, restaurant-owning hands. Maybe he thought I was a piece of steak. He kissed my cheek then lumbered on toward the bar for a drink but I forgave him. I could tell he was stricken. He had tried to smile but couldn't. Dora kept a sharp eye on Robert and Elliot and they stayed close to her. Robert kept walking back and forth between rooms, avoiding engagement. I worried that he would explode, kick something before the night finished up. But after a while I understood that his restless moving kept him afloat. Elliot accepted the hugs of strangers. He answered their questions. He nodded. He looked older than all of us at his young age.

I went into the downstairs bathroom and threw up glasses of ginger ale. I wiped my mouth with a paper hand towel, the kind Mother and her friends used for parties. This one had an "S" printed on the border for Stein. I went to find Peter.

I think people expected me to cry openly but I didn't. I was full of tears that surfaced only when I was alone. I didn't want these people to feel satisfied by my pain. Crying in public would fulfill their expectations of a tragedy — those country club women, the ones with firm thighs, deep summer tans, the ones who laughed loudest at the pool, who clicked their teeth against crystal rims of Martini glasses.

"Excuse me a moment."

Upstairs, I located Peter on my cousin Kenneth's bed. My brother balanced a pencil and paper on his knee, and was smoking a cigarette.

"What if Dad sees you?"

"Fuck if I care."

The room was dark except for one small reading light next to the bed and a fat, burning candle set on a plate on the floor.

"I'd like one," I said reaching for a cigarette. I wanted to smoke like Mother, become her.

Peter threw an unopened pack to me and I fondled it. All the times I had opened the top for Mother while she was driving in the car.

"Honey, there's a fresh pack in my purse. Can you get it for me? Thank you, sweet."

I folded back the cardboard top. Usually, Mother smoked mentholated, extra slim, long cigarettes. I tugged a regular, unfiltered cigarette from the pack and placed it between my lips. Pieces of tobacco fell onto my tongue, bit like bitter salt.

"When did you start?" Peter asked.

"Today."

I watched Peter suck on the cigarette, then vent the smoke through pursed lips. I tried to do the same and coughed.

"Don't swallow it," he said.

I tried again, holding the cigarette as Mother did: thrust out between two fingers as if it were a magic wand, a tiny spotlight for showing off her best hand. When the cigarette grew an ash, I went over to the window, opened it and tipped off the end into the winter night air. I leaned over the windowsill and looked down at my aunt's side yard. A squirrel ran across a branch at my level, twitched and cawed then scurried down a familiar route to the rhodo-dendrons that lined the yard. Old fall leaves clung from branches, stiff and lifeless. The cold turned my breath white.

When I drew on the cigarette, the ash turned red as burning leaves. I was ten the last time families on our street gathered outside to burn leaves. Air pollution was a new concern. Mrs. Brenwald's leaves turned black and wet around her car but our leaves rose in big, fluffy humps as Father pushed them into the street, the metal rake scraping against asphalt and sand, pulling our entire front lawn of leaves into his mound.

Once lit, the pyres spit and popped unruly acorns high as the telephone wires above us. It was only at this time that the children, even the youngest, were allowed to light the ends of sticks. I remembered inserting a twig between my lips, watching the end burn as I was doing now with the cigarette. Peter wasn't there. He had started a band with two friends and was at the drummer's house practicing.

All afternoon I poked at the simmering nest with Mickey Fineburg. Slow afternoon shadows stretched across our yards until we disappeared with the trees and darkness, slowly merging into a single netting of dusk. I puffed on my twig and tried to exhale with finesse, the way Mother did — as if smoke streams were tails of kites that could take me away on a breeze. Mickey's mother walked out to the street and said, "Be careful what you're doing, you two. Time to come in." She stood in a long wool coat and watched for a minute before going back inside.

Mother didn't come out that day. She said she didn't like the cold. I wondered, looking up at her lighted bedroom window. Was it something about us or me that caused her to stay away?

~~~~~

"How long do we have to stay here?" I asked Peter. Still leaning out the window, I saw more headlights driving up the road beaming my way.

"The rest of the week. Man, this place is swarming."

"She knew a lot of people," I said, thinking of the country club crowd.

"Yeah. But did they know *her*?"

He lit up another cigarette.

"I'm feeling sick, are you?" I asked.

He nodded.

The house made different noises from the clots of people going in and out. The doorbell rang. The telephone rang. Downstairs, a renewed crowd wandered through my aunt's large living rooms. Cigarette smoke, burned coffee, cherry-filled candies, coffee cakes, damp winter coats all tossed together. I could have leaned out the open window all night, staring at the sky, waiting for the moon. But the fog stole my view. I couldn't spot a star for all the density in the clouds.

"I wish we could go home tonight," I said.

"I don't," Peter said. "It'll be hell when we do."

"It's hell here."

I was sick of listening to those glossy tones of strangers one floor below.

"Honey, how are you, dear? I'm your mother's cousin, Margie," a woman with pearl earrings and a black hat the size of a Frisbee said to me. She bent down and squinted at my face as if my eyes were on display at a jewelry store. Then she touched my arm to further inspect the goods.

"Father's in the other room," I said, stepping around her.

Downstairs, our neighbor, Mrs. Fineburg, wore the same black coat as that day of the burning leaves. "Take care, Sarah. Take care," she said, sipping on a cup of black coffee. I wasn't sure I could. Take care of what? My brothers? Myself? Beside her, Mickey stood mute, inward like a little, lost boy. We were preschoolers when he pulled out his penis and showed me how his urine rose in a smooth arc across our driveway. Ancient memories. At funerals you think of these things and say nothing. What did it matter now? "Have some food, Mrs. Fineburg, we have too much." I pointed to the buffet of casseroles before walking away.

I tried to picture myself walking into home-room, a new person now. A person without a mother. Margaret might steer me to the girls' room to find out what had happened. What would I say? I didn't know what Sophie would do, or the teachers. I saw Anthony meet me and walk me to class, then put his arm around my waist as if I were his.

"Do you think anyone at school knows?" I said, turning from the window.

"The whole friggin' town knows. The entire *state*."

I heard someone coming upstairs.

Kenneth walked in. He looked around as if he expected to see others and when he didn't he turned and closed the door.

"What a fucking circus," he said. He peeled off his black suit jacket and unplugged his tie from his shirt collar. He truly was huge, his head nearly touching the overhead light in the middle of the ceiling. The bedroom seemed to shift when he entered. "I've never seen such a collection of bullshit, have you?"

I always liked Kenneth but now I loved him completely. I turned from the window and went to sit on the bed, to be closer to him. He was one of the few people who spoke honestly and it came naturally to him. People thought him inelegant, the opposite of his brother, Edward. Mother once said it would be nice if he could be more polished. She thought he said things just to be provocative.

"I really can't tell where he's coming from," she said a few days after one of our seders.

But I saw that he didn't have the patience for manners. It confirmed my observation that good behavior offered a way of telling lies. Downstairs was a perfect example. I had observed *Miss* Delgarno sitting next to Father on the couch as if her new mission in life was to keep vigil, but I suspected her vigil was much more than that.

"I couldn't take another minute down there, although I think your mother would be happy so many people showed up," Kenneth said.

He pulled out two odd-shaped cigarettes and handed one to Peter.

Peter struck a match and puffed until the cigarette flared red. He inhaled and held his breath then exhaled a long stream of marijuana smoke.

He passed the joint to Kenneth who sucked on the cigarette three times. Kenneth's cheeks puffed out like a bad trumpet player. He bent over and hacked violently.

"Good, good stuff," he said. "You're not going to tell, are you, beautiful?" he said, wiping a tear from his eyes.

He knew I wouldn't.

Very soon after, fatigue pressed against my shoulders. I lay down on the bed and listened to Peter and Kenneth talk about the music scene in San Francisco. The vibration of their voices grew loud and soft or both, as if I were listening to an amplifier while someone invisible kept fiddling with the dials.

I woke up in the middle of the night in my aunt's attic bedroom. My room smelled of old wallpaper, a stale odor of paste, plasterboard and radiator steam. I was still in funeral clothes, a black skirt and sweater that I wore for choral performances.

I didn't know what would happen to us. Sobbing, I clutched the pillow and curled up into a cramp, trying hard to squeeze her vital presence into myself. I had lost her forever. She had driven into a deeper light without me.

Chapter Twelve

Escape Route

I returned to school after a week, not knowing what to expect, nervous and scared in a different way, hugging my books to my chest to protect myself as I passed the town library, the Five & Dime. Everything was altered now.

My heart jumped as I approached the schoolyard. I saw Anthony smoking with a group of boys near the fence.

"Looking good, Sarah," he said in a low voice, his hand curling protectively around a cigarette.

I breathed his smoke and tried to smile as I passed him, some part of me wanting him to walk with me into the building but he didn't. Inside the corridors, kids pushed. Shoes clattered. I moved through heavy double doors, following the building's smell of warm paint and steam. The first bell rang. Its stark, impersonal sound took me right back to the old routine. In homeroom, I looked for Margaret but her seat was empty. Mr. Giles started the roll call. He called my name, his eyes settling on me for just long enough that I knew that he knew about

Mother. I didn't want it to be this way. I wanted to erase this terrible feeling. Return to normal, make it stop.

Mr. Giles looked at Margaret's empty seat. He called name after name on his list, his pencil flickering over the attendance book, his subtle shaking a constant companion. The bell rang again, shrill vibrations like a cold rain as I darted upstairs to biology, Sophie waving from her seat.

Mr. Bingham told us to keep in mind what we learned about molecules and to turn to the section on ecosystems and the evolution of swamps. He looked at me, but then he talked in his usual stern way about beavers, and trees and water interacting as one system. "The deletion of one affects the processing of the others," he said. "Mr. Beaver makes his dam, the water pools up, the tree roots begin to rot." He lifted his bearded chin, perused the row of students then looked at me again and said: "all things connected," in a surprisingly gentle voice. On the blackboard, he wrote "degeneration" and "regeneration" in blue chalk.

I also wrote down these words in my notebook, neatly, in pen, but I couldn't think about those things. Instead, I drew a beaver's nest, leaves and sticks heaped round as an igloo. I felt my skin rippling as if it sensed stares I couldn't see behind me. Mr. Bingham said that beavers had an exit and entryway and a special escape route leading underwater in worst-case scenarios. Where was my escape? Where could I disappear? The classroom darkened. Outside, rain clouds clotted up the sky.

Mr. Bingham hunkered over his tiny desk, calling out our homework assignment and a short test for tomorrow as the bell rang. Sophie waited for me while I shuffled my papers together. I was stalling. What was she going to say?

"This will be an easy test," she said. "He likes to sound tough but he's not."

"I know what you mean," I said, relieved that she had said something typical as if nothing was wrong.

The long hallway had a life of its own. Twelve minutes of chaos. I walked into Margaret standing outside the girls' room.

"You're not sick," I said. Sophie stood beside me.

"Did Giles say anything?"

"Nothing. He marked you absent."

A blond girl with dark roots swung open the bathroom door, releasing a cloud of smoke. She looked hard at me but said nothing when she saw Margaret.

"I had to take my baby sister to school." Margaret held open the bathroom door. "Come on. I need a smoke."

I followed her in. Sophie came with me. Toilets flushing in succession sounded violent, small humping explosions of water. Another dark-haired girl leaned over the sinks to blacken her eyelids. She smudged white lipstick on her mouth, powdery confectioner's sugar.

"I had to help my mother," she said, her eyes shifting when she said, "mother." The sound careened into my heart's canyon, falling into darkness.

"I'll have a drag." I held out two fingers and she passed me the cigarette. I puffed, blowing smoke in a stream as I had watched her do. I would pretend. It was the only way. I blew another stream at the grimy ceiling. I liked this place that never let in light. The green windows dimmed the room at all times of day. She watched then took back her cigarette.

"You've been practicing. I don't know if I should tell Giles," Margaret said. "He won't believe me anyway." She took another drag.

"Tell him. He'll believe you."

Margaret blew smoke and offered her cigarette to Sophie who surprised me by taking a puff. She coughed. The girl at the sink looked over at her. Sophie passed the cigarette back to me. I put the filter to my mouth. It was hot and sweet as flavored lipstick. I tried inhaling this time and coughed too.

"You both need a lesson," Margaret said, smiling.

She took the cigarette and lifted her face, sucking in a long length of the cigarette then hissing it out. She directed the stream up like a singer reaching for high notes. Then she went into the stall and threw the stub in the toilet. The thumping and crash of the flushing toilet resounded again.

~~~~~

After lunch, Sophie and I went to gym and shimmied into hideous green uniforms, ironed and washed and starched to a harsh cardboard texture. In the dressing stall, I worked the pleated dress over my hips, snapped every button. I slid my nylons down and put on socks and sneakers. Water stains the size of squished cockroaches marked up the cement floor. The room smelled wet, the air interminably chilled.

Miss Holloway paced the aisles yelling, "Get on it, girls! Hop to!" She cruised between the stalls and peeked over the tops of the curtains to hustle us out. Thick-thighed, her gym skirt pleats opened when she walked. She had an umpire's chest. Her breasts joined together as one. Her calf muscles stretched the elastic limits of her kneesocks.

Outside on the playground I stood near the splitting white lines of the basketball court where Anthony had played. We lined up for timed races. Miss Holloway sniffed and rolled her small eyes. She held up her stopwatch, the pride in her life.

"On your mark, girls. Get set, wheeeoooo!" She blew her whistle. "Go, go, go, go!"

I ran fast but Sophie with her longer legs beat me by two leaps.

"Next group up. Hustle. Hustle. Move it!"

The boys' gym door opened and let out a small crowd of older boys in gray sweat pants and tops that looked soft and comfortable, so different from what we girls had to wear. Anthony ran in the middle of the pack. His blond hair fell across his forehead as he headed for the grassy field a quarter mile away, off school grounds. A few boys whistled at us as they ran by. Anthony saw me and nodded. I felt a thrill.

"Girls! What are you looking at? Back in position, now!" Holloway clapped and blew her whistle. "We're losing time here."

This went on for the rest of the period until it was time for showers, which we had to take. Back in my changing stall, I stripped to a pink towel from home. I wanted to bury my face in the terry-cloth to escape and hide but Holloway was pacing the aisles. I tiptoed down the short corridor to the shower room, a chamber of cement subdivided into stalls with plastic curtains hanging from metal rods. Above, green mottled windows covered in wire mesh allowed anemic sprays of light. My showerhead dribbled lukewarm water. The feeble nozzle connected to a maze of thin piping that zigzagged across the ceiling. *All things connected*, Mr. Bingham said.

The floor was greasy cold. I pretended to wash with a scarred bar of soap as Holloway roved up and down, the Nazi Gestapo with her invisible dog and stick.

"Under the water, all the way, Sarah," she said, standing at my stall and staring in. I stepped back and covered my pubic hairs but she parted the curtain for a better view.

"Get under. You can't wash with air, can you?" I crossed one arm over my breasts. Cold air seared my stomach as she held the curtain open.

"Turn and get your back wet."

She waited until I turned and dipped one shoulder under the dribble.

"That's right. No exceptions."

She released the grip on the curtain and moved on to her next victim. What did she mean by that, no exceptions? That she would not treat me kindly because my mother had died? How I despised her.

By now the showers collectively let off a wheezy, thin layer of steam. One by one I heard curtains scraping across metal bars and Holloway barking her ignorant, prurient demands.

"Soap and water, girls, please!"

The deeper she walked into the steamy maze of naked girls, the happier she sounded. I reached for my towel and hurried back to dress.

Sophie and I walked to our next class in stunned silence.

Finally, I said, "I hate her."

"Me, too," Sophie said.

My art teacher, Mr. Wilkins — a tall, lanky man — skated between tables, gliding and pivoting when he emphasized a point. It was my last class of the day. I had almost made it through.

"You're here to break rules," he announced. He took a sharp turn at the windows then stopped in front of them as if he expected to see something out there. "There's no absolute right. Understand?"

I nodded, breathing in his sanity compared to Holloway's sick, strangulating antics.

He loped toward the opposite wall and turned off the lights. "See if you can create something." He slid back over to his desk and succumbed to his chair to see what we would do.

The room quieted except for pencil scratching and the tapping of wooden rulers. I drew lines across a dinner table, crisscrossing them until the dining room looked imprisoned like one of Robert's creepy, space-time alternative worlds. Wilkins got up again and moved through the room to glance at our drawings. He sat down again and began reading a novel.

At the bell, he hiked a backpack over his shoulder, and called me over.

"Tell me about your drawing."

I shrugged. "It's a table."

"I got that. Tell me about those lines."

"Maybe they represent conversations."

He nodded. "Good start."

Sophie waited for me in the hall and we all walked out together to Mr. Wilkins's car in the school parking lot. He was the owner of the dented red Saab.

"Did you have an accident?" Sophie said, and I could tell she regretted it because she looked away from me.

"Life's an accident," he said, opening the car door.

I saw Mother driving away in the snow and it made me understand that I had entered a blizzard of other people's discomfort as well as my own. I had to figure a way through it. So, I forced myself to pretend that cars and accidents had nothing to do with me or Mother.

"What happened?" I asked.

"It's not important. Get in. I'll give you two a ride home." He tossed his backpack into the backseat, along with empty soda cans, old mail, a pair of sneakers and a stack of drawing paper.

But Sophie and I had decided to go to a football game.

"We're going to the game," I said.

"Waste of time, ladies."

He folded himself into the front seat and rolled the window down. "Waste of time." He smiled and drove out, honking once as he turned onto the main street.

A few blocks away, I heard the syncopated clapping of the cheerleaders. The game had started. We hurried to the field and found a remaining spot on the bleachers. Rows below and behind us were full. Down in front, eight cheerleaders in pleated skirts and thick sweaters skipped on a running track, scattering black dust. Two girls wore ponytails with ribbons. They smiled as if their mouths had been ripped open. A group of boys in leather jackets and pants sat in the upper rows of the bleachers, hooting back. Directly behind us, a row of Italian girls were snapping chewing gum.

"Kike," one of them said to me.

"Hey, kike. You deaf?"

Someone tugged on my hair. I turned around.

"Excuse me?"

The girl behind me had bleached blond hair with obvious black roots. She looked vaguely familiar. She wore blue eye shadow and patches of rouge on her cheeks.

"Excuse me?" she said, imitating my voice.

I leaned forward and tried to focus on the game. I refused to be intimidated by this. Anthony shot out from the group and ran diagonally across the field to catch the football. The ball wobbled, broken-winged, and fell yards short from where he stood. He ran back to the huddle. Sophie nudged her knee against mine, signaling me that she wanted to move away but I didn't. I didn't want them to know that I was scared. The huddle broke up. Then the quarterback ran back and sent the ball into the air again. This time Anthony caught it. He ran out of bounds.

"Dirty Jews."

"Do you have a problem?" I asked the blond. The other two cohorts looked stone-faced, their pale skin framed in straight, black hair.

"Do you?" the blond asked.

I turned away again. My shoulders braced, anticipating abuse.

Someone nudged my arm. "We didn't say you could sit here. You're blocking our view."

I swiveled back around.

"I don't need your permission."

The blond smirked then broke into a smile. The cheerleaders started clapping to a specific, irritating beat. "One, two!" Clap! Clap! "Let's go for more!" Clap! Clap! "Three, four!"

Sophie nudged my elbow again. "Come on," she whispered.

"Five, six!" Clap. Clap.

Still, I wouldn't budge.

"You should listen to your skinny friend. She's smarter than you," the blond said.

I cupped my hand over Sophie's ear. "Stay here."

The blond pulled my hair. I shrugged the hand away.

"You better do what she says," one of the cohorts said.

I turned.

"I'm not moving. Okay?"

"Stupid-ass Jew. Don't ever let me see you alone."

The blond rose from the bench and began heading down. The other two followed. "Kikes!" They hopped onto the grass and started across the field toward some pine trees.

I gripped the edge of the aluminum bench. My knees locked. I couldn't move.

"Oh, my God," Sophie said.

We both looked behind us to see if anyone else had come to replace them. I felt suddenly exhausted. Home. I just wanted to go home. Even if home was empty. Where was my escape route? Anthony ran across the end zone. Everyone stood up and stamped on the bleachers. The metal vibrated under me.

"Tone-knee. Tone-knee!" they shouted.

The cheerleaders formed a T formation, throwing ribbon shakers over their heads, then catching them before they fell to the ground. In the midst of this jubilation, Sophie and I huddled in our tiny cave. The Italian girls disappeared into a grove of trees and when they were gone, I breathed. I wished Margaret were here. I wished Peter were here, but he hated these games and stayed far away. Sophie pulled up her kneesocks. "How are we going to walk home?"

"We walk out with everyone else and stay with the crowds."

"This is a disaster," Sophie said. She looked down at her feet and shook her head.

The game continued around us like a swirl of leaves while we hovered at the core, trying to pretend that we belonged. The cheerleaders screeched and worked themselves into near hysteria. Anthony crossed the end zone, securing the win for the school. Then it was over. The crowd began to disperse.

I looked toward the woods. I couldn't see past the first line of trees.

"What if they're waiting for us?" she said.

"We'll stay with the crowds."

The players gathered at the benches, slapping each other's backs, sucking on water bottles. Anthony stood in the middle of a group talking, one eye toward the bleachers looking for someone.

I waved my arms. "Anthony," I shouted. "Anthony."

He said something to the boy next to him and hiked up the bleachers to my seat. The cheerleaders headed back to school, punching the air in syncopated rhythms. "Two, four, six, eight, who do we appreeshe-y-ate? The Chargers!"

He stood in front of me, one hand on his hip. His wet jersey pressed against his chest, his shoulder pads bulging. He looked wonderful.

"These girls were trying to pick a fight," I said.

"They called us kikes."

"Who?" He searched the field, which had emptied except for the team.

"I don't know them."

"They pulled Sarah's hair."

I touched my hair, the memory.

"They went into the woods." Sophie pointed to the faraway trees.

"Girls, follow me." Anthony took both of our hands, as if he knew I might balk but I didn't because he was protecting Sophie, too.

"Hey, Tony," one teammate shouted. "Going for two? Nice going!"

"Get lost!" he said, then smiled at us. "See. You girls are already getting me in trouble."

"Tony, my man!" another uniformed kid called.

He waved dismissively and slowed down until the rest of the teammates had gone ahead of us.

"Giselle ain't going to like it, Tony," another boy shouted.

"I don't want to get you in trouble." I slipped my hand out of his and wrapped both arms around my books.

"I'll take care of this. I'm going to walk you girls home. You wait for me outside the gym."

"It was wrong what they did," Sophie said, also removing her hand.

"The blond girl wore a metal bracelet on her wrist," I said.

"Yeah, yeah, I know her," he said.

"Who is she?"

"Leave it to me," he said, and I knew he didn't want me to probe for more.

When we reached the playground, one of the cheerleaders, a girl with long legs and pretty mouth called to him. "Anthony. Come over here!"

"Wait here," he said, loping across the pavement to greet her. He kissed her once, then again, longer.

The cheerleader stood with a knee bent, her arms crossed, which she uncrossed during the second kiss. I turned away, disappointed. I didn't know he had a girlfriend. Margaret hadn't told me.

"Must be Giselle," Sophie said.

I shrugged, still not wanting to look. I heard the clacking of his cleats coming towards me. "Hey!" He stopped beside me and touched my chin. "So, you care?"

"I don't like to watch people kissing."

Giselle had already walked away with her friends to the far side of the playground and was crossing the street. "What are you worrying about her for? We're breaking up." He looked at me with sleepy, violet blue eyes.

"Doesn't look that way."

"Tony, man, you coming? Enough with the girls!" someone yelled from the gym door.

He dashed up the steps and at the top he turned around. "Stay right there." He went inside.

Sophie and I stood at the bottom of the stairs waiting. The playground grew silent and vacant. The sky, too, looked indifferent to our dilemma, trapped in an empty schoolyard. A few cars remained in the lot — probably the coach's car and the janitor's. If the blond girl came back, they would have to cross the empty lot and by then Sophie and I could run inside and get the football coach.

Sophie made half-hearted pliés and stretches. I leaned against the iron rail. An occasional car passed on the street. The sky dulled to a frying pan gray. It was getting late. Ten minutes went by.

"He won't desert us, will he?" I asked.

"No," Sophie said. She scuffed one foot back and forth, sweeping it up, pointing her loafer.

"I wish he would hurry."

The heavy metal doors opened. Anthony came out in street clothes, black pants and a Varsity jacket in school colors. His name had been sewn on the back. He had combed his hair off his forehead.

"Let's go, girls. I need a cigarette."

"You'll get kicked off the team."

"Oh, so you do care." He hurried across to the sidewalk, outside the school boundary and handed me a matchbook.

"Light it for me, Sarah."

I shook my head. "Not here. The coach will see you."

"He's inside. Come on, Sarah, light me up."

"I won't." I scowled, feeling both embarrassed and manipulated. I owed him something but I grew stubborn.

"Do it further down the street," Sophie said.

I pointed to a large, leafy elm tree. "At the corner there."

I ran ahead and stopped behind a tree trunk. Anthony sauntered over with Sophie, who looked grateful to him that we were not walking alone. Well, so was I. When he walked up to me again and put his cigarette between his lips, I struck a match, but the match head crumbled and failed to light. He leaned closer, testing me, his shoes almost touching mine, his cigarette dangling from his mouth. I worked on another match and this time it lit. The flame made a sucking sound as the dry papers crinkled under the heat. The smoked smelled sweet. I wanted to take a drag.

"I'll have some," I said.

"I think you like me."

He handed me the cigarette and I took a short, awkward puff. I could feel myself flushing again from embarrassment. I handed the cigarette to Sophie but she didn't want it. So, I handed it back to him.

"Show me the way, girls."

As it darkened outside, I walked between Anthony and Sophie, who talked about her upcoming dance performance for the "Nutcracker Suite." I was glad for her chatter. I was too nervous to talk. I kept thinking about Anthony and Giselle. He had a girlfriend. I was alone. I had to seek protection. That was what mattered. The sky lowered and touched the trees. We walked through the town and headed for the hilly neighborhoods where Sophie and I both lived. A black Cadillac slowed and stopped beside us. The electric window slid down. A plump, pretty-faced woman with a bun in her hair turned to me.

"Hello, Sarah dear," my aunt said.

I walked over to the car and leaned in to give her a perfunctory kiss. She looked over at Anthony and Sophie and started to say something but changed her mind. "Everything okay?"

"Fine. We're just walking home." Saying the obvious sounded silly but it was true, almost. And I didn't want my aunt or anyone in my family to know I had been called a kike, or suspect my interest in Anthony, or see how dejected I felt that he had a girlfriend.

"Send everyone my love." The window closed and she drove away, the tires barely making a sound. The car bounced smoothly over the next hill.

"Nice Jew canoe."

"Jew canoe?" I turned to face him, all my thwarted desire turned to effrontery and discomfort. "That's my aunt's car. Why did you say that?"

He put up his hands. "Didn't mean anything. It's just an expression. Okay? Jeez. Girl's got a temper."

"No, she doesn't," Sophie said. "It's not a nice thing to say, like your friends calling us kikes. Haven't we had enough of this today?"

"Hey, hey, hey, turn it down. I like Jews. Okay?" He flicked his cigarette toward the curb and made slow circles in the street.

"It's not right," Sophie said.

"Are you girls going to forgive me or what?"

"Just don't say that again. Ever," I said.

He walked up to me and stood so close, I smelled his cologne and the smoke on his breath, and his clean sweat. "I won't. I promise. Okay?"

We stopped at Sophie's house first, a white Colonial with blue shutters. She ran up a flagstone path to a side door and waved good-bye. Inside, her pretty mother awaited her. Her surgeon father would be coming home late. But Sophie's family was a two-parent family. Complete. I wondered if her father could have cured Mother's bent fingers.

I didn't like that thought. It hurt and it made it hard to breathe and I didn't want Anthony to notice. But he too had grown pensive in the dark as we walked down the hill and back up another, toward my house. Street lamps lit our way. It was that time at dusk when people put the lights on and haven't yet pulled down their shades. I could see clearly into strangers' expensively furnished rooms. Crystal chandeliers. Fancy, flowered wallpapered walls.

"Pretty rich neighborhood you live in," he finally said, lighting up another cigarette and curling it into his palm. "You're lucky."

"It's not what you think," I said.

He nodded and I believe he gleaned my thoughts about Mother because he lifted his left hand and touched my hair.

"I'd kiss you but I have a girlfriend," he said. He didn't smile when he said this. He didn't joke. I stopped at the end of my street. I wanted to kiss him too. But I looked away. I didn't want him to know.

"This is it." I pointed to my side of the street.

"Which one is yours?"

I pointed to my house. The downstairs lights were on. Robert's room was lit up, the dining room windows and the round, white ball glowing coldly. Mother's room was dark, a cavity of pain that Anthony couldn't see. I looked down at my feet, pushing away tears.

"You okay?"

"I feel safe, now. Thanks."

He nodded and turned. "See you at school."

I watched him walk off. I watched him until he reached the bottom of the hill and then he blended in with the dark, like someone stepping into the wilderness.

3

Chapter Thirteen

Amorphous

My youngest brother came into this world bearing the unseeable of unseeables: faith. He came into the world with knowing. From birth Elliot rode the emotional currents that stirred up our household. He did this instinctively and innocently, as if each swell in the familial sea were a natural occurrence. He didn't know any other way. I guess none of us did. But he was more accepting.

His entrance into life deepened Mother's reticence. If I was used to her retreats, whether in the garden, or on the phone, or at the club, after Elliot her absence became customary. We were entities whose biological threads connected to something amorphous, which we called Mother. So, instead, Elliot tied himself to his dreams and imaginary friends.

Love was something distant that retired to a room on the second floor.

Mother was beautifully ethereal and because of that Elliot sought that which he could hold in his hands — tactile things, touch. So it was that he first came to love miniature toy animals. He embraced them. He entrusted them with his emotional survival. To these things he grew attached.

He coveted any kind of replica. He collected small china elephants, dogs, tigers, sea lions that came inside cereal packages. He ferreted them out of tea boxes. In this imagined world he tended to injuries and set his second family on his windowsill for repair. He understood explicitly that living beings needed sun and air, wind and rain. They needed tending to. They needed love.

The amazing thing about his animals — and the numbers grew so that Dora complained and said it was impossible to dust his room — was their ability to listen. A mere glance on his part and all his animals knew his feelings. A slight tilt in his arm, an unsuspecting nod and they figured things out. Elliot told me his animals could do this. They knew him best. But as I saw it, they expressed his ability to intuit and emote.

He felt things. At the same time he did not feel compelled to verbalize what he felt or saw the way Robert did. With Robert, words were not necessarily transports of emotion but detached observations, descriptions of actions and things. Definitions kept Robert in control. "The reason why they have *shiva* is because *shiva* means seven in Hebrew and that's why *shiva* lasts for seven days."

He didn't take the meaning beyond that.

In our house that roiled with shouts and protests, Elliot understood the value of remaining quiet, unperturbed and imperturbable. In our house, voices tangled like sewing thread at the back of the drawer. To avoid the squabbles that formed into tiny, ever-tightening knots, he retreated too, but unlike Mother who moved through the house edgily nudging and pushing to her destination of remoteness, Elliot exuded softness. He was putty in the family's hands. He slackened the rope and in so doing, released tension around him. In this way Elliot eluded Father's incisive glare, and appeared nonplussed by Robert's inexhaustible outrage: "I don't like all those people looking at me. Tell them to leave me alone."

It's why I liked to sit with Elliot in the afternoon, after school, after Mother died. He turned to his toys as a way to communicate the angst he sensed in me. When he explained the relationships between his ceramic elephants, or the history of a lion's chipped foot, it was as if he were reciting. I relaxed. I felt safe again, or normalized to some extent.

"It doesn't hurt him," he explained to me, turning the glazed lion in the sunlight. "He's learned to walk just fine. He doesn't even notice it anymore."

"How do you know?"

"He told me."

His animals heard him, every note and chord in his body's internal harmonic gathering. It might be that he didn't like the way Father spoke to Peter. It might be that he didn't see the sense in Robert's needling and insouciance — Robert's ability to create barriers on the smallest scale — not letting Elliot touch his fish tank, for instance. Nevertheless, Elliot absorbed these insults and sponged them out somehow in his psychic conversations with toy animals.

"The cows stand in the field and watch because they understand better than the others," Elliot said.

It might have been easy to think that Elliot didn't notice unruly behavior precisely because it was all he had known. But I knew that wasn't so. He simply chose to ignore certain aspects of others' personalities. Robert treated Elliot poorly whenever Elliot came in to look at his fish. The fishbowl was a magnet for Elliot. It held a transcendent light that captured a silence and intensity that Elliot identified with. Robert, wholly caught up in the concrete details of fish and tank, fish food and filter missed the nuances behind what Elliot saw and barked at him to go away, or not touch the glass. But as harsh as Robert sounded, Elliot understood this about his older brother and eluded his ragged edge. He still chose to touch the glass upon every visit to Robert's room, knowing each time that Robert would launch into silly protests but that's just what they were: silly, inconsequential. In this way, Elliot possessed weight, self-knowledge, and a natural understanding of the multiple ways other people responded to the same stimulus.

So it was that Elliot also had a way of accepting Mother's death, albeit, not without a sage's wisdom and sad face. He accepted the illogicality of it. In his nine-year-old mind that had matured emotionally beyond the clumsiness of his body, he said that God was like clay and that all things on earth came in different shapes — including Mother — and that Mother had simply been remolded, but still remained a part of us. He was certain of this.

"Mother visits me after school," he said.

I sat on the floor of his room, next to the windowsill, and watched him line up a group of dogs and cats in a circle. He alternated cat, dog, cat, dog. I didn't know what to say to this. What he said scared but comforted me.

"How?"

"She came with the wind."

"That's beautiful, Elliot."

"You don't believe me."

I didn't know if I did but I felt her puzzling silence, her complexly muted presence, an unspoken puzzle I had not solved.

"Yes and no. I don't know. It's confusing."

If these vespers, these harbingers of changing weather added up to some kind of ghostlike substance, then I did believe. But I doubted. Doubt obscured me. The question mark would remain. Yet sitting next to Elliot calmed me. If he could manage so could I.

What I began to learn, though, is that the question mark — my mother — stayed with me, followed me wherever I went. She floated inside, a buoy without a boat.

~~~~~

With each school day I was pushed along by an invisible contract, a Code of Avoidance, an uneasy social rule that said I would be better served by silence. No one said anything about Mother, and neither did I, as if I had been sent out to space where sound didn't travel. I heard nothing in the darkness; saw only hints of distant lights, darker reflections in Sophie's eyes, a flicker of tension in Mr. Giles' shoulders; a determination on Margaret's part to share a cigarette.

If no one talked about it, then the tragedy would go away, and that would help me deal, as if this silent code had the power to remold Mother, and me. It did in a way. For it governed every conversation. It defined the way some kids looked away from me or turned nervously when they saw me walking down the hall. I lived inside a capsule, a massive, unspoken bubble of muteness, until I grew so accustomed to it, I hid inside it.

With Mother gone, Father seceded from the daily machinations of home, letting Dora take over despite the financial strain that paying her full-time put on his finances, or so he said. He dropped the country club, in the name of saving money, but I believed it was more than that. He never cared about it. The club was Mother's domain; moreover, the family business was flailing under Uncle Max. It seemed it wouldn't last.

And, what did six o'clock really mean anymore without Mother descending the stairs to greet him, without her implacable face reflecting his? We started to eat in the kitchen, lining up on our bar stools, Father standing by the window eating distractedly, dropping food like pieces of him falling apart.

Robert and Elliot still walked to school together. Peter still came home later each day, caught up in the gyrations of his last year in high school, his band, his impending graduation in the spring. The day after Anthony walked me home and the day after that and more days following, he became remote. So, I studied harder to block out what hurt. I practiced piano, marching through scales, stamping out thoughts, thinking musically so as not to think of anything else. Harmonies guarded me from a wandering ache.

~~~~~

Then one afternoon in the spring I came home from school and found Father and Miss Delgarno drinking tall glasses of vodka in the den.

"Sarah," she said, standing up too quickly as if she were sitting on a pincushion full of prickly guilt.

"What are you doing here?" I said.

I surveyed her face. She was the sort of woman who overdid her makeup. Her lipstick had a greasy look to it, not the soft, powdered touch that Mother had mastered. Miss Delgarno's miniskirt was a kneecap too short and as I stood in the den wondering what I thought about all this — I didn't want to be a fool — I watched her tug at her hem, then cross her knees as if that would make up for its poor design, its awkward stitching, not at all tailored and fitting as the clothes Mother chose. Miss Delgarno was much younger, too, trying too hard to be hip.

"I've asked Sherry to join us for dinner," Father said.

I nodded. Mother had a way of phrasing her outfits, layering silk tops with colorful scarves, or a pin that offset the square look of a three-piece suit so that the lapel danced with glints of gold. Not Miss Delgarno. She was messy. Her large smile, overly solicitous.

"Can you sit with us for a moment?" she asked.

"Sit where?" I said, looking around the room. She had taken up Mother's chair and the couch, though empty, looked miles away from the chairs by the window. I had no intention of making her feel at ease. And I didn't like her use of "us." What was she doing here?

Father's smile looked more like an ache. I hated the weak look in his eyes telling me, *please, Sarah. I don't have the strength*.

I turned and left the room, oddly triumphant in my desire to hurt her, not thinking of him. But her — I didn't want her here. She was not welcome. She would have to try harder, that I promised, and with this resolution, I became a notch lighter, useful, a woman of purpose.

At dinner, Dora circled the dining room table. We didn't wait for Peter. He rarely ate dinner with us anymore.

"Robert, sit up. Put the book down. Not at dinner. Sarah, help Elliot with his chicken. Cut it into smaller pieces. What would you like to drink, Miss Delgarno?"

"Nothing. I'm fine. Call me Sherry, please."

Dora tightened her lips and looked at me. The flash of disapproval galvanized us. She too did not like what she saw sitting in Mother's chair. I had grown so used to Dora's sharp eyes confiscating the flaws she inevitably saw in me that I reveled in her new focus of reprimand. Dora was circumspect and that made Dora my accomplice. I felt a quick thrill, a rare sense of unity.

Father said, "Sherry, you ought to ask Robert about his time series."

"I'd love to hear about it."

"Nothing to tell. You can read it," Robert said.

Father grimaced. He would have shouted a few months ago but the shouting had turned into lugubrious expressions, his eyes liquid as the vodka glasses filled to the brim; his cheeks sodden, still chapped from crying. Father took another long swallow of his drink, then resumed eating his chicken.

"Your father asked me to join you," Miss Delgarno said. "I hope you don't mind. I'd like to help out any way I can."

I did mind, obviously. Who was she to take on this task? Why, of all the people I knew, from teachers and friends, should she be the one to finally speak up? Dora left the room, shoving through the swinging doors so that the hinges squeaked and the doors clattered.

Elliot decided to tell us about rattlesnakes.

"Did you know that some rattlesnakes lay eggs and others have live babies?"

"That's weird," Robert said. "They're caught between evolutionary cycles."

"I had no idea," Miss Delgarno said, looking at Elliot and Robert. She put her fork down. "I'm going to have to think about that one. What do you think about it?"

Elliot shrugged. "I like snakes," he said, twiddling with his peas. A few popped off his fork and spun off the table. He smiled and I might have laughed but not today.

Dora reentered.

"I'm done," I declared, handing her my plate.

"Can we be excused?" Robert asked.

"What about dessert?" Father said, looking at Dora.

I stood up. "I don't want any."

I didn't want to spend another moment with Miss Sherry.

Robert pushed back his chair. "Me either."

"If you want, I'll show you my animals," Elliot said to her.

Sherry looked over at Father who nodded.

"He's quite the collector."

Then she looked at Dora. "Can I help?"

"I've got it all taken care of here."

I went to my room to finish homework but heard every footstep Delgarno planted in our house. From her jaunt upstairs to Elliot's room, because Elliot who didn't judge, who accepted you if you were kind, was willing to listen. I heard her go back downstairs to Father's office. For a long time she stayed in the office. I heard records playing somber, melodic Frank Sinatra tunes, then the brighter voice of Ella Fitzgerald. I waited and waited for her to *leave*.

While I was in the shower, Dora knocked on the bathroom door to tell me to save some hot water for my brothers. I could tell she was connecting with me by her softer tone. I grunted, "Okay!" because I was so accustomed to sequestering my feelings from her, not wanting her to have an edge, but I felt lifted up by our alignment and doused my eyes and head under the water spray, lost myself in warm liquid, and forced myself to turn off the water before the heat ran out simply because she requested it.

Delgarno wouldn't leave. She stayed after I tucked in Elliot, and after he fell asleep; after Robert's light clicked off; after the dishwasher cycle had stopped. The buzzing of Dora's television remained and streams of Glenn Miller's band seeped under Father's office door.

She stayed after Peter came home. I smelled beer on his breath. His army jacket exhumed a pungent dose of cigarette smoke laced with a planty, sweet smell of hashish. I sat on my bed with the night light shining.

"She's still down there," I said of Delgarno.

"What do you expect?" Peter said.

He left to go upstairs. I lay in the dark listening to pop 40 hits until I fell asleep. I didn't hear Father come upstairs. But I heard her car roll down the street.

The next afternoon I came home, intent on checking a few things. I went immediately to Father's office and dumped an ashtray full of Delgarno's lipstick-covered cigarette butts into the kitchen wastebasket. It surprised me that Dora had not done so but it looked as if Dora had decided not to go into the office at all. The room smelled of stale perfume and carbon paper. Father left open his sleeper couch, blankets tousled like seaweed washed ashore.

He slept there every night now. A cadre of clean shirts and two sports jackets hung on the office closet door. His shaving bag lay open on the desktop. I checked the downstairs bathroom and there it was: his toothbrush still moist from morning use, stored in the medicine cabinet.

Upstairs, the master bedroom door stayed shut. When I opened it the room smelled and felt like a cabin that had been vacated for the winter season. The windows had been vacuum-sealed, stale air devoid of dust and microorganisms. I edged open a window. Mother would not want her room cut off from her beloved outdoors. The grass was greening and that smell of new growth was everywhere: in the bark of the trees, the buds on thorny bushes. You couldn't avoid it.

Her clothes hung in her closet, still wrapped in dry cleaner's plastic. I stood in front of the dresses and waited for something, I didn't know what, pressing my face into the pink dress she wore to a New Year's Eve party at the club, inhaling her. I started to reach for the violin case on the shelf but changed my mind. I took her makeup case from her dressing room drawer instead.

The next day I wore her eyeliner and mascara to school, and a light layer of lipstick. Dora noticed. She started to say something as I walked out the door but I was ready. I was ready to tell her that I was wearing Mother's and she couldn't do a thing to stop me. No. So Dora hesitated, like people do when they sense something different and are surprised by it and powerless. I had never talked sharply with her, usually meeting her directives with stares and grimaces, but instead of berating me this time, she reached her hand out and touched my shoulder.

"Looks better on you than that Sherry woman," she said, affirming our partnership. I think I could have embraced her, lifted her up in my arms had I not spent the entire year learning not to.

I also discovered several unopened packages of real silk stockings and a garter belt in Mother's dresser. I didn't wear these; I wanted to save them for a special occasion. So, I stored them in the back of my underwear drawer wrapped in a paper bag. I stole another, cheaper pair of pantyhose from the Five & Dime later that week.

Chapter Fourteen

Moon in the House

To prepare for the high school spring concert, "Springtime on Broadway," as Mr. Edwards called it, I stood on the raised stands surrounded by a chorus that was finally knitting together. Mr. Edwards pointed to me and blithely asked me to sing the solo verses in "Aquarius," from the musical *Hair*.

I adored this song.

Harmony and understanding,
no more falsehoods or derisions.

The song skipped and hopped, mixing colors and jewels with bigger ideas about revelation and freedom, about the zodiac and the universe. Words about dreams and visions spun around me, clothed me in feathers and silk.

After practice, Mr. Edwards gestured for me to wait. I waved to Sophie and watched the choir file out of the large room, some in pairs, until the last person, a girl in a plaid skirt and red sweater, left. Mr. Edwards sat down at the piano bench.

"Let's play this once through together. Do you have time for it?"

I nodded.

He shuffled the sheets of music, penciling in notations above the lines, then placed his thin fingers on the keys.

"Start softly now and let it build. Imagine a cone widening — the beginning of the song is at the narrow tip of the megaphone. As you sing through the verses, think of the sound filling the widest part of the mouth." He played past the introduction and dipped his head to indicate where I should begin.

"When the moon is in the seventh house —"

"Good. Keep it going to the stars. Next two lines, please."

I sang about peace and planets. I sang about Jupiter aligning with Mars. I saw myself soaring through space, sailing across rings of stardust.

He stopped playing and swiveled around to face me. The room without music felt cavernous. I became small, tiny all of a sudden.

He straightened the music sheets again. "This is good. Very good. What do you think, Sarah? How's everything going with you right now?"

"Fine." I nodded quickly, too quickly, and looked at the stage as if something important needed watching over there.

He smiled and glanced at the stage. "I was thinking that singing's not just about the music, it's about your life. The whole package. Your mom, your family. That's why I'm here. Not just to play these notes." He trilled a few keys. "Make sense?"

"Sure. Okay."

I might have spoken sarcastically as I had to my uncle and those people who came after the funeral, but he was different. I had not expected this. I could tell it wasn't about how sorry *he* was, he was sorry about the situation. I could hear the sincerity in his voice — not urgent, not cloying.

"My father died when I was a little bit older than you — your brother, Peter's age. So, you and I know about losing the most important person in our lives."

I nodded again but I didn't feel like escaping, as I usually did.

"He died of cancer. Big family secret. Not good to have those kinds of secrets." He tapped his chest with two fingers.

The far door flung open and the girl in a plaid skirt ran back in. "Forgot something," she said, huffing.

"Red notebook?" he said, pointing to it on a chair.

She ran out again and he turned back to me. "So if you want to get anything off your chest, come see me. Anytime is a good time. Just knock on my piano." He smiled. "Okay?"

"Okay."

"You sound terrific. Now memorize those words and you're there."

I collected my books and headed out more or less dazed. First, that he had spoken personally to me, and second, because of what he said about his father. I walked home in a dream that lasted all the way past the stores and trees, our driveway — a feeling that I was not alone. He had been on the same train of this unwanted trip, taking in similar views.

After my private talk with Mr. Edwards, I hummed the song everyday between classes, in the shower, walking home. I became it.

~~~~~

On the night of the choral performance, I wore a long black skirt and white blouse, but underneath I carefully hooked Mother's garter belt to a pair of her sand dune-colored nylons. These had a sumptuous feel, entirely different than the coarser pantyhose sold at the Five & Dime.

Everyone at the school came, including Anthony, who sat in the far back. He caught my eye and nodded. I smiled and quickly looked at the crowd that was growing boisterous, a funnel of hysteria as the semester wrapped up, capped by this evening. Giselle sat on the opposite end of the room with friends. Margaret told me she was no longer with him. She didn't tell me why he stayed away from me, only that he was dating lots of girls and was stupid for not asking me out. Boys were idiots sometimes, she said. The blond-haired girl who had harassed me sat next to Anthony. She was his sister and this is why, since the day he walked me home, she left me alone.

All the parents showed up. The auditorium was packed, echoing with the voices of the entire high school, grades 10-12; nearly three thousand people warming the room. The lights dimmed twice.

When they blinked on again, I spotted Father in the middle center with Elliot and Robert on either side. Robert, of course, plunged in his book series on time travel. He was on book eleven now. According to the series, eleven was a mystical number with vibrations that opened the soul to yet another dimension, a parallel universe where people like us lived, only differently, without the noise and disturbances. Imagining myself in this alter world, I saw our house in a perennial springtime with Mother's roses blooming, the coriander smell of the Korean spice bush filling my bedroom. Daylight would be lush as a field of dandelion flowers. The sun, never hurried, would drift across the horizon in early summer. Of all the books that Robert had read in this super fiction collection, this one intrigued me the most. The idea that something abstract as a number could transport you to another world was something I wanted to believe in. I saw the power of sound, the physical way a note vibrated and made the brain shimmer with joy. Music took me someplace else. Perhaps numbers worked in a similar way for Robert.

Elliot waved to me. I nodded from my spot on the second row in the soprano section. Sophie stood behind me. Peter was also performing: a guitar solo of Bob Dylan songs near the end of the program. Mr. Bingham would open the program singing three art songs. The lights dimmed and the auditorium grew dark and quiet. Time to begin. All eyes of the chorus focused on Mr. Edwards, who smiled and lifted his baton. A flap of his elbow and we were off with a lively "Everything's Coming Up Roses" from the musical *Gypsy*.

We sang through our medley of songs. The nerves in my stomach settled down and focused. When "Aquarius" started with its quiet beginning, Mr. Edwards turned to me and raised his eyebrows: ready, Sarah? The orchestra launched into its intro, repeating the main melodic line, adding a series of harmonies, then slowing down to meet my part. I inhaled and sang.

"When the moon is in the seventh house," at first softly, cleanly, exhuming the ache and promise of the phrase as it filled the empty tank that had become my chest. Everything in me rose to the crescendo in the music, like a plant to sun. I tilted my head higher, looking first over the heads of the school body to the red exit signs all the way in back. The chorus joined in, adding layers of notes, a rippling of sails responding. I sang again, leading the fleet, always lighter than the chorus, able to float above the room. By the time I reached the last lines of the first stanza, *and love — will steer the stars —* I had left the auditorium on a solo ride, as if I were in a hot-air balloon drifting over high branches and the chorus like leaves rustling below. Together, we sang: *"This is the dawning of the Age of Aquarius."*

I stood taller, turning my palm out, offering up my heart. It was here, in this moment of singing, that I shed my shadows and ghosts. I forgot about Anthony and Giselle. Father's face cringed in another bout of tears but it didn't register in me except as purity of emotion, his lost desires embodied in the song. As I reached the final stanza and the chorus joined in again in a celebratory shout *"this is the dawning of the Age of Aquarius,"* we brought the melody to its exuberant end. Mr. Edwards swept his arms up in a final punch to the ceiling and the people in the first rows stood up in a paroxysm of applause, followed by the rows behind them and more rows again, hooting and shouting their approval, a room shaking with illusions of joy.

I rubbed my thighs to feel her against my skin and remembered how proudly she talked about Mrs. Janson's daughter, Justine. I didn't know if I measured up to Mother's standards. This wasn't opera I was singing. As the program went into intermission, and the second half came and went, Father squeezed my hand and refused to let me free. I was his prize for the evening and Peter too, for he had sung Dylan's "Times They Are A-Changin'." In this short evening, Peter and I became known to the entire school. I became visible again.

Students whom I knew only from sight came over to congratulate me. "You're really talented. I didn't know you sang. You sound professional. When are you singing again? What grade are you in?"

In bed that night, relief and exhilaration splashed against another layer that stayed ever the same inside. Alone, the music that had filled me, that had temporarily patched up the cracks and holes, drained away, like streams after a flash flood. I was left with darkness again.

I lay awake listening to the heat in the radiator as it sent off cryptic messages of pings and pangs knocking against metal. The house rattled like a broken toy. Downstairs Father shuffled down the hall from his office to brush his teeth. He had been proud. For that short time, he too had risen above himself and glowed. But Mother's absence dimmed that too.

I turned over but repositioning my body didn't help at all. I turned back over. Mother's death became my life sentence, a different kind of imprisonment, and I realized that Elliot might be right about ghosts. This one had slipped inside me, pacing for public recognition, seeking that salve of music, a restless, circular longing for condolence and release.

Chapter Fifteen

Stonehill

Peter planned to stay at our cousin Kenneth's apartment for the summer but he didn't tell Father about this and he didn't tell me until the night of his leaving. It was what Peter dreamed of: getting away. Far, far away. Kenneth lived in Los Angeles.

As I sat on Peter's bedroom floor, my back against the wall, I watched my brother roll an extra pair of jeans and flannel shirt and wedge them into his backpack; his toiletry bag and notebook for songwriting, he tamped down on top. The magic of his cross-country trip flamed inside me. I wanted to go, too. His bus was heading west at midnight, passing through cities sparkling in the dark.

"Do not say a word until I call tomorrow."

I nodded and followed him downstairs to the basement. It might have been a regular weekend night, Peter off with friends, his guitar slung on his shoulder. He walked down the driveway to the end of the street, where a friend picked him up to take him to the bus station. By sunrise, he would be well on his way to something better than here.

The next morning, I woke up to a bright summer sun, feeling slighted and cold. Why had Peter not included me in his secret plan? My room felt empty and small, the air trapped in tiny capsules hard to inhale. But, my brother did what he promised.

Late afternoon, Peter's telephone call from Ohio yanked Father out of his stupor.

"You better tell me what this is all about," Father shouted on the phone.

In a minor, perverse way I was glad to hear Father raising his voice, shouting again as if he was remembering who he was, who we were. He squeezed the receiver and paced the kitchen floor listening to Peter, who had called from a gas station a thousand miles away.

"Jesus Christ. What's Kenneth's number? I ought to have him arrested. Does your aunt know about this? When did you come up with this scheme of yours? You call me as soon as you get there." Father nodded idiotically, his eyes knocking around the room like trapped flies. He didn't wait for a response. He hung up and swiped the counter top, covered in daily newspapers, onto the floor. The pages skidded toward my feet.

"Did you know about this?"

I shook my head.

As I stood at the doorway, half-paralyzed by too many emotions sinking to my feet, Father looked at me and decided that I needed to attend summer school. He didn't want me wandering off as Peter had done.

"You are not going to hang around this house all summer, young lady. Get yourself in trouble."

Peter was eighteen but I was still controllable at sixteen, so Father imagined.

By the end of the week I was enrolled as a day student at the academically rigorous Stonehill Academy in Concord, Massachusetts. Father insisted I attend for the entire summer. He would have signed me up as an overnight boarder but money was too tight for that. Uncle Max's business was closing down, which meant that Mother's inheritance no longer existed.

Sophie had gone to the Berkshires to a dance camp and Margaret was working for a hair salon. So, I was glad to go. The idea of doing nothing all summer was a numbing prospect, an added punishment for losing a mother, a family business, for losing it all. With extra credits earned, I could graduate early. I put my mind on this.

On my first day at Stonehill, a girl named Betsy James picked me up in her aquamarine, Thunderbird convertible — it was her mother's — and sped on the highway at seventy miles an hour.

"It's twenty-six minutes of highway," she told me. "Twelve minutes of country. You a summer student? I go all year."

"Yes."

I held on to the car door handle but soon felt reassured. She drove well, with confidence. Once she turned off the highway, she slowed down and wound through old farms and wooded hills until we bounced up a dirt road, passing under evergreens and maples, to the entrance of the school. Betsy was in her last year at Stonehill. She was working as a paid intern, assisting the photography teacher.

"He's an old man. He likes to take pictures of me. I mean, they're creative pictures."

Except for details about her mother's car, how the car had 82,000 miles on it, how she had picked out new tire rims, and how she loved to drive; I couldn't get past the surface of her. She talked as if police were chasing her words; the ends of sentences rounding sharp corners, or skidding to sudden stops. She applied and reapplied her lipstick while cruising in the passing lane. Oddly, she was pretty except for the ticking of her head — she shook her thick, long hair repeatedly as if to make sure it were still there — and the overzealous way she smiled and talked. She wore open-toed sandals and miniskirts, which she tugged and pulled as she pressed her painted toes to the gas pedal. Her shaved legs glowed with suntan lotion, filling the front seat with coconut scents. She chewed wintergreen gum.

During the ride to school, she told me that most of the students came from the New York area and many were "fucked up," an expression I didn't expect from her. She warned that drugs were commonplace on campus.

"You'll see kids going into the woods. Check their eyes. Red? Glazy? Yup. They're smoking marijuana."

She twirled the radio dial and settled on an oldies station. Leslie Gore's "It's My Party" shouted from the speakers.

"I don't do drugs," she added. "Do you?" She looked at me in a way that told me she wouldn't approve and that I might jeopardize my ride if I did.

I shook my head.

"I mean I drink. Beer, that sort of thing," she said.

She turned the dial again and leaned back in the seat, so that her toes tapped the top edge of the gas pedal like a ballerina *en pointe*.

~~~~~

On first impression, Stonehill appeared orderly and genteel. The main campus was a cluster of white clapboard buildings with green shutters — all classic New England — sewn into wrinkles on a hillside that sloped down to forest-lined fields and flattened into marshland. Summer students stayed in the newer and plainer brick dorms down the hill from the center quadrangle. The campus acreage included tennis courts, a photography studio, and two soccer fields.

Betsy parked in a grassy lot and left me to make my way to the dining hall where seventy-five students gathered for introductions. The glass-enclosed room smelled of varnished tables and chairs warmed by the sun. The pine floors glowed with new wax.

A woman with short hair and a suit greeted me at the door. She fished out my name tag from her folder. Each tag had an assigned table number. I sat at table six, next to a boy named Gregory Brown. He looked older because of his dark beard. He was lanky, his shirt loose on his bones. He wore a white, button-down shirt, rolled up to his elbows, revealing more dark hair on his arms. His shirttail hung over well-worn jeans.

Instead of saying hello, he immediately informed me that he had flunked French, and that it was his father, an attorney, who insisted he come to Stonehill. Gregory was from Scarsdale, New York.

"At the moment I'm my dad's failure but this could change." He winked when he said this, which immediately dismantled his intense appearance. His voice was friendly and sunny like a clarinet, musical but not overpowering. He smiled wistfully, as if the horror of spending a summer at this toney, New England private school was something he could tolerate just as he had put up with everything else in his life: with a smudge of irony. His red lips looked sunburned next to his beard.

"Foreign languages just aren't my forte. It happens to the best of us."

"I can help you if you want," I said.

"Deal. You can start now." He smiled in that appealing way again, his eyes both piercing and sleepy. "You fail anything?"

"No."

Mrs. Corey, the woman at the door, introduced herself as the headmistress. She had a stern face and wide forehead.

"Follow the rules and your time here will be a pleasant experience for all. There's always one or two who don't and for those I can promise you there will be stiff consequences. Any questions or concerns,

I'm here to answer them. Have a good semester. Study hard." She smiled, but smiling did not become her. She gestured for us to head on to our first class.

It turned out that Gregory and I were the only two students taking advanced French, which is probably why we had been assigned to sit together at table six. In the classroom, we sat at a long wooden table in a room with tall windows and dusty wood floors, flanking Madame Fallon who initially looked old enough to retire but whose quick-eyed, energetic personality made me forget her age. She wore a long, pleated skirt and a pink shirt with round collar. Her perfume had strains of mothballs and honey.

The class lasted the morning. Gregory and I took turns reading out loud from a textbook. Gregory spoke softly, often mumbling, which drove Madame Fallon to stand up behind him and unhunch his broad, bony shoulders. She often asked me to repeat what he tried to say.

At the end of class I waited for him to put his book in his knapsack. I carried my text in my arms. He opened his camera and checked the settings, then lifted it up and took his first picture of me.

"I'm not stupid, you know. Ask me about anything else, just not French."

I laughed. "Ok." I had yet to meet someone my age who wasn't trying hard to be someone else, except for Gregory.

"History is a subject I can handle."

I made a face. It was my least favorite subject.

"Hold on," he said. "Here's what's interesting about it. You can't go by those facts they teach you.

Historians skewer the facts." He made a twisting motion with his arm. "Did you know that?"

I shrugged. "No."

"Yep. Depending on their political or religious or economical perspective, but that's the fun part, interpreting perceptions, determining the historian's persuasion."

"I never understood it like that. Anyway, it's never about women." The textbooks I read in school rarely featured women, except for Betsy Ross types — flag sewers and pie makers — and the men seemed stiffer than dead animals. "I don't believe in history," I said. "What's the point? It's the present that matters."

During lunch, we kept our debate going about history's value — or nonvalue — as I saw it. It was so much fun we agreed to meet up again during free period at the end of the day. Stonehill might turn out okay, I thought.

I took a literature class where we read *The Bald Soprano* by Eugene Ionesco. A dozen of us, including Gregory, sat around a conference table in the library. In this play, the main characters talked in non sequiturs. No one made any sense but I liked this about the play. To me, the disconnection in the language, the odd behavior between adults, made perfect sense to me, reflecting that impenetrable world of my father and mother I so often witnessed, living in separate spheres, joined only by drinks and lighted cigarettes. But the play angered some of the students. They thought it stupid, a waste of time. I didn't think so.

When free time came, some students played tennis. Others read under oak trees or grouped together on the lawn or snuck cigarettes. Others went to their rooms or for walks. Since Gregory was a boarder, he wanted to explore the campus. We crossed the soccer field and walked into a dense border of trees toward the marshy area. The sun was hot and dry. A breeze kept the bugs away. We sat under a stand of mature pines and Gregory took more pictures of me. He explained that a group of his photos, portraits of old people from his town, hung in the town's main library.

"My father wasn't impressed."

"What's wrong with him?"

"Maybe he thinks I'm gay." He lifted his camera. "You're very beautiful."

I looked into his lens and began singing the refrain to "Aquarius." The song flew out of my mouth like a surprised bird. I looked up at the sky, through an opening in the trees. The wide spaces looked back approvingly. *"When the moon is in the seventh house."* I kept singing and then stopped and said: "Did you ever wonder what that means?" I felt happy suddenly, unleashed for the first time all year.

I swooped my arms up, singing: *"this is the dawning of the Age of Aquarius."*

"You've a voice for the world," he said, leaning toward me. He stroked my lips with his fingers, as if touching a photograph, then kissed me gently pressing his lips to my nose, then my cheek, then finally my lips, opening his mouth and offering his tongue, at first uncertain, waiting for encouragement. I gave him my tongue in response, and leaned toward him until my breasts touched his chest. He rested his hand on my knee and our kissing grew more urgent. He slid his fingers under my skirt touching skin beneath my underpants. The sensation was absolutely liberating, as if I had awakened to a place that offered my very own secret getaway. Waves of summer wind and the smell of pine melted in my brain.

In the Thunderbird on the way home, the wind tangled my hair and covered my face from whatever lingered from Gregory's kisses. Betsy, so enamored with herself in the mirror, failed to notice my distracted voice, the disorientation I felt inside my limbs.

At home, I ran upstairs to change into shorts. Elliot and Robert were outside playing on the old swing set in the backyard. With Mother gone, and now Peter, who had started playing at beach coffee houses in California, the house felt bigger, emptier in the shadow of my changing world. The air inside smelled unlived in, the way I imagined Mrs. Brenwald's house might smell. Next door, a grocery boy continued to deliver her bags of food on Saturdays. Occasionally, I still saw her curtains rustling in the windows.

In my bedroom, I could hear squeaking from rusty chains as my brothers flew back and forth into the sky. Robert loved the swings and could spend hours, it seemed, cutting a sharp arc into the summer air. The pendulum calmed his overactive mind.

I looked out my window to the yard. Two stories below, Mother's roses bloomed haphazardly while some wilted. Father had no sense about plants and no one, including me, knew what to do with her thorny bushes. To approach them meant approaching her and that spooked me. As a result, the flower-beds lost all sense of order, became overgrown and weed ridden. Tall stalks of unwanted shoots took over, robust and vengeful, to make up for all those summer days Mother patiently clipped, snipped, weeded, shaped the spiky growth until the garden obeyed and responded with a stunning mélange of color and perfume. Not anymore. The wild animals had been loosed from their cages.

~~~~~

When I came down for dinner, Dora called me into the kitchen and there I found the kitchen counter with only three place settings not four.

"What's this?"

"Your father is out tonight."

She made a disapproving look to let me know that he was with Miss Delgarno, then she turned back to the sink to wash dishes.

I didn't pursue this. I didn't want to know more. If Peter could escape to California, so could I, in my own way.

I sat down and unfolded the newspaper, flicking past headlines on Vietnam, Nixon and economic re-cession, to the comics section. The world of comics completely satisfied. Problems remained contained.

Life was something you could laugh at. Inside the squares, characters revisited the same woes day after day. They performed for me. Charlie Brown was a favorite. He tried relentlessly and hopelessly to lift his spirits; yet, week after week, he grew despondent while his classmate, Lucy, screamed, ranted, even hit him at times, without accruing results. No matter what unpleasant events occurred in the world, Charlie's depressed yet searching personality lived on. I could rely on him.

Dora plunked three paper napkins onto the counter and helped Elliot and Robert settle in with cold tuna sandwiches and glasses of milk. Next to my two younger brothers, I sat taller, my body no longer a child's. Dora fussed over them, insisting that they eat, nudging them to drink up, promising ice cream for dessert if they obeyed her. But at the kitchen counter, the rules of etiquette changed. Robert read while he ate. He had finished his series and was onto another. All his fantasy books came in groups of three or more as if to put off endings. Elliot fiddled with a pocketful of small, plastic horses, lining them next to his plate, talking to them. I tried to listen to what he said, but it was hard to follow. It was as if he were in the middle of a much longer discussion. I started filling in the crossword puzzle.

After dinner, I went up to Peter's room to play records and sing. I played Joni Mitchell's "Blue" over and over and Jimi Hendrix's "Crosstown" and Laura Nyro's "Timer." I missed him. These well-worn melodies we listened to on so many nights brought him back, made his presence palatable. Sometimes, my house felt raw like a broken blister.

"I like the one about ice cream," Elliot said in the doorway.

"Come sit down," I said. "*And ice cream castles in the air —*"

I sang Joni Mitchell's words again and he came in and went over to the record player, lingering as if my singing might bring Peter back to his world, too.

"When is Peter coming home?"

"Maybe after the summer, I don't know."

Tonight he looked older, less inward. Maybe he had grown a little. I knew he was asking why Peter had left us. He probably wondered if I would be next.

"Peter's older. All his friends went someplace this summer."

"I know. I want to go to Australia when I grow up."

I laughed. "That's far. I would miss you."

"You'll come and visit."

"Okay. I will." I pulled him over and hugged him.

"I think she'll be happy with Dad. Sherry's nice," he said.

"She's okay."

Once again, I was thrown off kilter by his foresight. Elliot knew things; he knew that Sherry might shape his life more than mine. But I tightened up when he said this, and turned to the record player, which had stopped, to flip the record over.

"You want to hear that one again?" I asked him. I poised the needle over the vinyl and lowered it until the diamond point touched the wide, dividing groove.

~~~~~

Later, I lay in bed thinking of Gregory and his hands touching me. My room dissolved into a glen of trees. I could think of nothing else. I rubbed my fingers between my thighs as he did until the melting in my brain returned and the feeling of diving into a warm pool filled my chest. The house grew silent and remained silent. Dora's television shut off. The dishwasher's cycle complete. I stopped waiting for Father to come home.

The next morning Father stood over the kitchen sink distracted again, sucking on slices of oranges, spitting out seeds into the drain. Dora moved stolidly about the kitchen, a muscular presence carving a triangular pattern on the linoleum floor between the refrigerator, sink and counter. She wrapped lunch sandwiches for my brothers; tempered the gas flame on the stove to keep Father's coffee from boiling over. She moved impatiently.

When she first came to our house, I thought her ugly and stout but I knew differently now. She was tough and steadfast; more importantly, she cared.

"You have everything?" she asked, as if she heard my thoughts. She turned from the stove and waited for me to answer.

"Yes. See you tonight. Right?" Betsy honked twice out front. I grabbed my books.

"Where else am I going to be?" She pretended to be insulted and we had our first laugh together.

I felt grateful towards her.

~~~~~

As the summer wore on, I grew to like how insanely fast Betsy drove on the highway; grew accustomed to her world of perkiness and glossy lipstick. I loved how my hair snapped in the wind, the air currents thrashing against my blouse. For the first time since needing a bra, I began to go without. I didn't leave the house this way. I got in the car and it became my ritual with Betsy to unbuckle my bra and slip it into my book bag. My breasts had grown another cup size and pressed harder against my cotton shirts.

We each had our secrets to bear: Betsy wore a bikini under her skirt. She posed every afternoon for Mr. Donald, the photographer teacher. The old man had a perverse obsession with her. Each afternoon, new versions of Betsy in glossy, 8 x 11 black and white photos filled the backseat of the Thunderbird: Betsy leaning over a tree limb, Betsy sitting with her legs spread on a school bench; Betsy bending over with her back to the camera.

"He says it's for art," she said, nonchalantly. "And he pays me. Hey, if it gives him a thrill who cares." She slid her palm up her thigh. "Thank God I don't have any cellulite."

I said nothing. I didn't have to.

At school, I went through the motions of classes until Gregory and I slipped away during free time in the afternoon. We went to the marsh. On the second day he pulled a rolled joint from his pocket and lit up as soon as we walked deep enough through the trees and grasses.

"You want to try this?"

I nodded and watched him pinch the joint between his lips, then studiously light the cigarette until a smoky perfume rose out of it. I remembered how Peter and Kenneth did it, holding the smoke and coughing and now I watched myself do the same. The sun was veiled and this made the oak leaves deepen in color. I walked toward the marshes. I wanted to stand in the tall reeds, where the cattails stood high as my shoulder. I wanted to become a field of cattails, dance with the reeds.

"This is where history happens," I said, taking Gregory's hand and pulling him with me. I walked toward a thick bush of cattails and stood in the middle, surrounding myself in the greenery. "Let's say you're fighting in the Civil War." I pulled a stalk off. "Are you thinking about dying? Your favorite, home-cooked dish? Or kissing your sweetheart?"

I turned and kissed Gregory.

"Let's say this is Paradise," he said. "You're Eve. I'm Adam. Let's take our clothes off."

~~~~~

This became our ritual. Every afternoon from then on, we crossed the soccer field to the remote end of campus, split a joint, and returned to the same small clearing by the marsh. It was far from the center of the campus and sheltered. Except for small animals rustling and a bird's disturbance in the twigs, no one paid attention to us. Gregory took pictures of me lying on the ground with my arms raised above my head. Then he lay down beside me on the pine needles. Each day we shed another piece of clothing: my blouse, his shirt, my underwear. He kissed my naked breasts and slid down my stomach, licking me where no boy had ever touched before. Layers of gloom peeled away. I abandoned myself to this lightness, opening my legs as Betsy did on the bench in her bikini, a feeling of wings fluttering between my thighs until I swam into another explosion. I touched him too, until his legs shuddered and his breath exhaled in a strange rhythm. Then, we became quiet and still.

When it was time to go, I dressed and walked out ahead of him, crossing the soccer field that grew hotter and drier as summer wore on. Brown grasses flattened to the ground. I climbed the small hill and passed the quadrangle where kids hung out, either on a bench or in small couplings in the darker shadows of the trees. I knew everyone's faces but few kids by name. At the end of the day, I returned to the parking lot and waited by the Thunderbird until Betsy sauntered between the crossword puzzle of cars and nonchalantly threw another stack of photos in the backseat.

~~~~~

The weekends were hardest. Day students stayed home while the boarders went on trips. I told Gregory not to call me at home. I didn't want Father or Dora asking questions. I didn't want Gregory connecting to my old life. I didn't want to explain myself or ruin the Eden we had created for ourselves. I never mentioned Mother. I only wanted the present, everything as is, no worries, no darkness and ambiguity. No past.

On Saturday mornings, I went to the Soquaset library or the music store and bought Top 40 singles and sheet music with my weekly allowance. I memorized songs by the Byrds, Neil Young, Carole King, Simon and Garfunkel, The Doors. I bought yards of cheap flowered cotton material at the sewing store and made ankle-length skirts for Gregory to reach under.

I sewed in the cool air of our basement, pushing the pedal of the simple Singer sewing machine. Father still had not moved back upstairs. He taught summer classes during the day. At night, he went inward, drinking tall glasses of vodka with lime, retreating to his office to listen to Frank Sinatra and Tony Bennett. He listened to the same songs over and over. Or he stayed out with Delgarno. I stopped practicing piano preferring to sing in Peter's room, to my invisible audience or Elliot, to Gregory in the marshes.

Peter wrote to say that California was a dream. Mountains. Pacific waters. Seals lounging in rocky coves in San Diego. "I belong here. Writing songs, sidewalk gigs. Love you. Peter."

Because of Gregory, I didn't notice the weeks passing until it was the final week, and then, on my last night at Stonehill Father said I could stay over. The headmistress assigned me to an empty room. One of the boarders had gone home early.

Despite a foggy night and threat of rain, the buffet dinner was held outside on the tennis courts. Tables covered in red cloth offered pasta salads and barbecue chicken breasts. Gregory and I took a nostalgic walk around campus. We crossed the soccer fields for the last time.

Once the daylight dimmed, the clouds grew dense and settled low to the ground. It was eerie and thrilling. I couldn't see past a few yards. I wanted to walk deeper into the fog as if plunging into the middle of it would allow me to capture its haunting soul, delay my inevitable return to school in September. Fog bleached away the sensation of time, melting its edges. I didn't want the night hours to end.

Gregory took a joint from his pocket and lit up. I drank up the smoke, the ether substance that lightened me like breathing helium. The weather obscured everything, even smoke, and the smell from the marsh flooded the air with a sticky stench of rotting grasses. I inhaled and waited for the oozing sensation to lift me up on the fog floating in layers all around me. The sound of distant laughter, a student calling out reached us as if from a neighboring town.

We claimed the swampy edge as our own and found a stump of a tree to sit on, searching for specters. A scarf of fog moved in circles. Gregory hugged me. I leaned into him. He reached for my shirt and pulled it over my head.

Tonight, we left our clothes next to the tree stump. The grass was dew soaked, tickling between my toes. Gregory came up behind me and leaned his hips against my buttocks. I had felt him so many times like this, but had not let him in and time was running out.

I turned and nudged him closer between my thighs.

We heard more distant calling.

"What are they saying?" he asked, pausing.

"It's nothing."

I pulled him closer.

"Remember this," he whispered.

We stood together, not moving except to close the gap between us until he was all the way in. He groaned, his knees easing down. Then he slipped out and slid down my thigh.

"Sarah —"

I knelt beside him.

"You okay?" he asked.

"I'm okay."

We reached for our clothes, got dressed and smoked another joint, folded together on the moist ground. No worries about time. I could have been anywhere in the world, queen of my own country. We heard voices shouting again and then it grew silent. I fell asleep.

I awoke to an urgent sound, someone calling my name. It was early morning. My mouth dry, I nudged Gregory awake.

"Go ahead of me. I'll meet you in the cafeteria for breakfast."

I walked back across the soccer field, to a small, grassy knoll just beyond reach of the dormitory windows, most of which were dark, except for one. Mrs. Corey paced outside, smoking, calling my name.

I stood behind a tree debating whether I should answer her or wait until daylight.

I walked down the hill and crossed the driveway.

"Sarah! Come here, now! What do have to say for yourself?"

I looked at the ground, at her shoes clotted with moss. "I was walking with Gregory. I'm sorry. It was such a beautiful night with the fog. I'm sorry. It sounds crazy but I fell asleep."

"Not good enough, Sarah. I'm very disappointed."

"I'm sorry. Nothing happened."

"I was about to call the police. I'm calling your father to pick you up — "

"Betsy can drive me home."

"Don't say another word, child. Come with me."

I stood and waited for more. But she turned and I followed her into the dorm lounge. She went into another small room and called home. On the one hand, I knew how very stupid I had been. And what about saying good-bye to Gregory? This would be impossible. I turned to look out the window as the dawn light brought the trees out of their shadows. On the other hand, Mrs. Corey and this school seemed already in the past like everything in my life. I didn't care. It seemed inconsequential, stupid that a walk in the woods — and I didn't think my sex life was her business — warranted a call to the police. This wasn't a dire situation. No one was dying or dead. I knew about that.

"It's my fault, Mrs. Corey," Gregory said, knocking on the door.

"It's mine," I said.

"Gregory! I'm calling your father next."

Mrs. Corey ordered him out. She led us both outside and instructed me to sit on a bench. Then she pointed Gregory toward a path that led to his dorm. I watched him walk away. Mrs. Corey sat on the bench beside me and we waited in silence. We had nothing left to say to each other. I was sorry to upset her but facing Father would be much worse. I dreaded his arrival.

While I waited — and Mrs. Corey did look pitiful — she chain-smoked, her hair was matted, her face oily from lack of sleep, I sat contrite, accepting blame. I understood my fault in this, but life was important and on this night I made a decision I didn't regret. The night held its warmth and I cradled it on my skin, steeping in the pleasure of Gregory's touch. Around me, pine trees lining the fields understood me. They didn't stir or twist like Mrs. Corey. Nature was accepting. I felt calm until I heard him. The car sped up the gravel road in a crash of pebbles banging against the car fender, tires scratching the road. The car stopped. The door opened and thumped shut. Silence and then he was in front of me.

"Get in, Sarah."

"It's not as bad as it sounds."

"Get in before I smash you!" He tugged on my elbow and pulled me across the driveway and into the front seat, then slammed the door. I leaned as far away from him as I could. He ignited the car and started driving out.

"Goddamn it, what were you doing?"

"Walking."

"Who's the boy? Who's the goddamn boy?"

"No one."

"Who's the boy you were with all night?"

He lifted his hand off the wheel and smacked the dashboard.

I shrieked. "Stop this! Stop this car. Now! You're scaring me!"

He lurched out the main entrance to the country road but as he slowed to turn a corner, I opened my door, leapt out into the soft wooded embankment, and ran.

Father honked and caught up to me, yelling to me through the window to get back in the car. I kept running alongside the road, until my lack of sleep started to weigh me down, and the road ahead began to look endless, a long line of fir trees and pale, white-dotted lines. No houses in sight.

"Put your head on and get in this car because I'm going to follow you until you do. Do you understand me?"

I slowed to a walk but I refused to look at him. "Get away from me." I kept walking.

He accelerated and drove ahead then turned sharply off the road and braked. He opened his door and got out.

"Sarah, get in the car." He pointed to my side of the car. He started walking toward me.

I turned around and ran again but then I tripped on a tree root. As I got up, I saw the sun rising. I could see its shoulder as it wended its way up through the vegetation. Not a single car had passed us.

He touched my arm and grabbed me, spinning me around and holding me by the shoulders.

"Don't touch me!" I screamed. "Get out of my life!"

This punctured him. He didn't let go but everything in him sagged to his knees just as that day with Peter at the dinner table. He looked at me but I looked away, at the sky turning orange and blue. The fog had been a temporary thing. Now the sky showed itself; a huge streak of colors over the trees that touched distant lands. I wanted to go to there.

He huffed, coughed, and spat into the dirt.

"Ach." I turned away.

"Please, Sarah," he whispered. "I am begging you as your father. Let's go home. We'll talk when we've both calmed down. I'm not going to leave you here."

I knew he meant this and I was tired. I nodded. I got back in the car.

We didn't speak the rest of the ride home. At home, I pushed open the kitchen door, passing Dora at the sink, and Elliot and Robert, their legs wrapped around bar stools. They had just come down for breakfast. I pulled myself up the stairs. I wanted sleep. A shower. Gregory. The smooth protection of my childhood sheets.

Chapter Sixteen

Saving the Fish Tank

So beautiful and lonely here in the house.

Dora made the rounds upstairs with the vacuum cleaner. She opened and closed Mother's bedroom door and when she plugged in the machine it punctuated the silent morning like a backhoe digging up a tree root. Back and forth the noise scooped under and around furniture as Dora strong-armed the vacuum further into Mother's dressing room. Dora vacuumed so long the whining pitch seemed like a new version of silence.

I lay in bed wondering what to do about the family beach outing. Certainly, I did not want to go.

"Sarah! Robert, Elliot!" Father called up from downstairs. "Get your swimming suits on!" His insistence on a Labor Day trip to the beach, one we took every year, almost made me forget — that delicious wisp of forgetting before remembering — that Mother had died so many eternal months ago.

No one answered except for Dora who turned the vacuum off. Now the house itself seemed to listen with me. A few minutes passed and he called again.

"Let's go! Everyone up!"

Dora turned the vacuum back on and the reverberations washed through the house. A grid of shadows from the sun and windowpanes cast a fence on my bedroom wall. I watched it carefully to see if it moved.

Elliot would want to go. He liked the beach with its glut of sand fleas, crabs, stones, shells, and circling gulls. Elliot was not one to refuse anything. That was not his way.

Robert opened and closed his bedroom door.

"Not coming!" he called with a slam.

Again, no one responded but the mood had been set.

"Everybody goes!" Father called up again after a short delay. This was followed by thudding footsteps.

He knocked on my door and opened it abruptly.

"I'll stay with Robert. He doesn't want to go," I said.

I propped up on my elbow. Father looked around my room. Unlike his office downstairs, I kept my bedroom neatly tucked in; my clothes stacked in careful layers in drawers, the way Mother liked it.

"Robert is coming. I will see you both down in twenty minutes."

Father went to Robert's room and opened the door to a hurricane of objections. My twelve-year-old brother threw something against a wall, a small object like a sneaker. Another object hit the wall. Father slammed the door again and charged downstairs.

Hearing this, I resigned myself to the trip and got dressed. I put my bikini on under a yellow cotton sundress. I slipped into leather sandals.

Dora headed back downstairs, the vacuum thudding on the carpeted risers. She would go to the living room next, then the dining room — she liked to work the enclosed rooms first, finally ending up in the front hallway before wrapping the cord and storing it once again in the downstairs coat closet.

Then I heard Sherry quietly padding upstairs from a night of staying over in father's pull-out couch in his office, her feet light as a guest's exploring a new house for the first time: toes politely touching the floor, legs moving quickly but with measured distances so as not to appear anxious or overeager. I heard her open and close my parents' bedroom door.

I peeked out my door and went into the hall to listen. Robert was silent in his room too, except for something scraping on the floor. I moved closer to my parents' bedroom door until I heard shower pipes cranking open in the master bathroom, the swishing of water behind closed doors. How dare she! With the shower going full blast now, I knew Sherry would not be able to hear me sneaking into Mother's dressing room. I stood, forehead pressed against the locked bathroom door while Sherry hummed "Begin the Beguine" by Cole Porter, a favorite of Father's. The humid, warm air crept under the door. I felt little breaths of moisture on my toes, the smell of minty soap.

I opened Mother's closet, still filled with her dresses in plastic wrap, and took a beach hat — straw with a green ribbon — from the shelf next to a box of shoes. I put it on and viewed myself in the full-length mirror on the closet door. Sherry stopped humming; suddenly, the water turned off. Frightened, I snuck back out, forgetting to close the bedroom door. I hurried downstairs to the kitchen.

"That's your mother's," Dora said.

I touched the hat rim and stood taller. If I were going on this beach trip with Sherry, who had the audacity to use Mother's bathroom, I would take Mother with me to keep Sherry in her proper place.

"I know."

I opened the refrigerator and took out a carton of orange juice. Sherry entered the kitchen, her cheeks red, flushed and moist from Mother's hot water. She wore white hoop earrings and a purple skirt wrapped tightly around wide, bony hips. Her bare midriff had a small curl of fat. Breasts, her crowning jewels, pushed out of a matching scarf-like cotton top. Shiny lipstick framed her square, thick teeth. I wondered how many times she had fucked my father.

"You look smashing in that hat, Sarah," Sherry said. She smiled handsomely, then turned to Dora for collusion and agreement.

"It's my mother's," I said.

Dora poured a cup of coffee and grudgingly handed it to Sherry.

"Cereal is in there," Dora said, pointing to the cupboard over the counter.

"Did you eat breakfast?" Sherry asked me. She looked at me in a way that said: *please give me a chance. Don't kick me in the face.*

I shrugged and looked away.

"Robert doesn't want to come," she said. "I'm sure he doesn't want to go with me. You, too. Sarah. I know you don't like that I'm here."

Her honesty stunned me. For a moment I softened toward her.

"Robert doesn't like excursions," I said. "Well, any kind of change really."

She nodded and sipped on her coffee, leaving a half moon of lipstick on the cup. "Could we try nonetheless?"

Nonetheless. I was listening to her until she said this. None the less?

Something hit the ceiling, an object much larger this time than a shoe. Dora and I ran over to the stairs and looked up. Robert's door was closed but Father was standing outside it, pushing on it.

"Stop. You'll break it!" Robert shouted.

Dora started upstairs, punctuating the carpeted steps with her commando feet, until she got to the top. Then I followed. Before I got to the top landing, Father managed to shove Robert's door open and the bureau that Robert had pushed in front of the door toppled over. Robert screamed.

"Murderer! My fish! My fish!"

He screamed again, as if someone were poking him repeatedly. I ran into the room. The bureau had caught the corner of the fish tank, cracking the glass. Water streamed out in a thin line, soaking the carpet. On the floor, Robert rocked on his back. The bureau had knocked him to the ground but I quickly saw that he was not injured. He flailed his legs hollering.

"My fish! You're killing my fish!" He jumped up and hugged the fish tank; the water level had plummeted to half while the fish — all six of them — blue and red tetras circled wildly in the shrinking pool.

"Get a pot! Save them! Help! Help. Help! Help! Help!" He wouldn't stop.

"Please, everyone, stay calm," Sherry said at the door.

The fact that she had the audacity to enter a riotous family scene silenced us all. She stood tall in the doorway, embracing a large lobster pot. "Let's pour the water in here. This will hold them until we get another one."

She put the pot on the floor, then looked at me for assistance. I took the end of the tank and tilted it. The water gushed over the corner and spilled into the lobster pot. The half dozen fish spun over the edge like splatters of bright blue and red paint then collapsed into tiny, two-inch drops of color again. They swam erratically as they tried to orient themselves in the black speckled lobster pot.

"The pet store is open today," Sherry said. "We'll drive down and get a new tank. Will you come with me, Robert? I'll need your help."

Elliot stood quietly in the hallway.

"You too, Elliot," she said.

Robert knelt next to the lobster pot. His shorts, wet from the spilled tank, stuck to his wiry legs. A dark hint of hair shadowed his upper lip. He had grown inches over the summer. At five feet, four inches, he and I were equal in height now. His bent legs looked gawky but the angles in his face surprised me in the morning light. Elliot looked a foot shorter than Robert, soft, round and vulnerable; whereas Robert had become physically threatening, his shoulders widening like a shield, his jaw cutting a sharper line. Robert talked into the lobster pot, moaning. "Don't die."

"I'll watch them," Dora said.

By now Father had crumbled into a tiny pile of himself. But it was hard to tell if he felt sorry for what he had done or simply sorry for himself, a state he coddled since Mother died, as if he were a bottle of wine that needed occasional turning but otherwise did best in chillier temperatures or benign neglect.

"Len, we'll be back," Sherry said to him. "I'm not going to worry about the beach. All right? We have all day." She turned to him and passed on a private, silent message to him, a lover's promise of reward if he behaved himself. My father deferred, his shoulders sagging now, his lip turned down into a defeated pout. I wanted to shake him when he did this, tug and yank him into a person that I could respect and like.

"I'm going to clean up this mess," Dora said with renewed confidence. "You go. I'll be right here. I'll add more water."

"No, don't!" Robert barked. "You can't meddle with the nitrogen process. We've got to hurry. They need to be *reintroduced*."

Elliot and Sherry followed Robert down and impulsively I decided to go too, last in line as we filed down to the driveway where Sherry had parked her car.

"Robert, sit up front with me. I want to understand what we need to do and I won't be able to hear you from the back."

Once again, her words had effect. Robert stood by Sherry's small hatchback and waited for her to open it for him. I sat in back with Elliot.

Sherry cupped her hand around the gear shaft and reversed out of the driveway. "Here we go."

"What's going to happen to the fish?" Elliot wanted to know.

"Nothing," Sherry said. "Fish are hardy creatures."

Robert rocked in his seat to ward off random misfires in his body, neurons spitting emotions haphazardly inside. The morning sun drilled a hot tunnel through the open windows. It was summer's last burning before fall would set in. I leaned my head out as Sherry started down the small hill, easing around the corners until she fed into the main street that led to town.

A car behind her honked impatiently. She ignored it, sticking her left arm out the window and waving them around her.

"Speeding won't get you there faster, Buster," she said.

Robert kept his eyes on the road. "Charles, Neon and Dimension, don't worry." His fish had names: Blue Tail, Angel, Flutter.

Pet Planet, located on a dead-end street off the town center, was empty when we walked in except for a tall, thin young man who wore his hair in a ponytail. The dim lights of the aquatic animals lit up one side of the room. Other small cages were grouped by animal type: birds at the farthest end, hamsters and gerbils in the middle and a litter of Labrador puppies sleeping in a furry gnarl in the front window.

The room was air-conditioned but fans blew from all four corners, roiling up the smell of shredded newspaper and puppy urine. The odor was a tangle of life — threads of eating, shitting, pissing, and breathing. Mother had not wanted a dog or cat, fearing the messes they made. Only after Robert had badgered her for months, checking out piles of library books on aquarium care and maintenance, did she finally relent.

"So long as you clean the tank," she said. "Dora has enough to do."

On the short ride to the pet store, Robert said to Sherry: "Fish waste products break down into ammonia, a highly toxic poison. But the natural biological process produces bacteria that convert deadly ammonia into benign nitrogen components. The cycle requires the right combination of water temperature, food, and monthly replenishment of new water." He breathed hard and continued: "The exact concentration at which ammonia becomes toxic to fish varies among species; some are more tolerant than others. In addition, other factors like water temperature and chemistry play a significant role." He talked as if he were reading from a movie screen in his mind. His brain photographed passages from books and if you interrupted him mid-sentence, he would start over, as if paragraphs fully emerged in his mind and popped up whole.

"You know," Elliot said, "they're not so different than we are. Fish have five senses. They smell and hear and taste, and see and feel." He counted the senses with his fingers.

"I know that. Additionally, they pick up vibrations in the water," Robert said. "Electrical impulses. They're extremely sensitive."

"I think they're better than humans!" Elliot said, his eyes opening to this idea. "They feel things we can't feel. They're super animals!"

"They're fish," Robert said.

~~~~~

In the store, I inspected different tanks of fish: ones filled with tetras, mollies, goldfish, catfish. I tried to imagine their liquid world. A printed sheet on goldfish explained that goldfish were intelligent, could even recognize the person feeding them when the person approached the tank. Elliot stood near me, placing a finger on the glass and staring at the graceful loops of fins. In one of the more crowded tanks, one fish nipped at another fish's fins until the chased fish fluttered to another corner of the tank.

Initially, when Robert had set up his tank, Father tried in his usual annoying and pedantic way to be philosophical about them.

"Why domesticate fish? What's the fascination?" he asked Robert at the dinner table.

"To pretend we're God," Peter said, half-closing his eyes, arching an eyebrow; his beautiful blond hair and smooth face looking purposefully arrogant. "So we can be masters of their tiny universe."

"Be quiet," Robert said. "It's evolution. Fish are our ancestors."

Remembering this made me ache for Peter, the ironic observer who was still in California with no plans to come back. I could practically see him singing folk songs in bars and street corners, a bandana around his neck. Maybe that's what I would do when I graduated next spring.

I moved through the pet store, passing shelves of small aquariums arranged according to their origins — fresh or salt water, warmer or cooler climates — and stopped at a cluster of small fish bowls, each with single Betta fish, also known as Siamese fighting fish. The data sheet on the tank said Bettas had an extra breathing organ called a labyrinth. The labyrinth allowed them to sip oxygen directly from the water's surface. In their natural state, Bettas lived in shallow puddles commonly found in rice fields in Southeast Asia. The puddles had limited oxygen supplies, thus the labyrinth gave them that extra boost to thrive.

Sherry came over and said, "Labyrinth organs. Can you imagine if humans could do that? Breathe in and out of water?"

I bent over and stood close to one glass bowl. The tiny, blueberry-colored Betta fins flowered at the sight of my approach. The fins splayed and rippled to warn me away. I stepped back. The Betta relaxed.

"People like fish because they're beautiful," Elliot said.

At the back of the pet store Robert engaged with the attendant, and discussed details of purchasing a new fifteen-pound tank, new pills to dechlorinate the tank water. The attendant told Robert: "one inch of fish to one gallon of tank."

When Robert first set up his fish tank in his bedroom, Mother liked to stand at the tank.

"Did you notice that Domino likes to stay near the bottom right corner, Robert? Why is that?" she asked.

She leaned over the rim and watched quietly until her neck ached, her narrow frame shadowing the lighted tank.

"I believe I'm growing attached," she said, surprised by her own revelation.

Robert freshened the tank every two weeks. He did this by draining a portion of the water using plastic tubing, siphoning it out into a mixing bowl. One time the old water spilled on the kitchen countertop and left an odd, dank smell. Mother scrubbed and scrubbed that spot. She needed everything to smell right and look right; her compulsion to rid the house of stains and streaks ongoing. She tried every new countertop cleaning liquid. Products that sprayed and wiped off, scrubbed, soaked, dissolved came home in weekly grocery bags. She walked into rooms, bending and turning on lamps in search of streaks on the wood furniture. "Dora," she would say, pointing to the dining room tabletop. "This needs to be wiped again. Look — "

Together, she and Dora tilted their heads, convening in earnest over another imperfection in the house.

~~~~~

At Pet Planet, I tired of fish watching. Though each fish had a unique path, a distinctive way of feathering across the watery plain, these fish had what they needed. I walked over to the four puppies available for adoption. They slept soundly in the arms of God waiting for someone, like me, to take them home.

"Come on, Sarah," Robert said, the edge returning to his voice. "We need to get my fish home."

A new fish glistened in a water bag dangling from his hand.

"What did you pick?" I asked.

"A Tetragon, Tetra for short. That's what I'm calling him," Robert said. "I have room in my new tank for one more." He marched out the door.

Sherry followed with the new tank and filter in hand, a big smile on her face. Elliot carried a bag of

food and fake tank scenery. I left the sleeping puppies. I wanted badly to touch one but didn't.

In the car, Sherry said, "What did you think
about the puppies, Sarah?" She talked to me in the
car's rearview mirror.

"What?" I didn't want to answer her. She had
caught me aching for something. "Cute. What else?"

In the front seat, Robert cuddled the plastic
water bag on his lap. "Easy. Don't bump. Watch it.
Yikes. Low, low, low, easy. Sorry, Tetra boy."

"How do you know it's a boy?" I asked.

"He told me."

~~~~~

At home, our procession inched back up the
stairs to Robert's room. Dora had kept watch, as
promised.

"Everyone's fine. Swimming like fish are supposed to do."

Father had retreated into his office downstairs,
though he didn't have any college papers or student
exams to correct. School had not started yet. Robert prepared the new tank, and added chemicals to
balance pH levels. He placed the tank on top of his
bureau, away from the door. The mirror behind the
bureau doubled the fish tank and reflected light.
This pleased him. He rarely sang but the sonorous
clarity of his speaking voice, its clean tone and pro-
jection echoed in his room as he sang the Beatles'
"Good Day, Sunshine."

Sherry's lobster pot rescue gave her a sure grip on Robert's slippery slope and easily won Elliot's devotion — Elliot who wanted to please, born with a readiness to be loved, embraced her from that moment on. We didn't go to the beach. Instead, Sherry coaxed Father out of his office and managed to get Dora, despite my silent disapproval, to unload a stack of hamburger patties and hot dogs from the freezer for an early supper barbecue in the backyard. The small round base of the grill sat on a tripod stand with wheels, which Dora rolled to the back porch steps so she could keep an eye on it from the kitchen.

While Dora squirted the lighter fluid in zigzags across the top of the charcoal, I sat on a chaise lounge and plucked on Peter's old guitar. I worked on easy chord changes and thought about taking a cross-country bus to California to visit my brother.

Dora struck a match and dropped it into the basin. The fire charged, leaping up in twisting fins of heat. Elliot and Robert flapped back and forth on the swing set, though Robert had clearly outgrown his swing. Father turned the stereo speaker from his office so that it faced the open window screen. Out came the popular song, "Little Green Apples," *it don't rain in Indianapolis in the summertime*. Apparently, our family happiness or the appearance of it managed to attract our neighbors, the Fineburgs, who sauntered over to join my father and Sherry for an impromptu, neighborly glass of wine.

"How quickly our children grow up," Mrs. Fineburg said to Father. She was a pleasant, comfortable-looking woman who favored sneakers and tennis skirts in warmer weather. She explained that Mickey was away in Europe, junior year abroad, then opened her mouth in disbelief. "Why, look at Robert. He's unrecognizable!" she said.

Father stood close to Sherry, his elbow touching hers. The Fineburgs smiled a lot, as if seeing Father reconnected as a couple returned him to a world they knew.

The charcoals in the grill glimmered red. The smell of burning grease, the sweet and sour scent of ketchup and mustard imbued the yard with odors of suburban normalcy. While all members of my family, except Peter in absentia, and even Dora appeared relieved, pleased with the results of the fish tank fiasco, I sat on the porch step nibbling at my hamburger bun, not hungry for food, chewing on a morsel of suspicion that Sherry in her optimism and hope had finally won something from us, but in the process taken something away from me.

Chapter Seventeen

The Beautiful Daughter

The doorbell rang and I went to see who it was.

"You're the beautiful daughter! I'm Mrs. Gore. Suburban Realtors!"

She held out her hand. Despite the humid day her hand was arid and cool, still fresh from her air-conditioned car. I saw her sapphire blue Continental parked in front before closing the door.

"Nice to meet you!" she said. "Your aunt told me you're a singer."

"Something like that."

Mrs. Gore took a step into the front entranceway. She looked like those older women at the country club — someone who marched around puffed up in the chest as if she had designed the club herself. I could see her in golf shoes, click-clacking across stone tiles, her golf visor perched like a tiara, confident and oblivious to others — a country club duchess. Her strong perfume stitched my nostrils with threads of old carnations, cinnamon and vanilla frosting.

"Is my father expecting you?"

"Oh, yes. We have an appointment."

In fact, I knew this. Mrs. Gore had just sold Aunt Annette's house. September was nearly gone and my aunt and uncle's impending move to Miami, Florida, in December, spurred Father to see what kind of money he might get for our house. Father planned to rent something, then buy something smaller.

As soon as the Klines' house sold, Uncle Max officially shut down the shoe company. He announced this development during Sunday dinner at his house the week before. I hadn't been to the Klines' since Mother's funeral and upon entering the Klines', I grew morose. The mahogany paneled walls in the entry room, the dark furniture and heavy furnishings brought ugly memories back into being. I ached for a joint to lighten my head but Kenneth and Peter were not there to distract me. The Klines' house felt enormous, silly in its overreaching grandeur. No majesty, only the resin of failed Passover dinners and the hangover of Uncle Max's lusting eye. Even my aunt — plumpness and smoothly swept back hair — seemed out of place in her endless rooms, as if her impending relocation had unbalanced her too.

Mary, their housekeeper, served meatloaf casserole. She carried a bowl of green peas around the table, cradling the china in both hands. It wasn't necessary. The table was too long for our small group. Mary wore a maid's uniform and I wondered if it was something that my aunt had supplied? The white dress buttoned in front like my gym uniform. Uncle Max sat at one end and my aunt on the other, leaving a gap in the middle of the table for the pared down

Kunitz family. Elliot, Robert and I sat on my side. Father and Sherry sat opposite.

"If you know how to turn a key, you can sell a house," Uncle Max said to Father. I sat closest to Aunt Annette. The house sale had absorbed all of my uncle's attention. He showed little interest in me.

"It's not that easy, Max, you know that," my aunt said.

Uncle Max released a guffaw. "Sure it is. With the money from the house sale, we've enough to retire. Florida is the next frontier. Look," he went on to explain. "It's cheaper living, certainly cheaper than the northeast. Even in this bad housing market — you can buy good, solid — I mean very good — houses in Florida for pennies."

The Klines had owned their mansion for twenty-seven years. The sale would give them enough to buy a beach home outright, he told us. "Unimpeded water views!" Uncle Max made his point by dabbing his face with a linen napkin.

"I may get into this sham of a business myself," he added. "List a few properties. Why not?"

"Max, I think we've been lucky," my aunt said, again.

"What luck? A beautiful home doesn't need anyone to sell it. It sells itself."

"You've been blessed with a beautiful home," Sherry said.

Sherry's presence, along with Peter's west coast migration and absence, created a low-grade tension in the room. Peter was in the process of moving out of Kenneth's condo into a house with four others near Venice Beach. He had enrolled in the California State College system to avoid the draft. He wrote me letters on stationery so thin his handwriting made bumps on the pages. I liked running my fingers over the indentations. He always drew a picture of himself, a stick figure of a man with hair grown to his shoulders. And he included lyrics to new songs he wrote, scribbling guitar chords like E6 and A minor so I could hear them. "This one's for you, Sarah," he wrote.

Satellite Heart
See you flying through space
Can't leave yourself behind
'cause the world's a circular place

I carried his latest letter in my pocket, a talisman of our bond, proof of purchase for hope, for my future. If he had made it out, so would I.

My aunt made an effort to talk to Sherry at dinner.

"And you said you teach women studies? What is that exactly?"

Sherry wore a pale blue pullover sweater and plaid slacks. Each time she put the fork to her mouth a jangle of bangle bracelets chimed in. She looked over at me and tried to smile but I looked away. Unlike Mother, who charged her outfits with surprising dashes of colored scarves, Sherry inevitably forgot some critical detail — as in the case of today's outfit: a crooked blouse collar. She just couldn't get it right, or maybe she didn't care, as if something in her was set free, willing to get messy in her bare feet.

"I'm looking at gender roles in nineteenth-century literature. But that's just one example."

"Sherry has been a great family friend," Father pronounced. He sat up suddenly after not moving for most of the meal. He looked contracted in his chair, crunched as if suffering stomach pains. His head bent away from the conversation, from words that hurt his ears. He resented Uncle Max's flush state of affairs, my aunt's seamless life.

I couldn't help rolling my eyes. Did Sherry think studying gender roles made her a family expert? A mother substitute?

Uncle Max nodded and peered at Sherry as if he were looking through a mask or darkened spectacles, though he wore no glasses. But, he didn't say anything. The unmentionable was Mother. Her absence lodged in my ribs, a cramping ache that I couldn't expel. Everyone felt it.

Aunt Annette prodded Sherry to tell her more.

But Sherry didn't want the attention and turned to Robert and Elliot. "Tell your aunt about your newest fish," Sherry said. Robert and Elliot had returned to the pet store with Sherry after Robert's fish tank fiasco to get this newest fish for Elliot.

"We have a Betta fish." Elliot looked at our aunt to see if she recognized what this meant.

"Betta Fish? I have no idea what that is."

"His name is Only Boy," Elliot said. "But he's everybody's fish."

"That's marvelous," my aunt said. "I'm glad to hear that."

"I've allowed Elliot to keep Only Boy in his room," Robert said.

"He's got beautiful scarves for fins," Elliot said. "But you can't put him in with other fish. Bettas fight. They eat other fish. Sometimes they're called Siamese Fighting fish."

"They're territorial," Robert said.

"That's why we named him Only Boy," Elliot said.

I liked to watch Only Boy in Elliot's room. Drifting to the bottom or easing up to nibble the surface, the Betta flickered around his small glass bowl on Elliot's night table. When I approached the bowl, Only Boy puffed out his lungs readying for attack. But as soon as I retreated from his sight, he relaxed and floated mid-water like a miniature blimp.

"He's really nice," Elliot said.

Maybe we were like Bettas, too. Bettas lived in shallow pools of water in rice paddies in Thailand. We lived in shallow pools of separateness in our bedrooms.

"A happy Betta makes bubble nests," Robert said.

"You'll have to explain that to me, dear," Aunt Annette said.

"That's a cluster of bubbles that the fish makes," Robert said. "It forms on the surface to attract a mate."

"Only Boy makes bubbles at night," Elliot said. "He's happy."

Uncle Max twisted his lips. "Very good," he said.

He resumed talk about the great new Florida real estate frontier. Who needed the winters? It's a wonder he hadn't come to this revelation before. He refilled Father's glass of wine. Father remained bent over the table disinterested, taking short gulps of wine. Elliot mashed his potatoes, peas and meatloaf into one big lump.

~~~~~

All this whizzed through me as Mrs. Gore stood in the foyer waiting for me to let her in. Her cropped silver hair bubbled out as if frozen mid-air.

"You're the oldest girl, I understand?"

"The only girl."

Tiny curls twisted around her earlobes. Bangs trimmed just above her penciled eyebrows, exaggerated arcs that created a surprised face even when she stopped talking.

"And your father, he's here?"

"Yes."

She smiled again. I found her large, conical-shaped breasts irksome. They burst against a white cotton shirt. She wore black pedal pushers that made her appear chunky at the hips. I loomed over her to block her view of our house but that proved difficult. Her eyes automatically and coldly found a way to photograph her potential listing. I saw her mind clicking away.

"Lovely home," she said.

"Thank you. Wait here, please."

"Glad to meet you!" she said exuberantly as I turned away, as if she were the party and she needed to make sure I knew how much fun she could be.

I went upstairs to get Father, who was talking to Robert. They had reconciled about the fish and now Father visited Robert's goldfish every day. I went back down to the living room. I didn't want to miss what Mrs. Gore had to say.

She was petite yet I could feel the enormity of her judgment as she sized up the hallway, living and dining rooms. She sidled closer to the piano. "Will this be for sale?"

"No," I said.

Father turned to me.

"No," I said. "It's not."

Pausing again, did Mrs. Gore see the worn spot in the rug at the bottom of the stairs? What about the paint lifting off the wall near the front closet? Did she smell the odor of our missing mother, the listless air, the home's chronic desuetude? Father trailed her. The forced peppiness in her voice hurt my head. Who was she kidding?

Mrs. Gore walked back into the living room, saw me staring at her and smiled impulsively. Her eyes grew tight as they circled the rooms, taking in furnishings. She nodded and they moved on.

"Will you be including *anything* in the purchase — light fixtures? Larger pieces? The dining room set for example?"

Father shook his head. "I don't know."

"We're not selling furniture," I said.

She turned and gave me a sewed-up smile this time.

"I understand. It's terribly disconcerting, isn't it? This moving business."

They disappeared upstairs to the second floor. I heard them stopping in each bedroom, including mine, then returning to the upstairs hall again. I hid our good silverware in the closet.

Their footsteps paused directly above me. I heard Father's voice. More steps as they moved through Mother's room, around the king-sized bed, into Mother's changing room. Would she open the closet doors? I couldn't hear.

"Elliot!" Father called up to the attic.

Again the footsteps resumed upwards to the third floor. Mrs. Gore's voice rose above Father's and off they went to the top of the house. A breeze blew outside. In the *Wizard of Oz*, Dorothy's house spins to a distant place. I held on to the arm of an imaginary couch waiting to land.

They came down again and went to the kitchen. She oohed and ahhed. "How convenient for a family," she said, referring to the eat-in counter with bar stools.

On her way out she walked into the living room and touched a blue, ceramic plate that mother had brought back from Mexico on one of their adult vacations.

"Careful," I said. If I were a bird, I would have pecked her.

"Nice to meet you." She turned to me, all smiles once more — the experienced, older woman who could set things right. She had shell-colored teeth, sharp, brittle at the edges, a wet-looking tongue.

As soon as she left, Father came back and sat on the other end of the couch.

"It's the best thing to do right now."

"You know," I said, getting up. "It's all your fault." I suddenly hated him. The feeling surged like an open water hose. "This mess. Everything."

"What?" He reached to touch my arm.

I twirled away from him.

"Don't touch me!"

He stood up.

"None of this would have happened if you had gone with her. Why didn't you go? Why didn't you *drive*?"

We looked at each other, locked in an emotional paralysis until plumes of grief started spilling out. I didn't want to inhale them so I fled.

I left the house.

I walked to the town pharmacy and called Gregory from the pay phone. The first week after Stonehill, we talked a few times. Twice, Dora had taken the call. But since starting college, I hadn't heard from him.

"That boy from New York, he lives too far away, don't you think?" Dora had said. She looked me up and down like a doctor giving an exam. "Be careful," she said. "You've got plenty of time for men in your life."

"Look. He's nice. It's not a big deal. He's just a friend."

I pretended boredom with the subject. I even tried to pretend to myself that he didn't matter because it was too hard to live in this in between. I was old enough to drive but I hadn't yet gotten my license. Maybe I was afraid to. Gregory was far away, and a phone call didn't replace or compare to walking in the woods, or getting photographed, or having sex.

At the pharmacy, I stood in the phone booth fiddling with the change slot. Gregory's dormitory phone rang and rang. No one answered. In a panic, I hung up and called Margaret.

"Did you hear?" she said, after she answered and heard my voice.

"Hear what?"

"Anthony's been drafted."

"What?"

At the end of the school year, I had watched Anthony drift away from sports and grow his hair. I sometimes saw him smoking joints across the street from the school. I felt indebted to him for walking me home after his sister's friends harassed me. The girls never bothered me again. After our walk, Anthony broke up with Giselle. But then I saw him with different girls, lots of girls. Whatever seemed ready to happen between us didn't.

"He's leaving in two days for Vietnam. Someplace south. I know how to find him if you want."

"Yes. I want to."

"I'll come get you now," she said.

Chapter Eighteen

Gooseneck Lake

I left the drugstore and walked back home. Father had retreated to his murky little fish tank of an office to correct students' papers. No doubt his true love, Sherry, would soon be over to cheer him. While I waited for Margaret to pick me up, I went to Peter's room or what was left of it since he had fled to California to seek his fortune, and took out his old guitar from his closet.

As soon as I held my brother's instrument in my arms, a tunnel opened up for me and took me through a mountainside. So easy to sing. I started with The Weavers' familiar folk tune. *If I had a hammer.* I curled my left hand around the guitar frets, the way Peter taught me. The pressure of my fingertips on the strings renewed a deeper purpose. Melodies took me out of the house, away from my father's romance, far from my own dark place of losing Mother. I sang new words for old songs.

If I had a car, I'd drive across the country. I'd visit my brother, far far from this land.

A car horn honked twice. I ran downstairs, across our long front yard, to Margaret's car. She looked different sitting behind the wheel in her uncle's Dodge Dart. Her legs were pale, her dark Italian eyes ringed with smudged mascara. She had been inside all summer working at her cousin's beauty parlor. But she smoked as elegantly as ever in her mini yellow dress.

"He shows up when the sun goes down," Margaret said. She pushed her dark bangs from her forehead, shiny with sweat.

"It's dark, now."

"That's what I mean."

She offered me a cigarette and I lit up expertly. I had smoked all summer long, taking on the habit completely. She steered a look over at me, surprised by my nonchalance, which I had first modeled after her.

How glorious to be out: my elbow resting on the window, a breeze riffling my skin. I wore a tight cotton top and long, flowered skirt, my tiny Jewish star around my neck. It gleamed nicely against my skin, still tanned from lying in a grassy field with Gregory. But already Gregory was slipping into long ago.

Margaret drove slowly through my neighborhood, past brick estates, then down the hill where smaller houses sat on the flat part of town, to the ice-cream store.

"See him?"

I recognized the gait, his shoulders leading the way as he walked toward a small clique of boys smoking in the adjacent parking lot. Margaret circled the lot and parked. We got out. I flipped my hair back over my shoulders. It was awkward, this sauntering over to a group of boys I didn't know, except for Anthony who spotted me and nodded in recognition. I waved to be friendly and he left the group to meet me. Margaret headed for her new beau waiting for her inside.

"You grew up," he said, sizing me up and down, eyes to ankles. He had a dreamy but inanimate smile on his face. "You seeing anyone?" he asked.

"I was."

"How far did you go?"

"As far as I wanted to."

I looked into his blue eyes but they were screened in, hard to see beyond the marijuana glaze or what appeared to be his general disinterest in anyone or anything in particular. He had changed.

"You're different," I said.

"You too."

He stood in front of me and touched my chin then leaned in to kiss me. I let him press his lips against my mouth.

"You're not a virgin," he said.

"And you?"

He smiled and shook his head.

"Come on. I'll buy you a coke."

We walked into the bright ice-cream store. A group of long-haired boys sat on counter stools smoking, waiting for sodas, French fries. Their bangs fell past their eyes. One boy hung over the counter stabbing a straw into his coke, poking for hidden answers. Margaret was sitting in a far booth making out with a blond boy that I didn't recognize. Maybe I had made a mistake, calling her, setting this whole thing up.

The store had a frosty, crystalline glare from an air conditioner that pushed too hard. I was cold. Anthony sat beside me and lit up a cigarette. He wore a blue tee shirt and black jeans. He looked at my blouse and ran his finger along the edge of my neckline. He touched my star.

"I remember this."

"I won't forget what you did to help me."

"Kids are stupid."

I took his cigarette and sucked on the filter, then blew the smoke away from both of us. He twisted on the stool and placed his palm on my thigh. I didn't flinch. I knew he was testing me.

"Let's take our drinks out."

The waitress handed us cokes in plastic cups. She was a high school student like me. Her hair was pushed under a hair net, her pink uniform soiled with chocolate ice cream and splattered hamburger grease. Anthony left her a huge tip. "Come on. We'll talk in the car," he said.

I looked over at Margaret but she was still at it. The manager of the store, a medium tall man with thin, dark hair and brown-rimmed glasses was standing over her booth. Her new boyfriend turned and asked the manager what he wanted.

"Are you ready to order?" the manager asked.

"All set here," the boy said.

"Ready to pay then?"

"I'm still drinking."

Margaret lit up a cigarette and smiled at the manager.

"We're almost ready," she said. She looked over at me then and tipped her cigarette good-bye.

At the take-out counter, a mother in blue striped shorts and navy shirt carefully handed her young daughter an ice-cream cone.

"Watch the drips, honey," the mother said.

The little bronze-haired girl held her cone high, her love torch for all the world to see.

"What's the matter?" Anthony asked, brushing my chin.

I shook my head. It hurt to see that child with her mother, but I didn't want to tell him that.

In the car, he reversed and swung out of the parking lot, bouncing over the curb onto the main street. I thought about Mother driving alone to Gooseneck Lake on a summer night. Too much drink. Too many pain pills. Her thin figure slapped against the dashboard when her car tripped over the embankment. Did she feel as I did now: wanting to break away but not knowing how?

"Let's drive to Gooseneck," I said.

He smiled. The lake put our heads toward a common goal, a destination, a feeling that we had purpose and it put me in a better mood. I opened the ashtray in the car and lit up the half joint lying inside it. It tasted stale, muddy.

"All this time I thought you were a prude. You fooled me," Anthony said. He put his hand on my thigh again.

"People change." I lit up and smoked languorously as if our time would never run out.

On the way, he drove just under the speed limit. He glanced at my ankles and sandled feet, and sidled a look at my torso and waist. I watched him take in the whole picture, bit by bit.

Whatever was meant to happen, I would let it.

"I regret not getting together," he said, taking the joint from me.

"Yes. Me too, and now you're leaving."

"Day after tomorrow."

He didn't say anything more about getting drafted but the danger of it was there, racing between us.

"Do you like swimming?" I asked.

"I don't swim."

I coughed out the remaining dregs of marijuana in my lungs and sat up in the seat.

"Why not?"

"No one taught me."

"Well you can sit on the beach and watch me." I slipped my feet out of my sandals and pressed my heels into the dash. We drove for a time in silence. The slow effect of marijuana squirmed through my body. I could tell he didn't know what to think. Perhaps the awareness that I was stranger was making its way into his thoughts for he became more formal, a bit shifty in the car seat.

"Where's your brother, the singer?"

"He's in California now."

"You're both singers. Runs in the family, doesn't it?"

"I guess. Yes." I didn't tell him that Mother played violin before arthritis set in, crippling her joy. I didn't mention my great grandmother's opera dream.

"You know what runs in my family?" he asked.

"Sports?"

He laughed. "That's good. Truck drivers. My father and uncle drive trucks."

"Is that what you want too?"

"Why not? Money's pretty good."

We parked in a rustic neighborhood with cabins, under tall, straight pines. This time when he kissed me I kissed him back, his tongue seasoned with cigarette smoke and earth. I kissed aggressively and then I broke off and ran into the woods toward the lake's edge. He sauntered alongside me, easily keeping up, the athlete in him emerging effortlessly. But I soon lost my breath and slowed down. Then I tried to run again. This running and stopping on the soft earth kept on until we finally came to the water. It was not the high bank where Mother had toppled the car and ended up in the hospital. That was on the opposite side of the lake, near the highway. I pulled my shirt off and tossed it back. It was dark under a quarter moon. Too dark for anyone except Anthony to see my breasts. The water lapped the sand and tall grass. Lacy curls of white broke the surface.

"Beautiful," he said.

I slipped off my skirt and kept my underwear on. Then I went in and felt the water in layers: the warmer surface, the denser, cool bottom. My toes tickled the cold; my breasts hardening, my nipples pointing out as if greeting the air. Anthony came to the edge but didn't go any further.

"Jesus Christ."

I laughed but I was getting cold and plunged in before I could stop myself. I dove again, pushing my butt up and circling under, then exploding through the surface.

"Come in, Anthony."

"No. You come here."

But I turned and swam away, paddling through water that numbed my skin. I dove under again, a strata of colder waters wrapping around my legs. I felt the soft bump of a fish against my ankle.

"Hey, come closer so I can see you."

I turned toward shore, then stood up in the shallows, hugging myself.

"Looking for this?" He dangled my skirt and blouse in his hand. I reached for them but he playfully pulled them away and started walking.

"Very funny," I called to him.

"You want it, you have to give me something in return."

"Like what?"

He stopped. He walked up to me and held my clothes behind his back. I stood still, the slow drips of water inching down my legs, settling into small pools in my underwear, on my lip and neck, in the crook of my crossed arms.

"I should have kissed you that day I walked you home."

"Why didn't you?"

"Didn't think I was good enough for you."

"I didn't think I was pretty enough for you."

I liked the way he looked at me now, full attention, his glaze dissolving so that I could see deeper. He took another long drag of his cigarette and flicked it into the lake. We both watched the red tip arc, dive suddenly. Gone.

"Kiss me now."

He stepped closer and peeled my arms from my chest. He stepped closer again until his hips pressed into my wet underpants. His erection soon made his pants irrelevant. We pulled off the rest from each other and I let him in for a quick, slippery ride.

~~~~

Long past midnight, Anthony dropped me off at the end of my street. I insisted on it. I wanted to slip in the house unnoticed. I barefooted up our driveway to the backyard but saw Father's office light on. I sneaked over to the window to peek in. There she stood in his office, much taller and broader than Mother, her arms around his chest. I ran into Mother's rose garden, so overgrown now that only the thorns seemed to have flourished. Mother would be beside herself if she saw how we'd let it tangle, the bushes left on their own. I knelt down, face against the dirt path, furious with Father. I wanted to run back down the driveway to get Anthony.

Too late.

Maybe he heard something because the office light turned off, then on again, and off. The whole house became dark. I walked into the kitchen and turned on the overhead light. I took out a pan and noisily placed it on the stove, then filled it with water to boil noodles. I was hungry. I had forgotten to eat. But I only heard silence thickened with heartache, and then a rustle from Dora's room. She came out suddenly, pink rollers in her hair, and shuffled into the bright room wearing a blue cotton robe that made her skin look blacker.

"What are you doing?"

"I'm hungry."

"You're all wet. Where were you?"

"Swimming."

"Lord." She turned to go back to her room but changed her mind and came closer to me.

"When did she come here?" I asked, referring to Sherry.

"After dinner. They went to a movie."

We looked at each other, Dora softening towards me, not by smiling but by acknowledging what we both knew to be true: that my father had pushed me too far, stepped out of bounds, broken my rules, rules I didn't know I had, rules about time and consideration. Time to adjust to this change without Mother. Consideration for letting a younger woman — any woman — take Mother's place.

"He doesn't care, does he?"

She sighed, then sighed again as if breathing could pull in better words or clear out the muddled ones that I struggled with. I could smell her hand cream and the perspiration on her temples. I stirred the pasta, impatient for it to cook.

"Listen, Sarah," she said, adjusting the flame under the stove. "Your father has his needs. You'll understand that when you're older."

I snorted. My breasts jiggled under my damp blouse. I felt sticky and hemmed in by my clothes. "Well, I'm not older. Okay?" I stiffened up, standing straight while I gave the pasta, overdone now, a few more rough twirls. I yanked the pot from the stove and emptied the hot water into the sink, including the pasta.

"Can I help?" Sherry said, appearing in the kitchen doorway. She was dressed in a yellow shift that hovered above her kneecaps. She had wide knees, sturdy legs. Nothing like Mother's slim calves. "Late night munchies?" She smiled, her lipstick faded on her lips.

"I didn't have dinner."

I hated her attempt to be teenage friendly and knowing.

"What's burning?" Father said, standing behind her, his hair wild in the summer heat. He didn't look at me. He asked Dora.

"Ask your daughter. She's cooking."

But he ignored this and came in and poured himself a glass of water.

"I've invited Sherry to stay over tonight. I'll sleep on the couch and she'll stay in my office, on the sleeper."

"Sure."

I left the room, the pasta, the pots and went upstairs to shower. I was disgusted, raging. I wished I had stayed out all night.

In the shower, I splattered my face in a downpour of water. Why had Mother plunged into Gooseneck Lake, gorgeous in her short hairdo and party dress? Was she leaving her marriage? Leaving us? Running away as I had wanted to, before Anthony delivered me back. Six months later, her new Cadillac failed to protect her. February's snowfall and a truck or was it the memory of Symphony Hall that conspired to kill her. I couldn't accept that she was not coming back.

When Anthony and I returned to his car, I made him hard again with my hand. I liked the control and power it gave me. He lay back in the backseat, his pants unzipped, his shirt on. But afterwards, after his groan and hump, he looked confused as if I had penetrated his private shelter without permission.

On the ride back home, I leaned against him and smoked, the car filled with a tenderness that comes when there's no future between lovers. No hope.

I stepped out of the shower and stood at the top of the stairs wrapped in a towel. Downstairs I heard Father's grumbling voice, a woman's sigh, and something knock over in the living room. Then the rest of the lights in the house went out.

Chapter Nineteen

Pure Mechanics

I took the train into Boston as soon as classes ended and followed the directions to a Planned Parenthood clinic in Beacon Hill. I had missed my period, which is not what I had planned, not what I wanted to think about. I woke up queasy in the mornings, feeling strange. But I forced myself to follow the school routine: science and the human body, English. Logarithms in Math. American History. I took aspirin, told myself I suffered symptoms of malcontent.

Between classes, I ignored the clans and cliques that had regrouped in the hallways since school began. After my summer with Gregory, my night with Anthony, all the boys at school seemed young, too young and impish.

But Sophie and I still had many of the same classes together. In the afternoons, she went to ballet lessons, tap and jazz. She started dating a senior named Benny Weiss. Benny's skin was pale and he had plump lips the color of apple cider. He worked hard to look old and wizened. He read French philosophers and talked about existentialism. He wanted to sleep with her but she resisted, though they went everywhere like husband and wife. He drove her to the movies and ballet on the weekends. It surprised me at first and then I grew used to seeing them arm in arm, kissing in his car.

Margaret rarely showed up at all, and twice had been warned by the principal to make an effort to come to school. We were assigned different homerooms. I was on the college honors track but I didn't feel much on track except that I completed my work, and never missed choir practice.

Mr. Edwards had asked me to sing another solo for the Thanksgiving concert, "One Hand" from Leonard Bernstein's *West Side Story*. The theme this year was America. We practiced the American anthem. This was not an easy song. Its range stretched high and low. He also urged me to try out for the school play, *Guys and Dolls*, but I didn't want to act. Every day I put on an act. I was the daughter who didn't care — but I did. I did.

I cared when Mrs. Brenwald finally died. Coming home after choir practice one afternoon in October, I turned up our street and saw a huge flatbed truck parked in front of her house and a man in brown overalls standing in her driveway. Dora, Robert and Elliot huddled at the curbside watching.

The man wore a plaid flannel shirt. A cigarette burned in his hand; his face dirt covered. Mrs. Brenwald's tall, brown weeds had been shorn. The electric weed cutter lay at his feet. I could see he had been working at it for several hours. But most striking was the car, without the sheet. There it stood, a memorial to a prehistoric life and now in her postmortem existence it would be moved again, carted away to an automobile collector, or so the man said.

"I send 'em off," he said. "Don't know more than that. Most folks take better care of their cars than their own family members, I can tell you that." The man talked as if he were used to such odd spectacles and circumstances. It was his business. He lifted his chin toward the house and shook his head.

"Pretty darn sad."

Years of rumors had been confirmed. Brenwald's house was a maelstrom of newspapers and brown paper bags, and a dead cat.

The man's eyebrows cast shadows on his face.

I turned to Dora. "When did this happen?"

"This morning. She's not in there," Dora said. "They took her out. A utility man called the police. A family member came while you were in school. A niece." Dora shook her head.

One police car and an ambulance without flashing lights drove up the street and parked. We inched back onto our lawn. The policeman opened Mrs. Brenwald's door revealing a peek at paper debris inside, a hint of the severest neglect. My chest felt punched. I didn't want to imagine Mrs. Brenwald like this, or the thought of her getting hauled out on some stretcher. I saw Mother's coffin. Overcome, I turned and ran into our house, bursting into tears.

I couldn't stop. Upstairs, I knelt at the window in Peter's room, his guitar over my lap. Downstairs, I heard my brothers clunking across the kitchen.

Dora called up to me. I strummed a chord but didn't answer her, so she started up. I plucked "The Crystal Ship" by The Doors. Still, she kept coming up.

"You all right?" she asked. She stood at Peter's door huffing.

I shrugged, hoping that would be enough. But my eyes hurt. I couldn't hide the swelling.

"You should cry some more," she said. "It will cleanse you."

"No it won't."

I turned back to the guitar, still hoping she would leave but she came closer. I hunched over the strings and felt her hand on my shoulder.

"You don't want to go inside too deep," she said. "Not at your age."

She ran her hand gently across my back, then told me she would be downstairs cooking dinner. When she had gone back down, I wrote a song.

Lost lady
Staring at circles
Staring at squares
Reads a book, plays solitary games
Seeks solace,
Seeks peace
Skips waves
Runs away

The train ride to Boston was forty-five minutes of fear stretching in my throat. Sophie had sensed something and asked several times what was wrong? I told her I didn't feel well, which was true.

Something was off center, atilt, pulled out of orbit. At sixteen, I should be getting a driver's license, not this.

I looked out the window to distract myself but I kept seeing ugly Miss Holloway standing in front of our sex education class.

"One time, that's all it takes, girls," she said holding up a stubby pointer finger. Her finger, white and fleshy as a limp penis, pointed lamely to the ceiling. She dangled a condom in her hand, tightening her cheek muscles as she rolled it over a plastic penis mounted on a desktop for sex education demos.

The boys were in another classroom, presumably viewing a similar demonstration given by the football coach.

"Gross," one girl from the back of the room called out.

Miss Holloway flicked up her head but ignored the comment. Once the condom covered the plastic penis, she handed it to one of the girls in front to pass it around.

"There's no mystery to this. It's pure mechanics."

If only it were that — if only I had understood what I was doing, if only I hadn't taken this chance.

On the train, a few high-schoolers and black housekeepers scattered in the rows down the length of the car. I guessed the teenagers might be going to the city for after school music lessons or jobs, or simple diversion, something to do beyond the boredom of classrooms and suburban life.

Miss Holloway didn't talk about love or worry or hope. She held up packages of birth control pills, packaged in plastic disks that turned each day of the month. She passed the tiny yellow pills around. She didn't talk about feeling engulfed, the thrill of someone wanting you. She displayed latex diaphragms, a god-awful looking contraption that looked like a rubber drain stopper for the kitchen sink. She had tubes of contraceptive cream the color of toothpaste.

The train clipped past suburban towns, past trees in autumnal dress. I passed backyards, still green and mown, and closer to town yards abandoned to the detritus of carelessness: walkways strewn with children's toys, plastic balls, old sneakers.

A man inserts his penis in the vagina, Mother said during our mother-daughter talk about sex. I was eleven. We sat on the divan in her bedroom, the sewing box at her feet. An early afternoon light shone on our knees.

"I know that."

"Do you have any questions?"

"No."

She opened the instructional pamphlet, touching it gently. On my page, she pointed to a picture of a naked woman; on her page: a naked man. The woman's vagina was shaped like an isosceles triangle; the man's penis resembled a pickle. Both man and woman looked like people waiting for a doctor's examination.

The most important thing to remember is that intercourse is an expression of love between a man and a woman.

I nodded.

Here, she said, handing me the little book. *You keep it.* I hid the book under my bedroom rug. *An expression of love.* An expression of love. What was that?

I opened my science book and reviewed the chapter on hormones. I liked the idea that separate organs in our body secreted powerful juices, as if we were many streams interlocking, a series of channels swirling, draining, filling up. Maybe Mr. Bingham was right. Everything connected. I thought how singing tied the network together. When I sang, all internal signals aligned, swooped into a unified flow up and down mountains, rivers and oceans. The tallest mountaintop became climbable.

The train racing past town after town lightened my *gravitus*. I grew hopeful again. Hopeful that I would clear the darkness that sponged into my mind since Mother died. If I were lucky, and I thought about God for the first time since Mother died, this nausea would be an instructive scare. Dear God. Please teach me not be so brazen

I had a good head on my shoulders. Pregnancy didn't happen to girls with good grades. I would go on the pill. It would soon be behind me. But if I were pregnant, I would have to go to New York. Abortion was illegal in Massachusetts.

Margaret knew about this clinic in Boston. She had been there herself the year before. After the miscarriage in the bathroom, she started on the pill. She said it was the century's best invention. Better than getting the vote. And if I were pregnant?

When the train stopped at South Station, I walked across downtown's shopping center, through the crowded intersection where Filene's and Jordan Marsh department stores dominated, past jewelry stores — so many of them — and the antiquarian bookshop. Sidewalks buckled with years of repaving, heaving cold, mud and ice.

I buttoned my coat and pulled it around my neck. The sun looked fetal, a tiny clump barely clinging to a rooftop, as if the earth had aborted it, and now shreds of light tangled in the sky, remnants of an unrealized future. I walked through crowds of black teenagers lined up outside a record store. Music blared into the street. The wind gusted. Crisp leaves collided with my feet and face.

The woman at the clinic who answered the phone told me to cross Tremont Street and head for the State house, its gold dome lackluster in the late afternoon light. I felt so terribly alone. She said, "take a right onto Joy Street."

Joy Street — the irony of it — was north of the Commons, on the corner of Beacon Hill, the historic neighborhood patterned with cobblestone sidewalks, gas lamplights, elegant four-story townhouses. "*You can't miss the sapphire blue door*," she said. And there it was, just as she had described. No sign, nothing but blue, this door that opened to young women, too young to be pregnant.

I stood at the door to summon my courage. This horror of ridding myself of child, a seedling of someone's future ignited by Gregory's impulsive burst of salty liquid one night in a misted wood or was it Anthony? Easy jack off while my lips kissed his, as if somehow this mingling of juices, this act of conception would transform us. Just one night. One day. Two stupid moments that changed everything. Where was I inside them? I missed my mother. Mom. Mommy.

I hesitated at the step outside the sapphire door.

I could barely utter these words to myself. Mother, I said slowly. I had a mother, a disappearing mother, a mother who was not here. I repeated this to myself. Not here. Somewhere. Out there. Like swimming in an ocean. The currents taking you without realizing it. You notice when you look back at the shore and see that you have drifted downstream, hundreds of yards away. Maybe thousands.

I reminded myself that I once had this comfort, this possession of having a mother, owning one. She was home, upstairs in her bedroom reading magazines, sipping her drink. She had been there whether I liked her there or not. The sight of her sitting on the loveseat in her bedroom, with the pleated lampshade by her side, blinded me for a moment. I swooned. I wanted her to see me. Stay with me Mother, please. It mattered. Who was it, Gregory or Anthony? I wanted to get this over. Start over. Start again.

Inside the clinic foyer, I stepped across black and white marble tiles. I hooked my jacket on a coat tree and followed a sign up a small stairway to the right. At the top of the stair, I gave my name to a woman with short, red hair. She wore a black sweater. Her thumb was pen stained.

"You'll need to look these over." She slid a sheaf of papers across the desktop. She glanced at me with hard but compassionate eyes. I had entered a private club, one where no one wanted to belong. She pointed to a room at the end of the hall. I passed an old dumbwaiter. Could the original owner imagine vials of blood instead of teacups?

In this room, another woman in a white overcoat tied a rubber band around my arm and took a vial of blood. She did this without looking at me. She unsnapped the rubber band and labeled it. She asked me to state my last name, then assigned me a number. 302. This was to insure privacy.

302. What if I forgot?"

She said my telephone number would do.

By the time I made it back to the train, it was dark, the kind of darkness that is cold and brown, like an empty oil drum. Cars honked up and down the street. Rush hour began its manic impatience. I lit up a cigarette, curled it into my palm, an expert at smoking now. I blew the smoke, inhaled, blew the white breath, then snapped the stub onto the sidewalk and twisted it out.

On the train, I rehearsed my excuse for arriving home late. I would say that I stayed late for choir. Not even Dora would question that.

The train filled with men in overcoats and heavy raincoats, men with leather briefcases and freshly folded newspapers. Men with wing-tipped shoes, and cuffed suit pants, and blue and red dotted ties. These men wore their hair short. They parted their hair in boxy, geometric shapes.

The man next to me excused himself when his bulging briefcase touched my foot.

"My wife keeps telling me to get a new one," he said good-naturedly. "Coming back from school?"

"Dentist appointment," I said.

I folded the brochure into my hands. It was full of questions. *Are you really ready for sex? What are your beliefs about sex? Are they different from your parents'? What kind of protection is best for you? Do you know the potential side effects of the pill?* Another brochure said, *No margin for Error: Why diaphragms succeed or fail.*

The train began to thin out as it went further north, stopping at commuter towns, until the man next to me got up and nodded good-bye. At my stop, I slid the curled-up pamphlets under my seat. I walked up the station stairs to the center of town and the familiar walk in the dark, under streetlights beaming misty halos in the cold air. I passed raked front yards, and finally turned to the house that from the beginning of my life had always been there.

The FOR SALE sign on our front lawn said: SALE PENDING.

I hastened up the driveway.

~~~~~

Inside, I met Dora in the kitchen stirring sweet potatoes and dishing additional chunks of broiled halibut onto a serving platter. She raised her eyes at the clock.

It was 6:12.

I thrust off my coat and hung it in the hall closet. Sherry's beige mohair coat was warming up next to Father's. Robert and Father looked up at me expectantly.

"Mr. Edwards asked me to sing another solo." I sat down next to Elliot at the dinner table and fussily filled my plate with fish and salad.

Sherry smiled pleasantly. "Congratulations."

Father nodded. "Very good." He scooped a forkful of potatoes into his mouth and waited for Sherry to take over. She had established herself here as a regular dinner guest.

"I'd be happy to pick you up after practice, sometime," she said.

"That's okay. I saw the sign," I said to Father.

"Sold it," Robert spat out.

"Not quite," Father corrected him.

Father put his fork down and in a calm voice that I rarely heard anymore, a voice that said he had everything in control and that things, despite appearances, would improve with time, told us that a family from Pennsylvania had made an offer. Loved the house. The garden. Saw the potential.

"Assuming everything proceeds, we will close on the house in December, during vacation, so as not to interfere with school."

"I don't want to move," Elliot said.

"Oh, Elliot," I said, affectionately. I touched his arm. I loved the way he said what we all felt. He didn't shout or lecture either.

I looked out the dark windows of the dining room, at the reflection of the round, globular chandelier shining back.

"Did they say they loved this light?"

Father smoothed his hair, ignoring the remark. He leaned back in his seat.

"It's not a good market. We're lucky to have this offer."

"Not according to Uncle Max," I said.

"You know," Sherry said, and once again it surprised us all the way she inserted herself into our business. "I moved when I was twelve. I can promise you that I didn't want to do it, like you, Elliot. Absolutely fought it. I told my parents I would sleep in a tent in the backyard. You know what? We moved and I liked our new place better. Life is funny that way."

"You mean like Dad meeting you because Mom died?" Elliot asked.

Dora came swinging into the room, the door thumping behind her.

"Who wants seconds?" she asked loudly. She looked determined and watchful as she walked around the room holding a dish of white rice mixed with mushroom soup. The mention of Mother changed the mood in the room. Father sighed. Dora flitted around the table, her Cardinal wings intent on keeping predators away from Father, who slumped over the table and reached for his glass of wine, emptying it in a smooth roll of his wrist.

Dora stood next to me holding a bowl of rice in her hands, waiting for me to scoop out a portion but I shook my head. My queasy stomach returned. Nauseous again. Dora noticed a shifting expression in my face, nodded and moved on to Elliot who plopped a scoop of the wet rice onto his plate. His unanswered question curled around the chandelier like invisible smoke and vaporized as if no one had heard him. Father plunged another forkful of rice into his mouth, corking up his son's question, his pure, unfiltered attempts to get at the truth. Sherry politely spooned another helping on her plate. I didn't understand her. She was earthy and awkward, insightful and intrusive.

"I just don't see why we have to move," Robert said.

Father rose from his dreamy state and looked at us with a threatening eye.

"When you're older, I'll explain it to you again. I don't expect you to understand. That goes for all of you."

Two days later, I called the clinic from the pharmacy pay phone and heard the words I dreaded. Positive. I was pregnant. I couldn't think but I knew I had to make a decision. The house sale loomed. My breasts felt tender to the touch. I wanted to hold someone. I leaned against the pay phone and called my brother. I needed an endpoint.

Peter answered the phone and I burst into tears.

"Sarah. Look. This is manageable. I swear it sucks but it's manageable. Call Sophie. She's a decent friend."

He kept talking, reasoning while I cried, sobbed, unable to calm down. I plugged another dollar's worth of coins into the phone. People walking in and out of the pharmacy passed by the glass booth but no one noticed me. Kids came in to buy bubble gum, longhaired trolls. Housewives came in for toiletries, nail polish and lipstick. An elderly lady walked out with a white prescription paper bag, like Mother's paper bags. Those pills. Why was it necessary? What had gone wrong?

"You are going to be fine," Peter assured me again. "I promise."

~~~~~

Sophie took charge in a way that completely surprised me, insisting that I sit in front while Benny drove us to the airport. We told our families that we were taking a day in the country, to look at the leaves. Everyone did that.

I was so thankful that Benny didn't judge me when I got in his Datsun. He looked kind and patient. I got in, holding my handbag stuffed with birthday cash I'd saved up over the years. The sun spread across a blue dappled sky. The air felt cold and clean. After today, I vowed to myself, I would start over. I would get a boyfriend like Sophie. I would learn to be happy.

The plane was full of well-dressed women in houndstooth woolen suits, off to New York for a day of the latest fall fashions. Lord & Taylor, Bonwit Teller's, Saks. It was something mother used to do. Down in the morning, back at night.

At LaGuardia airport, Sophie took my elbow and spotted the man in thin brown pants and leather jacket holding a cardboard sign that said Ranch River Estates. That was the secret code word. Sophie shook the man's hand. We're from Beacon Hill, she said. This is what the clinic told us to say to him. Connection complete, he nodded. I didn't speak. Sophie talked. She talked about anything. The flight. The weather. The airport. He nodded and led us to his car outside.

Sophie sat next to me in back. The man was listening to a radio talk show, a sports talk show and the announcer talked cleverly about the New York Giants, the quarterback, the wide receiver. The talk clattered in my ears. I looked out the window and followed the dashing white lines on the highway. I sat back. I told myself to stay calm. I was halfway there. It would soon be over. Over.

The car jostled and slowed and he swerved out of a lane to the side.

"Oh shit!" the man said. "Goddamn. Jesus. Shit."

"What's the problem?" Sophie asked in her chirpiest voice. She leaned over the front seat to see.

"Flat, flat. We've got a flat. Never mind. I know how to fix it."

"How long will it take you?" Sophie persisted.

He yanked on the emergency brake and opened the car door.

"Sit tight, ladies. I can do this in my sleep."

I closed my eyes, nauseous from car fumes. Hundreds of cars raced by, thousands of people couldn't care less about my dark world.

Sophie opened the back door and called out.
"How does it look?"

"Flat. Give me three more minutes."

It was a milder day, warmer in New York than Boston. Thin clouds streaked overhead. The trees were not as stripped here as they were at home. I wondered how far Gregory lived from this highway. I didn't call him. I wouldn't call him.

The car hiked up once then bounced.

"Want us to get out?" she called to him.

"Nope. Almost done here."

In a few more minutes he was back in the car, driving faster now, smelling of oil and rust. Once he exited the highway, he turned down a side street and parked outside a small, indistinct brick building called the Long Island Medical Center Association. He acted as if he had done this a thousand times. I knew he had.

Inside, I walked into a clean, brightly lit reception area full of women. Women sat in chairs, others slept in La-Z-Boy chairs lined along a hallway. At the front desk, a woman handed me a clipboard with more papers to fill out. When I handed them back, she told me to go into the exam room.

"Doctor will be right in."

Sophie walked with me. She hugged me. Her skinny arms held tight. "You know, it's almost over. I'll be here when you come out."

It was a small room. A huge, rectangular light shone from the ceiling. I shut myself up. I told myself, just get this over with. You are here. Remember this.

I undressed and followed the nurse's instructions. Put the apron on. Underwear off. Okay to keep your socks on. I lay back and the doctor came in. A man with a determined but pleasant face. I was in this place, an almost mother, lying on my back. I would get this over with. It was almost over. He put the needle in my wrist vein and told me to count to three. I didn't remember counting.

And then I woke up.

A nurse helped me up off the table, easing me across the hall to one of the La-Z-Boy chairs I had seen earlier. I fell back asleep. I woke again, sobbing, gulping hysterically, sucking in the loneliness, more regret, the soreness in my vagina, cramps, and relief.

"Look, Sarah, I got you a teddy bear," Sophie said. She placed a small, furry object in the crook of my arm. "We can go home now."

Chapter Twenty

Jewels

On Sunday I stayed in bed with a headache, cramps and fatigue. Father accepted this and left me alone. On Monday, he called up from downstairs.

"Sarah! Fifteen to eight. Let's not be late!" He started up to my room. I quickly tugged the quilts around my shoulders.

He knocked on the door.

"I'm still not feeling well."

He opened it and stood in the hallway looking in. My shades were drawn giving the room a sick brownish pallor.

"Women stuff."

This set him back. He started to close the door again.

"I'll tell Dora to call the school. See you tonight. Call me if you need me. All right?"

He raised his eyebrows, waiting.

I nodded, sliding further under the covers. "Shut the door all the way, please."

Downstairs, I heard him talking to Dora. The back door shut and he headed down the steps to the driveway. I looked at the clock. He had reverted to his old precise schedule: 7:45 a.m. out the door in the morning as if precision about time could put order back into our lives. The arc of Time prevailed over his mood swings, Robert's diatribes, Peter's absconding to the West Coast, Elliot's gentle emotional probing, and his daughter's insouciance. Sherry had something to do with it. She was there nudging him back to life.

I waited to see if he took the car, but this morning his shoes scraped along the pebble-crusted driveway, down our short street, a right turn down the longer hill, another right to a flatter stretch, then left onto the main road to town and finally the train station, not far from the pet store. His overloaded briefcase filled with the day's literary rantings, some ancient author's forging.

Elliot and Robert went next. Robert chattered beneath my window while Elliot whistled. Something about early October made the sound of their voices clean and light. Maybe it was the thinning trees. Less leaves to absorb the vibrations. Robert told Elliot to shut up and listen. It was the usual morning fare. Elliot didn't hesitate to respond in an even tone. I admired Elliot for his ability to ignore Robert's prickliness and I think that Robert, despite himself, appreciated this. On some level, and he rarely occupied himself with what others thought, Robert suspected, he knew his diatribes and mental chomping harassed people and wore them down. It was why he had few friends. At the same time, Elliot toughened under the influence of Robert's insistent, repetitive talk. He grew stronger. He opened himself to the world and endured.

Once the house stopped rippling with sounds and the breakfast smells subsided, Dora came upstairs and knocked on my door. She set a warm mug of tea with milk and sugar on my night table. I didn't expect this. She put a small plate of buttered toast next to it, lingering until she saw me sipping and nibbling. She raised the shades to modulate the morning sun coming in and when she came back up to retrieve the empty plates, she lowered them so the afternoon sun wouldn't pierce my eyes. She felt my head for fever and took my temperature. I was normal.

"What kind of bug is this?"

"It's my, you know, my stomach. Period stuff," I said, hoping that would say enough, but say nothing as well. She pinched her lips, assessing something in the middle of the room looking for what to put in order, sensing something because I rarely stayed home. I much preferred to be out. But my room, as usual, was clean and neat, so she left.

Blood soaked my sanitary pads. I got up to change. The clinic in New York said to expect this. I had a sheet of warning signs and tips and ten days' worth of antibiotics. The nurse told me to take it easy the first week. Increased activity could increase the bleeding. She gave me a prescription for birth control pills. One pill a day. I had a tip sheet about this too. The essentialness of remembering, the danger of forgetting. I had a good head on my shoulders. I used to. I thought I did.

All these things I kept in my night table drawer, tucked in a box. I had another tip sheet listing numbers to call, including a follow-up appointment with the clinic psychologist on Beacon Hill. I had a handful of aspirins laced with codeine — to still the mild cramping, the uterine spasms. The pills quieted my head. I eased into a warm safe feeling. I lay on my back gazing at nothing, the tiny yellow birch leaves flickering outside my window, a squirrel skipping up a branch, then curling itself into a prayer's stance. I listened to my body whirring smoothly, thoughtless as a child, simple as days when the slant of sun or a color in the cloud was enough knowledge, more than enough to take me through the day.

I slept.

I wrapped the sanitary pads in wads of toilet paper. The tiny trash can in the bathroom filled up with a sour smell of old blood and dried body fluids. The same smell saturated my nightgown. I got up and took a shower to clean it away, push the New York trip further back in the drawer. I smoked two cigarettes leaning out the bathroom window. Long sucking smoke.

I didn't have these warning signs: *excessive* blood, clots *bigger* than fifty cents.

When the aspirin lost traction and the tugging in my lower abdomen started up again; a grinding twist in my stomach, I took a few more. The tip sheet said to expect this. Nauseous fingers played with the back of my throat. I breathed. I turned over in bed. I flipped the pillow to its cool side. I turned the radio on.

The trip might have been yesterday or it might have been last year. The way to New York where Gregory lived might have been across the ocean, Europe, a nightmare crossing a current of disbelief. And Gregory. He seemed like a stick figure now. An idea that hadn't worked out.

This wasn't me.

Except it was.

I struggled against this. I wanted to fold myself up, put me in a drawer neat as my room, vacuumed, dust free — life free. I was an intelligent girl, talented, the one who made the right decisions. I had made a terrible mistake.

But then, I had a mother once.

"Oooh," she said, her voice girlish and pleased. "Shall we sit up close?" She placed the popcorn container between us. Our fingers collided happily as we dug in and scooped handfuls. I followed her to the middle section of the theater, about twenty rows back from the screen and settled in beside her. On a rare outing together, she and I went to see a James Bond movie. Alone. Together. Not long after Grandpa's funeral. Not long after the first accident.

Diamonds Are Forever was playing at Soquaset's movie theater. Mother ordered a large buttered popcorn and two Cokes. The theater was half-full. We didn't see anyone we knew.

Up front, the red curtain opened and the movie trailers began. Wearing navy pants and matching jersey, Mother melded into the darkened theater, except when the lights from the movie brightened her exposed arms and face. Midway into the feature, she put her hand on my arm. We laughed, giggled, and gasped as our hero, James Bond, burst through a paper wall, threw darts into the chest of the British enemy and fist-fought his way out of an elevator. We traveled to prairies in South Africa and posh Las Vegas casinos. I inhaled the aroma of butter on her breath while James Bond hung dangerously from the roof of a skyscraper hotel. For a short time, mother and I were action-loving companions riding an invisible roller coaster together, leaning into our seats, not wanting the ride to end.

~~~~~

I tried to touch her absence. I lifted my arm and waved it across the undisturbed bedroom air. I opened and shut my fingers. She was palpable. She was out of reach. I wanted her now, here in my room, at the window, at night, looking out at my dark hunger, this vacuous wedge between my ribs. The farther she went from me, someplace out my window, past the birch tree and the Fineburgs' roof, to the plain vaulted room in the sky, her absence funneled deeper. I saw her sitting there. She was there. I got up and stood at the windowsill and tried to fit myself into the invisible envelope of her body. Time made things worse not better. Her leaving dug in, scratched and ached. I went back to bed. I saw her shoveling out the garden bed, clawing the dirt to make room for winter bulbs. Her fingers curled below the roots into the cold. Her pink fingernails protected by heavy, suede gardening gloves. The cherry tree had lost most of its leaves. The bulbous limbs reached across the patch of browning grass, saving its place for spring.

I wouldn't be here to watch the blossoms return. That angered me. It reignited grief. I wanted to scream. Get a hold of myself. My brain lobes vibrated. I turned the radio up. The 5ᵗʰ Dimension.

Up, up and away
My beautiful,
My beautiful balloon!

Shaky thoughts. On the way home from New York, the car, the plane, Benny picking us up. Dear God. Mother. Where are you? I held the little bear in my lap, sleeping as the plane shifted levels before making its descent. And then it was over in some way. All over. But beginning again. The carving was done. I was sore. I had come to the end of something. I had come to nothing. I lay in the backseat of Benny's car and we agreed that Sophie would come in to divert attention. Sophie had called Peter from the clinic pay phone. I was asleep, my head laden with medication and the frightening slice of regret that divided my life to before and after.

Life was full of before and afters. Before Mother died and after. Before Sherry came to the party and after. Before Peter left and after. Before Gregory slipped his penis between my legs and after. Before Anthony lifted me onto his lap and after. Before this abortion and after.

Except for music. Singing didn't have a before or after. It stayed and stayed.

~~~~~

I stepped into the kitchen and heard the television in the den. Robert and Elliot watching a Walt Disney movie as they did every week, and Father there with them. I smelled his cigarette smoke. Not hers. Sherry's coat was not in the hall closet. She went home on Saturday nights. The kitchen lights had been dimmed to night watch; the counters so clean a visitor would never suspect the confusion that prevailed, our spotted life. I heard Dora in her room watching TV.

"I'm home," I shouted to stave off suspicion.

This worked better than sneaking upstairs. My elusiveness would only tug at Father, who would want to know if I had something to hide, a list of details to prove where I had been.

I headed up to my room and changed into a nightgown and robe then eased into bed. I planned to say I wasn't feeling well. I planned to skip school. I planned to be alone, to change, to fix this mistake.

Sophie left, calling out to Father as she went out the back door.

"Good-bye, Mr. Kunitz. See you soon," she yelled cheerfully.

I listened to Benny back his car down the driveway. Sophie had made a good choice, a better way of loving.

The night drifted quiet as a merry-go-round when the music has been turned off and the carousel is coasting to a stop. Gravity slips its hold on you as you ride the merry-go-round horse, up and down, until the people around you are no longer a colorful blur but individual faces waiting for you to step down, come back to their world, but you don't want to let go of the pole or the height because up here on the merry-go-round horse, life looks better. I hugged my pillow and heard Robert and Elliot coming upstairs to bed, passing by my closed door. I had planned to take over Peter's room and have Elliot take over mine but with the house sale, it didn't matter anymore. I started to cry, tears spidering down my cheek. I squashed the drops into my pillow. I cried. I coughed the last drops out.

~~~~~

Tuesday, I lay in bed listening to the top 40 countdown on the radio. Emptiness flattened me as if I were lying under a mattress and another part of me lying on top of myself. In the early afternoon, Dora cleaned the second floor bathroom and emptied out trash cans. I smelled Clorox bleach. I listened to the shushing sprays of the window cleaner. Familiar smells wiping away history, wiping away this house.

I slept some but I heard her come in again and leave a cup of chicken soup. Later in the afternoon, before my brothers returned from school, she came in and sat on the end of the bed.

"Bad cramps?"

I nodded. I did my best to look calm but felt my face tighten. She would see the sanitary pads, the excessive number of them.

"You don't have to tell me," she said, looking at me in that way that penetrated my thoughts. "My middle daughter went through this."

I turned my head to the pillow. I didn't want her to see my tears but they dripped to the side, icicles melting.

"The most important thing you can do is get on with your life," she said putting her hand on my blanket-covered foot. "You're too young for this."

"I feel old," I admitted. I saw that she wasn't going to judge me. It was too late for that.

"Sophie's a good friend," she said. "Now you be a better friend to yourself."

That started me crying again and when she squeezed my ankle in sympathy, I shook with all that I gave up. Ashamed.

"It's a woman's burden, this business. Did you start the pill?"

I nodded.

She tapped my ankle again and went out.

I sat up slowly. The soreness between my legs complained. I remembered when I was eight, swooshing down an aluminum slide in the school playground, ramming into a boy's foot caught at the bottom of the slide because he had stopped abruptly, a joke to catch me on the way down. I ran around the yard clutching my pelvis unable to locate the specific point of intrusion. Streams of pain radiated into my hips and stomach. Muscle and skin throbbed an imprint of that boy's hard-bottomed shoe. It was the first time my vagina protested, the first time I was forced to think about a tunnel running inside me, a cavity of unknown life, a vessel filled with a universe too grand and dark, abstract and unreachable for my mind.

I turned the radio dial, spun it away from advertisements about cars and laundry soap. Dora returned with a warm facecloth, which she tamped lightly on my forehead. She placed a hot water bottle near my stomach.

"This will soothe you. I'll keep your father away when he comes home. He'll be no help to you right now."

"Keep her away too. It's uncomfortable."

She nodded, her stern face a measure of something tangible, a ruler of concern.

"I couldn't have told Mother."

"Tell her what you need her to know, now."

"What do you mean?"

"Talk to her now. She'll listen."

After she left, I thought about what Dora said, but it scared me. I felt confused. I moved out of bed and went to my closet to find Mother's picture I had hidden there. It was a framed, professional photo of her playing the violin. I rubbed the glass with my nightgown. She didn't dye her hair then. Shoulder length, her hair shone like lemon polish on wood. She was young, still in college. And there was that expression — a dreamy, happy look on her lips, and a dip of the head the way it perched on the chin rest of the violin, as if she were doing the sidestroke in a warm pool.

I couldn't talk to a photo. It was hard. What did it matter who she was *then*? That youthful part of her had left so long ago. *Here*, without her, it hurt. Maybe she did hear me. *Mother, are you listening?* The radio announcer chattered on, oblivious to me. I put the photo back in the closet and returned to bed.

~~~~~

For three days I stayed at home, sleeping for hours during the day, working on homework at night: algebra problems, biology chapter on the cell, a report due on Hawthorne for American history. Sophie came each afternoon with daily assignments and graded papers, then headed off to dance class. Benny drove up to the same spot on the driveway and waited in the car until my best friend returned to him, skipped back down the kitchen steps. Benny liked the rock station on FM. I could hear his car radio spilling out a low, sophisticated voice of a deejay, a torrent of words sounding sexy and angry; fermented in sleeplessness and drugs.

I piled my textbooks on the floor near the end of the bed. In the afternoon, Sophie knocked on my door, a few light taps, before entering. She brought the freshness of a school day, the way it might have been before Mother died, before Father fell apart, before Sherry attached herself to my life like a strip of bed sheets knotted and tossed over the side of a building, as if she were waiting for me to climb over the side or leap over imaginary flames, to her lifesaving arms.

I didn't despise Sherry anymore. She meant well but Dora meant better. And Mother wouldn't have approved. I remember how she noticed Sherry at the party, sidling up to Father in the backyard — Sherry, trying hard not to appear disheveled in her party dress and wrap. Her slathered lipstick. Her nipples. But Father and Shell, they liked something about her. She wasn't untouchable. Sherry ate potato chips from a greasy well in her hand. She wasn't prickly. She laughed at their stupid jokes.

Mother held back. She traveled inside an arcane orbit, spinning too quickly for any of us. Mother went out to the backyard that night of the party striving for something better, higher, so high she couldn't touch it and neither could Father. He couldn't grasp her core.

Where was she? Why couldn't I feel her? Why couldn't I remember who she was? Yet I saw her dresses, her chiffon pleated couture, her silk pointed shoes, the gold buttons on her coat. Please, Mother.

If this was growing up, I didn't want to go this way but I couldn't see any alternative but to move forward, to find something better. I reached for the sheet music under the night table. Mr. Edwards wanted me to sing. I held the papers in my hand; I held them tightly. I needed these notes, this music.

~~~~~

Dora finished vacuuming. She had stacked clean towels in the upstairs linen closet. After this, she went into Mother's room. Now that the house was under contract Mother's room became a packing room.

I felt well enough and got up to watch her unloading Mother's closet. She carefully folded chiffon dresses, wool suits, linen pants, shoes of different colors. She pressed them into boxes and labeled them. The violin case had been taken down, set aside with things that were going with us.

"You should be resting," she said, eying me severely.

"I'm feeling better today. What are we going to do with these?" I said, touching the cardboard flap of an open box full of sweaters.

"Take them to the new place."

Father found a two-family on a street just outside the center of town. The walk to school would be closer. We would live upstairs without Dora. An older couple that had rented there for twenty-two years would remain. Maybe they would be nice. Dora would commute four days a week from her daughter's house in Roxbury.

"Take some for your daughters. They don't fit me." I had broader shoulders, more height than Mother's petite frame. She wore narrower shoes.

Dora kept folding, ignoring my suggestion. "My girls are all set. Go look through your mother's jewels; they don't have a size for fitting. Bring them to your room. Look through them."

In Mother's dressing room, I opened the drawers of her built-in dresser. She kept items in separate boxes: golden tops, blue velvet boxes clamped tight. I opened and closed each box, one at a time, gently lifting a long, familiar string of pearls like cooked pasta from a boiling pot. She wore these pearls to all her club parties. The necklace linked twice around her collarbone. Day and night. Father said they looked like a dog's collar. But she wore them anyway as if to dare him to hook her up with a leash, take her to that better place she was seeking.

I guess he never did.

I went to sit on the floor but the soreness stopped me. I mounted the boxes in my arms and lay them out on my quilt. The sapphire ring, another string of pearls with matching earrings. A tennis bracelet of linked diamonds that she wore in the garden. She didn't worry about losing her jewels. Many came from her family inheritance. Grandma's ruby ring — it looked dull. I rubbed it on my nightgown and peered into it as I used to when I was a child. I loved to see the world break into facets and angles, the rooms turning upside down in the reflection, tacking into a direction that I didn't expect.

I put the ring to my eye again and saw the world reverse itself. I found this comforting as if the stone knew all along that I would come back to this moment ten years later, again, to see that not much had changed really, that the world did this. It spun and twisted and flipped and shifted in a silent, glittering slice of light.

Maybe Mother was in there somewhere. Possible. Possible to find her. But not in a way that I hoped or thought.

Long ago I had a secret place in the backyard woods. I had a place in summer when it stayed light long after dinner and Mother let me play in the woods while she smoked and talked on the phone. I hummed, watching the sky turn a deeper blue, spilling across the clouds, becoming a flood of colors until Mother called me. I waited for her to call me. I leaned on this.

I am calling for you now, Mummy. Please come home. Come. Be here.

~~~~~

On my walk back to school, I scuffed through a cascade of fallen leaves on the street curb. Back to the usual, full schedule, including chorus at the end of the day. At school, I passed the wall and cordially said hello to Anthony's sister. We had reached a truce.

"He's gone to 'Nam," she said.

"I know," I said, and I was going to say something more, but then, that would be like reaching for a plane that has already taken off. I nodded. Everything about it was sad.

Her boyfriend, a thick-muscled football player, squeezed her into his side while she smoked a morning cigarette. She didn't smile. Life was not a smiling endeavor for her or for me. It made me like her because of that. She darkened her eyes with black eyeliner, drawing thin lines across the top and bottom lids, drawing a map on her face as if to define its territories: eyes were off limits. Look from a distance but don't come in.

As I went through the day, walking with Sophie to classes, sitting with her during lunch hour, I had the feeling of watching myself, of being a witness to the present, as if I were already ahead in a future place waiting for myself to catch up. I had one more year in this place and if I planned it right, studied hard, I would graduate and get a jump-start on a musical life. Move to California, get hooked up with a studio producer, sing in coffeehouses with Peter. He had a small following now.

Mr. Edwards told me to feed my talent.

I could leave, go away from here, away from no longer having our house, away from a track of losses and pain if that were possible. Away from living in this semi-dark state, this tunnel that kept going and going. I had to choose to find my way out.

At choir practice, Mr. Edwards looked up from his music stand and smiled at me.

"Glad to have you back, Sarah."

Coda

I stood on the platform with the rest of the so-pranos and Sophie; and when it came time to sing my solo, I let my insides pour out into the empty auditorium. And now, as I step onto this pseudo stage, a photo of an elephant shining as my back-drop, my head fills with musical notes, this crowd-ed ballroom abuzz with concerned adults; everyone here for a good cause, martinis in hand, the odors of perfume and aftershave creating a jungle of smells. I adjust the mike and strum my guitar into tune, hush-ing this hip, California crowd. The overhead light is centered on me and in bright focused light, calls her forth. I begin. My throat releases. It happens when the amplifier and the lights and the shush in the room blends, and I am stronger than the shadow that I live inside. Alan is on his way, he has called.

I sing about a mountainside, and blue skies, and further up the scale, high notes vibrate in my skull as I go beyond places to where Mother sits, her flaw-less face enraptured with melody, urging me on. I sing, glancing at Mr. Edwards, who waves his arms gently to encourage me, tapping quarter notes, dip-ping his head in approval, a reverential smile lighting the corner of his lips. I sing until walls disappear, for my brothers across the country to hear me, for Dora long gone, and Father in Florida with Sherry who went with him, for Anthony Parelli who never came home from Vietnam; for Mickey and others who flicker online from my past, for all the people I have not yet met but who are out there — I knew they would be — even with this ineluctable hole in my heart, a motherless child, I knew they were out there to heal and embrace me. To listen and applaud.

O yes, I will sing.

Acknowledgments

There are so many individuals whose support I have valued and appreciated over these many years, and in moments like these — when thanks are more than due — it's tempting to list everyone I've ever met in my life. Where *Night Swim* is concerned, these people emerge most distinctly. There's the memory of Bill Emerson reading a first draft of *Night Swim* and loving it. There's Cis Corman of Barwood Films, who championed all of my work and never wavered for decades. Thanks to Karen Dionne and Chris Graham for introducing me to a wonderful community of writers at Backspace. To the Cape and Boots brigade: Susan Henderson, Robin Slick and Tish Cohen, your insights kept me floating at a critical time. Thank you, Caroline Leavitt, for your fierce enthusiasm, brilliance and heart. Patry Francis, your literary gifts and friendship are a blessing. Risa Miller, our connection goes beyond words. Thank you Suzanne Beecher, Eve Bridburg, Lauren Baratz-Logsted, Barb Aronica-Buck, Leora Skolkin-Smith, Billie Hinton, Mariam Keener, Sherrie Crow, and Robert Ellis Gordon. Special thanks to MJ Rose for leading me to Lou Aronica's door. To my publisher, Lou Aronica, thank you for sharing your vast experience and for extending your calm and steady hand to help me realize this dream. Much love to my "sisters band" Susan Keith and Jeanne Perry, consummate believers in every way. You shine a beautiful light on the universe.

To Anne Fischell: for your strength and inspiration.

Thank you, Dad, for taking my writing seriously from my first poem to all that followed. Your love and appreciation lives on in these words. To Mom, Anne, Lynne, Wanda, Frank and Lolly — finally at last!

To my small, unique family: Sam, your artistic soul teaches me every day; and Barr, husband and best friend in life and love: Thank you for believing, for staying with me and riding the waves. You embody faith.

About the Author

Jessica Keener has been listed in *The Pushcart Prize* under "Outstanding Writers." Her fiction has appeared in many literary magazines, most recently: *Connotation Press: An Online Artifact, Night Train, Eclectica, Wilderness House Literary Review and MiPOesias.* Writing awards include: a grant from the Massachusetts Cultural Council Artist's Grant Program, a Joan Jakobson Scholarship from Wesleyan Writers Conference; a Chekhov Prize for Excellence in Fiction by the editors of *Wilderness House Literary Review*; and second prize in *Redbook* magazine's fiction contest. For more than a dozen years she has been a features writer for *The Boston Globe, Design New England, O, the Oprah magazine* and other national magazines.

Please visit her website: www.jessicakeener.com. *Night Swim* is her first novel. She is also the author of the story collection, *Women in Bed*.